CAMELOPARDIS CASTLE

K J Houghton

MINERVA PRESS

LONDON
MIAMI DELHI SYDNEY

CAMELOPARDIS CASTLE
Copyright © K J Houghton 2000

All Rights Reserved

ISBN 0 75410 887 2

First Published 2000 by
MINERVA PRESS
315–317 Regent Street
London W1R 7YB

Printed in Great Britain for Minerva Press

TO BETTY.

CAMELOPARDIS CASTLE

ALL THE
BEST,

[signature]

An Introduction of Sorts

Long, long ago, when kings were kings and men were either knights, gentleman or plebs, the building of a castle in the region of Leopardis was mooted as an extremely good idea. It provided an ideal spot for hit-and-run raids on nearby realms, towns, villages, cots and houses. Anywhere, indeed, that might have women, donkeys and/or money in the near vicinity. Since money was plentiful, mainly from the prevailing violent forays and carpetbagging excursions into other weaker lands it was deemed that King Theodolite the Crusher himself should put forward a basic design for his dream home. His blueprint, being seen as having divine guidance behind it, was universally accepted.

Committees being only a relatively new concept at the time, life was ruled by two principles. First – follow divine guidance when it occurs in your neighbourhood. And second – self-preservation is next to godliness.

After only a few years, with the foundation stones of Camelopardis Castle not yet properly dry, King Theodolite the Crusher suffered the ultimate indignity of losing his crown to a mob of marauding barbarians. The fact that his head was still in close association with the crown when it was lost is of no real consequence at this point, except that it persuaded those former friends of King Theodolite the Headless, who still lived, to abandon the first principle and wholeheartedly adopt the second.

True to form they closed ranks behind the new king, barbarian though he may be. When Michael the Barbarian threw his own ideas into the pot, in the form of Romanesque pillars and portals, the populace were a little disconcerted. It came about that Michael, besides having a strange name for a barbarian, also had some very intellectually stimulating ideas about architecture. Some people believe that Michael was not in fact a real barbarian at all, but that he had simply been vaulted to power by a particularly nasty fraction of the PRAGBA[1] group as a joke. Be that as it may, when Michael's second proclamation outlawing pillage and rape was announced the populace were, quite understandably, incensed. After all, what else was there to do after the pub closed on a Saturday night and telly hadn't yet been invented?

The next king, Grob the Gross, was much more to the liking of the populace. He would throw 'Burn a Philistine' soirées and 'Lob a Brick at a Tart' cheese and wine parties. Alas, his idea of a castle tended towards the 'large blocks of flint and loads of cement' school of architecture. He was deposed (decapitated, dismembered, dissected, all the same root verb!) to be replaced by a forward thinking Tudor, in a time before Henry VIII was even a twinkle in his daddy's eye. When the populace saw his black and white façades rising above *their* castle they immediately condemned him as a witch (black being the colour of the devil) and burnt him at the stake.

During the following centuries kings came and kings went, each adding their own bits and pieces to an already elaborate structure. When finally complete the castle was so large and so well fortified that the populace found that without marauding enemies or invading armies life was becoming rather dull, so as one man they packed up their belongings, chattels, children, wives and sundry non-tax-paying-hangers-on and went off to invade Norway. Since none came back to tell the tale it is not known if they were successful or not.[2]

Camelopardis Castle then fell into a couple of centuries of decay, since there was no longer the money in any of the local kingdoms to run such a monstrous white elephant. Until that is, King Multiceros the Wise returned from a long trip to the East bringing with him several large white elephants carrying gold, gems, spices, tobacco and an extremely large quantity of opium. He set himself up in luxury, giving the ruins the only form of renovation they were ever likely to get. Walls were repaired and plastered anew, paintwork once more gleamed. Exotic Persian carpets, bought at extreme cost but sadly of very little aesthetic

---

[1]The Pillage, Rape and Gang Bang Association (affiliated).
[2]Presumably not. As a populace they were not all that bright.

appeal, were scattered throughout the salons and chambers.

Surprisingly enough, for an occupant of Camelopardis Castle, King Multiceros lived a long and fruitful life, setting up educational establishments for all classes and grades of intellect in the region, reorganising medical resources, building a sound, environmentally aware government and establishing trade links with previously antagonistic kingdoms and turned out to be 'a very nice genuine guy'.

His son and heir, Monoceros, was a bit of a let down. Quite a big bit of a let down it has to be said, if we're going to be honest about it. In the course of a few short decades he squandered the massive family fortunes on such futile ventures as a gas-fired spaceship, a horse-driven speedboat and imploding gunpowder.

In honour of his (failed) quest for space travel, Monoceros named his only son Vulpecula. As it turned out he got that wrong as well. If you're going to aim for the stars you have got to aim *high*, not far.

Our story, therefore, opens in a castle of stupendous size, kleptomaniacal design and astronomical (about as close to the stars as King Monoceros ever got) running costs and a close, interbred social hierarchy that is about to disintegrate into absolute chaos.

Confused? I know I am. Don't you just love it? Nevertheless, we carry on regardless. Welcome then, with fraternal greetings and all the luck in the world, to Camelopardis Castle!

And you thought that *you* had problems!

One

Even through the thick soles of his carpet slippers, Glimmergoyne could feel the cold seeping up from the bare stone flags in the passageway. Summer or winter the castle floor was always cold here, especially at five thirty in the morning. A velveteen dressing gown of lurid colours covered a long white linen nightgown. The pointed, drooping nightcap firmly fitted onto his scalp, with the bobble hanging over his left shoulder gave him the appearance of a mournful and tragic, if somewhat sartorially inept, ghost.

The flickering light from the candelabra held tightly in one scrawny hand caused the gown to flash and glitter madly but did little to lighten the deep shadows in the gloom of the passage. For the past twenty years as head butler to 'Family Vulpecula' Glimmergoyne had followed this route at this time in the slow measured tread that went with the job. He never faltered.

The trek to the bathhouse from his own room was complex and convoluted. First he passed the sleeping quarters of the senior castle staff, then third left, second right past a particularly obnoxious portrait of Queen Xenophobe until he came to the outer corridor that ran around this, the Servants' Hall level of the castle. Small lead-paned windows were set at intervals in the thick outer wall, but there was still too little daylight to help him along.

Idly his eyes swept over the heavy padlocks on the storerooms as he passed them confirming that all was secure. A welcome gust of warm air swept his exposed face as he crossed the entrance to the passage that led to the kitchens but his pace did not falter, not even to savour the warmth. The ludicrous Chef Bootes would be there, not a man Glimmergoyne particularly wished to meet first thing in the morning.

Shortly the windows ended and he was back in dark, black, slowly shifting shadow once more. Shortly the warm glow of light emanating from the Royal Laundry came into view, causing him to blow out the candles as he approached. Reaching the wide-open double doors, Glimmergoyne peered into the perpetual steamy fug.

'Good morning Mr Hydrus. Everything is in readiness for His Highness I trust?'

The deep sonorous tones of his voice penetrated the steam like a Lutine Bell.

'Good morning, Mr Glimmergoyne. Yes, everything is in readiness,' boomed a voice from somewhere deep within a steam cloud. 'So today is the anniversary then, is it? Twenty years as butler hey? You thought I didn't know, didn't you? Well, well, my heartiest congratulations, Mr Glimmergoyne.'

Hydrus, a giant of a man in a grubby apron and dirty jacket that belied the very nature of his profession, with a badly stained cloth cap perched on the mop of fiery red hair, emerged from the steam cloud with a hand raised.

'Well thank you, Mr Hydrus. Good of you to have remembered!' said Glimmergoyne nodding with practised diffidence, briefly taking the proffered hand. 'Yes, twenty years ago today it was. For fifteen years before that I was under-butler to old Sextans. Ten years before that I was doorman in this very—'

'Yes I know. I know all that, Mr Glimmergoyne,' said Hydrus hastily, belatedly wishing he had not started the old coot off. 'A long way from being boot boy, though, Mr Glimmergoyne?'

Hydrus winced as he said it, knowing the response off by heart.

'A long way indeed, Mr Hydrus. You know, I remember a time when the master said to me—'

'Your bath water is ready for you, Mr Glimmergoyne. Cubicle two. I've laid out your clean uniform for you,' said Hydrus hastily. The laundryman quickly shoved a towel and cake of soap into the claw-like hands.

'Oh. Yes, right. Thank you, Mr Hydrus. Very kind. As I was saying I remember when his Lordship said to me, now this is a very amusing story—'

'Oh dear is that the time? I must be getting on. Some pressing to catch up on. What you might call *pressing business* hah!'

'Oh, yes, very funny that, Mr Hydrus. Hah hah hah,' answered Glimmergoyne dryly. 'I shall have to try and remember that one!'

'I'm sure you will, you crashing old bore,' muttered Hydrus under his breath.

'Now, get along with you, Mr Glimmergoyne. We don't want the water going cold now, do we?'

'No, no of course not.'

'I'll give you His Highness's gear when you come out, all right Mr Glimmergoyne? Yes? Good.'

Hydrus shook his head wearily as the old man headed off to the row of bathrooms. Glimmergoyne was a nice enough chap but he could be incredibly *dull* at times.

The enormous grubby bulk of Hydrus the laundryman managed to make even the high-ceilinged Laundry appear small, as he plodded over to a long, wooden, much abused ironing table. Picking up a red-hot flat iron in his massive fist, he began to lovingly press an awful candy-striped dress shirt. He hummed happily to himself as he worked. Hydrus was not one of those who let his master's bad taste in colours and appalling dress sense adversely affect his mood.

Emerging a little while later from the bath cubicle in the immaculate black tailcoat, black bow tie, white waistcoat and striped trousers of the well-dressed butler, Glimmergoyne peered across the steam-filled room.

'Mr Hydrus? Mr Hydrus are you still there?'

'Yes Mr Glimmergoyne. Will you take His Majesty's first apparel now?'

'No, I shall return within the hour. After breakfast, to be more precise, Mr Hydrus. The morning suit. Grey with red and mauve stripe I think. Yes, the grey with the red and mauve stripe if you please, Mr Hydrus.'

'As you wish, Mr Glimmergoyne.'

The firm, measured tread of the immaculate servant carried Glimmergoyne through the vast wooden doors, first left, then left again, along the dismal, stone flagged corridors.

Now impeccably groomed, the figure of the head butler strode inexorably towards the Servants' Hall.

'Good morning,' he said curtly as he entered.

'What's good about it?' muttered Fornax the gamekeeper from

his appointed place by the blazing fire.

Glimmergoyne merely smiled the tooth-filled smile of the long-suffering father figure and ignored him. It was the smile of the wolf, the wolf that was trying to decide whether to bite first and ask questions later or just to give a friendly lick.

'Breakfast ready yet, Crater?' he demanded of the pantry boy.

'Twenty minutes, sir, if that's all right with you, sir?' whimpered a small pimply youth from the fireplace, cringing visibly.

'Yes, yes, all right,' answered the butler tersely, 'I shall return shortly.'

Glimmergoyne always found that children irritated him intensely. Taking the polished wooden staircase at the left of the hall, he trod heavily upwards, towards the Hall of Fire.

'What's so bloody good about it is what I'd like to know,' muttered Fornax to himself again as the butler disappeared from view.

'Shut up you old fool!' said Matron Beamish from the dining table. 'It's not everybody in this castle gets drunk as a fart every night and ends up looking like a reject from a mortuary first thing in the morning.'

'Shut your gob, you tiresome old biddy. Just go and give that Ortolan Apus of yours a good slapping. The little bastard put something in my beer again last night, I'm sure he did. I'll swing for the little sod, I swear I will.'

'You'll do nothing of the sort, you lecherous old drunk. My little Orty is just a high spirited boy, that's all.'

'High spirited?' said Fornax with a snort, 'is that what you call it? I'd call it being bloody obnoxious and downright puerile.'

'My little Orty would do no such thing.'

'Now then people, let's have no bickering please!' said Chancellor Antila, the official holder of the Royal purse strings. 'I mean, I'm sure His Little Highness meant no harm.' The little man giggled nervously.

'No harm? No *harm*? The little bastard tries to kill me and all you can do is sit there and say is "meant no harm"?'

'Boys will be boys,' said Matron Beamish, with a wistful smile.

'Hah!' said Fornax and sank deeper into his grubby tweed suit, glaring with bloodshot eyes at the gigantic matron. The throbbing in his skull was not conducive to arguing at this ungodly hour of the day.

★

At fourteen years old, the Prince Ortolan Apus was everything Fornax said about him and more. Using the immunity of being a Royal son as protection, he would vent his sense of dismay at being only second, third if you included Her Ugliness, in line to the throne on anybody and anything he felt deserved it. In other words, anybody and anything.

Quite unaware that his reputation was being maligned, albeit truthfully, in the Servants' Hall, Ortolan himself was at that very moment perched on top of a stool outside the Crown Prince Pyxis Vulpecula's room. He was involved in carefully balancing a bucket of iced water above the lintel. When it was positioned to his satisfaction, he gingerly stepped down from the stool, picked it up by one of the legs and tiptoed carefully across the scattered shards of broken glass to his own room. He smiled to himself as he gently closed his own door behind him.

It was always worth the bother of getting up early just to hear darling big brother Pyxie scream in agony. Ortolan Apus climbed back into bed and waited for events to take their course.

★

Glimmergoyne reached the top of the servants' staircase where there was a broad landing with stored tables and large walk-in cupboards for the use of the footmen and waiters who served table at the grander functions. He inspected the area out of habit more than anything for there were seldom the great parties and dinners these days. Not like there used to be in the old days. The lift shaft from the kitchen was the only source of sound in the deathly quiet of this level of the castle. Moving closer, Glimmergoyne could hear Chef Bootes shouting and swearing at some poor unfortunate down below. Glimmergoyne and the overweight, pompous Bootes shared a mutual dislike of each other that bordered on hatred. Glimmergoyne smiled to himself in satisfaction when he heard the deep, manly voice of Ethelreda, the pastry cook, berating the chef as an ignoramus lard-ball before turning happily towards the entrance to the Hall of Fire.

★

Chef Bootes strode across the kitchen to his tiny office fuming. She always managed to put him down, that stupid, fat cow, das verdamter pastry kochin. Slamming the frosted glass door behind him he glared out at the kitchen through the plate glass window, at the hidden smiles on the faces of the staff. He knew they all laughed at him behind his back. The bastards. Squeezing his enormous bulk between the handkerchief-sized desk and the back wall he glowered under bristling eyebrows and glared at them. Suddenly he smiled; a devious calculating smile. He needed a classy menu for next Friday night's Gala Dinner, a particularly lavish bash for the Duke of Philbert. The King wanted to impress him. Something to do with a loan, Captain Parsus had said, when he brought the instructions down. No matter. It would give him the opportunity to teach them a lesson. Teach them not to laugh at him behind his back. Reaching up behind him to the groaning bookcase bolted precariously to the wall, he pulled down a heavy tome entitled *Gracious Dining for Palace and Castle* and began to flick through its pages.

Chef Bootes had never really accepted the need for women in the kitchen. If he had his way they would be confined to the pot-wash where they belonged. *She* always managed to put him down, either by mimicking his accent or stuffing a pillow up under her jacket and waddling about in gross imitation of his own gait. It was not his fault he was so large. The doctors had told his mother that it was a gland problem. He didn't eat that much. Not really.

His eyes lit up as he read 'Aspic de lièvre en Brioche'. There was still some of that rabbit left from last week, it would be high enough by now that only the most discerning palate would know the difference; most of them would be so legless by the time the meal started that they would eat anything put in front of them anyway. Still, that would do for a start. And then how about some 'Truite du lac en papillote'? Fifty five trout to be boned out. Loads of vegetable julienne. That would keep the bastards busy. And then? What was the beef fillet thingy? The one with the stuffed truffles? Lucullus. That was it, 'Filet de boeuf Lucullus'. Marvellous. Couldn't let them use truffles of course, Antila the penny-pincher would throw a right wobbly. They could stuff loads of baby mushrooms though. Cockscombs? Well maybe not exactly but there must be something interesting in the store they could use. Right, and the next. Some of that smelly old Stilton. Powerful stuff that. The smell of that would strip paint at a hundred paces. All those peeled grapes and celery flowers too, another half-day's work. Bootes mentally rubbed his hands in glee. And then what? There had to be a spun sugar thingy in there somewhere. The fat slag of a pastry cook hated spun sugar. What about a 'Gateau St Honoré'? Fill the centre with spun sugar and candied fruits, then loads of petit fours. Very nice. The punters would love it!

Chef Bootes read down his list and smiled wickedly. On top of that of course, there would be two hundred and twenty turned potatoes, four hundred and forty pieces of turned carrot, four hundred and forty pieces of turned zucchini. They were *really* going to hate him for this one.

A sudden vision sprang unbidden into his mind. Large voluptuous thighs as smooth and white as alabaster, plump, heavy breasts with taut brown nipples, surmounted by the welcoming, inviting smile of Ethelreda, the pastry cook. He buried his face in his hands and tried to dismiss the image but with little success. The truth of the matter was that she had been the central point of his lustful fantasies for many years. The *real* truth of the matter was that Chef Bootes was madly and passionately in love with his fat slag of a flour-dusted pastry cook. The very thought of it terrified him. She must never *ever* find out. Never!

*

For Glimmergoyne, entering the Hall of Fire was always a moment to be savoured. To the right as he came through the servants' doors was the Great Staircase, a monument to many a grand and extravagant entrance. From the Reception Hall above one could look down upon the entire Hall of Fire. The huge fireplace that gave the room its name stood in an oval surround of quartz and marble with intricate gilt metal garnitures that dominated the middle of the floor. Fully twelve feet across, it had required a full-time fire-watcher just to keep it burning in its days of glory. Then it would have burned for fifteen hours of the day and have consumed several trees before it was doused.

Those were the days.

Today there would only be a small blaze set in the middle of the oval. One of the guard detail would carry out the fire setting duties in these days of straightened circumstances.

The tapestries depicting the heroic deeds of the many kings who had lived and caroused here in times past hanging around the walls had themselves seen many famous, and in some cases infamous, celebrities revelling with gusto. All the while the goings-on had been watched by the highly polished, shining suits of armour on black mahogany pedestals scattered around the hall. Helms and shields, misericordes and battle harnesses hung from the walls, mingling with the banners and pennants of a bygone, braver era. A time when honour had shone as brightly as the gleaming spearheads carried by the soldiery.

Sighing deeply, Glimmergoyne was woken from his reverie of times past by a bellow from the bandstand.

'Don't put that bit there, you imbecilic little moron. That won't bleedin' burn. To the left, man, to the left!'

'Good morning, Corporal Serpens!' called the butler wearily to the dapper little man in the bright red dress uniform smothered in gold braid.

'Good morning to you, Mr Glimmergoyne, sir. A nice day for it.'

'A nice day for what, Corporal?' asked Glimmergoyne, puzzled.

The little man just frowned, shrugged his shoulders and bellowed again, 'No, Private Second Class Gramm, you moron! Move the little log *there* to the *left*. Yes, that's better. Now that one. That one. No, not that one, the one I'm pointing at – look, do you *want* to have to clean the stables before lunch?'

Glimmergoyne shook his head in disbelief at the level of common sense in the soldiery of today. As thick as pig shit was a phrase that sprang readily to mind.

Glimmergoyne progressed up the huge, stately central staircase in his careful tempo one step at a time, between the exquisitely shaped marble columns that supported the highly polished mahogany banister rails. The early morning light was beginning to creep in through the windows on this level as he followed the balustrade, past the apartments of the Dowager Duchess Harmonia, to the florist's conservatory.

'Good morning, Philomena my dear,' he called pleasantly. 'Is it ready yet?'

'Ah, Mr Glimmergroyne. Always a pleasure to see you,' brayed a tall horse-faced woman who was watering the roses on a bench by the windows. 'Yes dear, the dianthus is on the table over there.'

'The white one?'

'The *dianthus floribunda*, yes.' She walked towards him, watering can grasped tightly in both hands. 'You really ought to know the names by now, Mr Glimmergroyne, you naughty boy you,' she said, braying with laughter once more.

'Look. All I want is a white carnation, Miss Philomena, not a lecture in bloody botany!' answered Glimmergoyne with more than a tinge of exasperation.

She brayed again showing him the full extent of her large, horse-like teeth, and said loudly, 'Oh Mr Glimmergroyne, you are a hoot. Shall I pin it on for you?'

'No thank you,' he said frostily, 'I can manage.'

'As you like,' she said and brayed again.

'I can manage, you silly cow,' Glimmergoyne muttered to her retreating back as he pinned the flower to his lapel. Why she had to use only stupid Latin names and not the good, strong common names for these things he never could fathom. She couldn't even pronounce his name properly for that matter.

The small fire in the Hall was well ablaze as he returned down the stairs. Mercifully the Captain had gone off about his duties and the vast room was quiet and peaceful once more. Glancing around at the polished suits of armour gleaming in the rays of the morning sun now pouring in through the vast windows of the East Wall, he took in the majestic ambience of the Hall. Stepping up to the nearest metallic mannequin, Glimmergoyne checked his tie and adjusted the white carnation in his lapel in the reflective surface of the breastplate before taking a turn around the room.

The glitter of the silverware on the long polished Great Dining Table gave him a thrill of pride.

Lacertus, the kitchen boy, was still buffing cutlery, giving the seven lonely looking place settings a final lustre before the arrival of the family.

'Ah, good morning Lacertus,' said the butler in his most affable manner. The boy was such an asset to the household, always working hard at something or other. His mother, Bessie, had been a chambermaid in the castle for a great many years.

'Good morning, Mr Glimmergoyne, and how are you this fine morning?' said the young man, smiling cheerfully.

Glimmergoyne, having been a bit of a ladies' man in his prime, secretly nurtured the fond belief that the boy was in actual fact his own son. Though this was an unproven, not to say unmentioned point, it gave him a feeling of paternal affection towards the boy from which both of them profited.

'Oh, I can't complain you know,' replied the old man, 'a few aches and pains but no more than normal at my age.'

'I'm sure you'll be good for many more years yet,' said Lacertus confidently.

'Well, I hope you are right boy. You know I have worked in this castle for over fifty years. I was only eleven years old when I came here as boot boy you know.'

'Is that so, Mr Glimmergoyne? Well I never!' said Lacertus groaning inwardly. Not the rags-to-immaculate-tailcoat story *again*! 'I imagine you'll be thinking of retiring soon then?'

'Oh no, not yet. Far too much to do first.'

'Not yet ready to be put out to pasture then, Mr Glimmergoyne?'

'Certainly not.'

With a smile the boy picked up another already shining spoon and began to polish it carefully.

'Is anybody coming to see…' he pointed to the ceiling with a jabbing motion of the spoon, 'today?'

'I believe so, yes. A Prince Scutum from some tiny out of the way realm. There is also the son of a tea merchant would you believe on the list. If either of them turn up today that is. I don't know. Traders in the family. Such a thing would never have happened in old King Monoceros's day, that I can tell you.'

'A bad business all round, Mr Glimmergoyne.'

'Indeed boy, indeed. Well, I can't stand here nattering all day. Time for breakfast I think. Will you be down?'

'Thank God for small mercies,' muttered Lacertus under his breath. 'Once I am done here, Mr Glimmergoyne, I shall be down.'

Glimmergoyne nodded happily, and strode off towards the stairway that led to the Servants' Hall.

Lacertus watched him disappear through the door with a great sense of relief. The old man was a fool. It was useful for an ambitious young man like himself to have an ally like the boring old coot of a butler, but he found the pretence of actually liking the man could be a real pain at times. Lacertus knew of the old man's secret paternal yearnings, but he also knew who his real father was. Many years ago his mother had let it slip. Things that were secret did not remain so for very long with Lacertus around. His *real* father was none other than the Duke of Vinatici himself. Lacertus was an ambitious young man, being the son of a duke when all was said and done, and in spite of the very minor point of the lack of actual proof of his legitimacy, his aims were high. He wanted to be King.

Nothing more and nothing less.

His plans, developed over long years of servitude and built on base cunning, had been carefully nurtured. The main objective would be getting the Princess Andromeda to marry him. Despite the fact that she was eight years older and rather ugly – well, very ugly if truth be told – he considered these things merely as drawbacks in the grand scheme of things. To this end he had so far managed to discourage, or otherwise deflect, about a dozen possible suitors for the Princess's hand.

The first real objective though would have to be the removal of the other runners from the field, namely the awesomely brain-dead Prince Pyxis Vulpecula, the son and heir, and his obnoxious little brother Ortolan Apus. Then, once the King either lost his marbles, was persuaded to abdicate or otherwise shucked off the reins of power, he, Lacertus, would move in and assume his rightful destiny. Her Ugliness, the Princess, could be dealt with at some later, as yet undefined, stage. She was, in a sense, the price to be paid for greatness. His intimate knowledge of the castle, both the public and private areas and all of the secret arteries connecting and interconnecting them in a honeycomb of dank and dismal passages, discovered through a single-minded effort to do just that, would soon prove to be invaluable.

In a few short weeks, on his eighteenth birthday the campaign would begin in earnest.

Lacertus stared into the depths of the blazing fire pit, rubbing the silver spoon on the cloth in his hands emphatically, an evil smile playing around his lips.

★

Breakfast in the Servants' Hall had been a dismal affair, as per usual, mused Glimmergoyne on his return trip to the Laundry. Matron Beamish had been nagging at Fornax again about his drinking, Columba, the under-maid, had been bemoaning her fate as the only under-maid over forty in the entire kingdom as she did with regular, mind-numbing monotony, and Antila, the petty little bean counter, had been moaning in his habitual high-pitched whine about the amount of food wasted to the fat, white-swathed figure of Chef Bootes who had studiously ignored him the whole time. He had studiously ignored everybody in fact. Morale was not what it had been when he had been a boy.

As Hydrus handed him the King's first clothing of the day, the formal but not too stiff grey suit with the subdued red stripes and diabolical mauve ones, Glimmergoyne found himself thinking of a small cottage by the sea. For the first time in his life he felt an intense desire to be somewhere other than Castle Camelopardis.

The very thought of such a thing frightened the life out of him.

Approaching the King's bedroom, just as he was about to rap on the thick, metal studded, wooden door, Glimmergoyne heard all hell break loose on the corridor above. Screams of pain intermingled with violent oaths and threats of bloodletting being imminent caused Glimmergoyne to dash, as fast as the butlers' regulated pace would allow anyway, up the circular staircase. There he found the ludicrous figure of His Highness the Crown

Prince Pyxis in his knee-length yellow and blue striped nightshirt dancing up and down on one foot, soaking wet from head to toe.

Calmly, the butler strode up to the hopping, swearing prince and slapped him hard across the cheek. Picking up the stunned youth, Glimmergoyne carried him bodily away from the broken glass that had mysteriously appeared from nowhere and set him down carefully in a glass-free space beside the wall. As he was examining the lacerated soles of the Crown Prince's feet he glanced up at the sound of a giggle and saw the Prince Ortolan Apus watching the action from the sanctuary of his own bedroom doorway.

'Ah, Your Highness? Would you be so good as to inform Matron Beamish that her presence is required here forthwith? Thank you.'

'You bloody little creep! I shall tell Father about this, just you wait and see...' shouted the suddenly conscious Pyxis at the retreating back of Ortolan, but he got no reply.

*

'Matron, Matron!' shouted the young Ortolan as he bounded down the stairs to the Servants' Hall.

'Why, mercy me, Orty, whatever's the matter?'

'It's Pyxis. He's hurt,' sobbed Ortolan throwing both his arms around the matron's ample waist.

'Oh dear,' she said, 'there, there now dear. Beamish is coming.'

'It's horrible, Beamy. He's blaming me for it. It wasn't me, honest.'

'There, there dear,' she said again in soothing tones, 'I'll get him sorted out. Never you mind. Here, have some hot tea while I go and see what's wrong.'

The smile on the face of the Prince Ortolan Apus as she picked up her small black medical bag and strode from the Hall was not as angelic as she would have liked to believe.

Arriving at the scene of the 'accident' with all the grace of a massive, blue cotton air balloon, Glimmergoyne looked up at the immensity of Matron Beamish from his crouched position on the floor and said with relief, 'Ah, Matron. Good of you to come so quickly.'

'No problem, Mr Glimmergoyne. What seems to be the trouble?'

'There are cuts to the soles of the feet here, and here. Well, all over the place actually. From that glass over there I surmise. There is a rather nasty bump and bruise on the side of the head caused by....' he looked at the boy pointedly and indicated, 'by that bucket I believe Your Highness said, is that correct?'

The miserable Pyxis grimaced unhappily.

'Let me have a look,' said Matron Beamish in her most conciliatory 'everything will be all right now' tone, and picked up one of the bloodstained feet to examine it more closely. 'Not as bad as it looks really. I've got some nice soothing cream in here somewhere,' she said brightly. Opening the bulky black Gladstone bag she started to rummage around inside.

'Um, Matron?'

'Yes Mr Glimmergoyne?'

'Why do you have a dead rat tied by its tail to your belt?

'Matron Beamish uttered a scream of such a piercingly loud, glass-shattering quality that Glimmergoyne was rendered totally deaf for several long minutes, while the King still safely tucked up in his bed on the floor below heard it quite clearly.

'That bloody Ortolan,' he muttered as he swung his feet out of bed, 'he'll have to go!'

Two

Through the early morning mist, the tall golden-haired figure of Izakiah Goldoor strode along the dirt track which, for want of a better word, was called a road.

There was a broad smile on his clean-cut, handsome features, not so much a smile of happiness, not so much a smile of anything at all really. It was the vacant smile of one who had discovered that it is easier to smile than to grimace. It required far less thinking about, far less mental effort.

The road led from his home village of Picton, a small isolated village in the middle of nowhere in particular, to the Mountains of Capheus which were most definitely a vast blue-grey shape right in the middle of the far horizon.

Goldoor had been walking for nearly two weeks by the time he arrived at the tiny hamlet of Borning Major, two weeks of living rough in hedgerows, barns and ditches, but the experience had done nothing to diminish the fervour of his stride, for Goldoor was a man on a mission. A man with a purpose in life.

Since he had eaten the last of the bread and cheese from his once cumbersome knapsack the previous day, he was feeling extremely hungry.

At a swift pace Goldoor walked down what appeared to be the main thoroughfare of Borning Major. The confident smile on his face wavered slightly, but only very slightly, as he passed the rows of cottages. All of the windows were covered or boarded up and the obviously once well-kept gardens were overrun with weeds. Some of the doors had large, crudely painted red crosses on them, though it did not occur to him to wonder why this should be. His simple mind was on a collision course with food.

An air of dismal decay, of lifeless dereliction, pervaded the genteel scene. Even the small village shop and bakery was as cold and empty as the rest of the street, not that he had any money anyway, but Goldoor was a sociable type and the absence of people unnerved him.

A dismal creak of wood from up ahead caught his attention.

The badly weathered inn sign swinging gently in the breeze looked as if it would fall down at any moment. There was a lamp burning in one of the grubby windows indicating at least the presence of an occupant, so Goldoor in the eternally optimistic high spirits of the slow-witted approached the entrance.

Maybe, just maybe, he could speak with the owner about repainting and re-hanging his sign in exchange for something to eat. The bright, hopeful smile on his face as he pushed open the rotting timbers that had once been a highly polished and perfectly serviceable door was received with only hard stares from the three occupants of the room.

'Good morning gentlemen!' he called cheerfully. 'Where is everybody? Not been a bout of plague or something in the area recently has there?' he said with a hearty laugh. A deathly silence fell on the already quiet room and the hard stares doubled and trebled their bleak intensity. 'Look, it was only a joke, I mean...' he began again but as his eyes met first one stony gaze followed by another glaring at him the laughter died on his lips.

'I say, look, um, I'm sorry. I mean, um...' he babbled, completely flustered by now. 'Is the, um, is the landlord here by any chance?'

The rat-faced, surly little man polishing glasses behind the bar stared at the tall, broad-shouldered newcomer for a long moment, 'An' who might be askin'?'

'I am.'

'An' who might "I" be?'

'I don't know,' said Goldoor puzzled. 'Who are you?'

The rat-faced man screwed up his eyes and looked at the boy again, quizzically.

'No, who might *you* be?'

'I know who I am,' Goldoor announced proudly. 'I am Izakiah Goldoor. From the village of Picton, away over yonder.' He waved his arm vaguely in completely the wrong direction. 'Who you are I don't know since I've only just arrived and you haven't told me yet.'

The winning smile he threw at the rat-faced man was so full of charm and so completely lacking in guile that the man put a hand to his eyes and pulled it slowly down his face. The boy was either exceptionally clever and hid it well, or a complete imbecile.

'Why do you want the landlord?' he asked, squinting.

'Well, I thought I might offer to repaint the shabby old inn sign hanging outside in exchange for a good meal,' said Goldoor enthusiastically and smiled again.

'You want to paint the sign?'

'Well, no, not really. I want something to eat you see, but since I don't have any money it seemed to be the most likely means of paying for some food. You see.'

Goldoor's pearly white teeth shone in the light oozing through the dirty windows. The rat-faced man took his hand from his grizzled chin and threw a sidelong glance at the two old men perched on stools at the end of the bar. He tapped his temple with his forefinger and made a universal gesture of disbelief before returning his attention to the stranger.

'So you want to repaint my sign in exchange for some food, is that it?'

'That's it in a nutshell,' said Goldoor nodding vigorously.

'I take it you have done this sort of thing before?' asked the rat-faced man suspiciously.

'Oh yes. Back home in Picton I am well known for "dipping my brush" so to speak,' replied Goldoor, still smiling.

A complete idiot then, thought the rat-faced man, shaking his head sadly. 'All right. You're on. There's some paint in the shed at the back. I'll get some food for you while you work.'

'Great!' said Goldoor. He smiled his most winning smile and waltzed out of the door.

'What were tha' all about Charlie?' asked one of the old men.

'Don't ask me,' answered the rat-faced man called Charlie. 'The boy's either a complete lame-brain, or a very good actor.' After few short moments, the cheerful smile accompanied by the rest of the blond head poked itself into the bar room.

'Excuse me?'

'Yes?' said Charlie with infinite patience.

'I say, um, could you tell me please, what's the name of the inn?'

'The name of the inn? "The Bishops Head",' said the rat-faced man called Charlie, with only a subtle trace of sarcasm. 'You *have* done this kind of thing before haven't you? I mean, you think you can manage that do you?'

'Oh yes. I've done plenty of heads. Back home in Picton. No worries,' said the smiling face as the head backed out of the door.

After a brief pause of total silence in the bar Charlie asked, 'So what do you reckon then, 'Arry? A nut case or what?' as he poured a stream of dark beer into a grubby old tankard.

'Dunno. 'E seems keen enough tho'. '

E can't possibly mek it any worse than it is now can 'e?' said the man at the bar.

'No. That is true,' said Charlie as he returned to the desultory glass polishing he had been involved in before the interruption. 'That is very true.'

An hour later, the voice of Goldoor called through the rotting ruin of a doorway, 'Right then chaps, it's done.'

'This I've got to see,' said Charlie, lifting the flap of the bar and walking towards the voice. The two old men exchanged a quick smirk and followed him. Outside, they found a happily smiling, paint-spattered Goldoor.

'There you are,' said the golden-haired young man smugly, pointing up at the now brightly painted square of wood. 'What do you think? Be honest now.'

Charlie looked up at the sign and shook his head sadly. He took in the bright orange, laughing face with triangular black eyes. A crudely shaped red mitre balanced precariously in the approximate position of the top of the head and splashes of purple in the approximate region of the shoulders clashed violently with a lime green scarf.

'What the *hell* is that? What have you done to my sign?' he muttered through clenched teeth. 'I thought you said you'd done plenty of heads. What kind of heads were they? Bloody scarecrows?'

'Well, yes as a matter of fact…'

Charlie buried his head in his hands and shook slowly in despair while the two old men from the bar howled with laughter and punched each other like a couple of school children.

'Is something wrong?' asked Goldoor, smiling innocently. 'Don't you like it? You don't like it, do you?'

The nasty hurtful words of the rat-faced Charlie were still ringing in his ears five miles later. It wasn't right for him to have said the things he did. How was a poor, simple woodsman's son from Picton supposed to know what a bishop looked like anyway? Life was so unfair.

Striding morosely over the rise of a small hill, Goldoor caught his first glimpse of the monstrosity that was known as Castle Camelopardis. The sight of it, sitting on its heap of granite with its many-paned, multi-faceted windows gleaming in the afternoon sun, cheered the downcast Goldoor immensely. The smile returned to his face as he took in the eclectic jumble of windows and the conglomeration of the many and various types of stone and masonry used in its construction. From this distance it had the look of a battered and discarded child's toy. Having been built by many hands at many different times without any kind of central game plan, Castle Camelopardis represented the refined, tasteful architect's worst nightmare. Goldoor thought it was the most beautiful sight he had ever seen in his life. Besides which of course, *she* lived there. The love of his life.

His mind, or at least that portion of it that was not directly involved in the day to day maintenance of the face-splitting smile, drifted back to Picton, to that fateful summer's day when the awful old pedlar woman who had caused all the trouble had rolled up in her grotty, smelly old wagon drawn by a grotty, smelly old pony. She had knocked most politely on the door of the little wooden shack he shared with his elderly parents, and the gesture had marked the turning point in his life. First of all it had been quite innocent. A bit of palm reading and a touch of the hard sell on some battered, second or third-hand saucepans. It was when she had produced the miniature portrait that his previously contented soul had changed. The pale-faced, blonde, high-cheekboned image had caught his imagination as nothing he had ever known before had.

'I *say*! Who is she?' he had demanded. 'Where can I find her?' At first the old crone had been reticent about telling him. It had taken all the coins he had in his purse to persuade her to part with the tiny picture. He then had to give the cart a complete overhaul, including greasing the axles and a paint job, before she would tell him. It was, she had finally announced, the Princess Andromeda of Camelopardis.

★

The argument with his parents lasted the next two days and nights as he tried to explain his need to find this girl. He smiled as he remembered his father's words,

'Izzy, Izzy my boy. Please, just think about this. Think with your head and not with your—'

'Eric!' his mother screamed. 'I won't have language like that in *this* house. And definitely not in front of the boy!'

'Oh. Right dear. Sorry.'

And that had been that.

The following day he had waved goodbye to them both, his heavily laden knapsack slung over his immense shoulders. Without a backward glance he had set off to find Castle Camelopardis. As soon as he was happily married and living in the splendid castle that his limited imagination made Camelopardis out to be, he would send for them both, to show them that he had been right all along.

Then they could all live happily ever after.

With a wistful sigh he tore his gaze from the awesome sight of the gigantic edifice, and turned his steps towards the small village nestled at the foot of the castle promontory.

★

The village of Leopardis had started life as the base camp for the early builders of the castle. As the years passed and the sporadic building work stuttered along, so the workers, faced with long years away from their families had brought them here, lock, stock and baby carriage. The very houses they built for themselves showed the same diverse stonework and architecture as that used for the castle itself. As each successive generation of builders had used any remaining materials for their own accommodation it came about that red brick mingled with wattle and daub, flint with marble slab and granite blocks with oaken beams, all in a confused mélange of styles and fashions.

As is common with settlements of this type, one of the oldest buildings was the hostelry, built only a few hundred yards from the Gatehouse that marked the start of the road to the castle.

Goldoor stood and looked up at the inn sign. 'The Artisan's Arms,' he read slowly, his lips moving as his eyes followed the words. He shrugged his shoulders despairingly and shook his head as he pushed open the door. Arms were a different colour of penguin altogether.

The early evening crowd around the bar appeared to have been the early morning crowd around the bar as well, judging by the raucous shouting and singing that was going on.

Striding confidently up to the bar Goldoor flashed his magnificent smile at the big florid man standing behind the counter and asked gaily, 'I say, are you by any chance the landlord?' The lamplight glittered on his brilliantly polished white teeth.

'That I am,' said the man cheerfully. 'Who wants to know?'

'Izzy Goldoor,' he said through the glittering teeth. 'I wonder if I might have a word with you?'

The very nasty and hurtful things shouted at him by the rat-faced Charlie kept Goldoor from mentioning his painting abilities as he asked the large man for a job of some description. A job and, more importantly, food. The rat-faced Charlie had given him only a measly lump of cheese and a mouldy piece of dry bread for all his effort. And that was over four days ago now.

'I'll do most things,' he said eagerly, 'all I need is a bed and lodging for a little while.'

'Can you chop wood?'

'Oh yes, at home in Picton I—'

'Lift barrels and crates?'

'Yes, at home I—'

'Scrub floors and whitewash walls?'

'Er, yes, I mean back home I—'

'You're hired. The woodshed's out the back. You can start there.'

'Um, yes. Thank you Mr… Mr…'

'Call me Fred.'

'Right. Mr Fred. I'll start now shall I? Tonight?' he began but the landlord had already bustled off to serve another customer.

With a shrug of his immense shoulders, Goldoor turned and left the bar.

Goldoor squeezed himself out of the rickety old back door and approached the ramshackle building that he supposed was the woodshed. He glanced upwards momentarily at the vast mass of the castle on top of its hill looming up towards the darkening sky. He sighed deeply as the windows caught the last rays of the dying sun. At least he was in sight of Castle Camelopardis. Close to *her*, to his love.

Lighting a long yellow candle, one of a pair he found on the workbench in the shed, and picking up the short-handled axe in his great paw, Goldoor began to hack away at the huge piles of logs littering the floor of the shed. Mr Fred appeared after about an hour with a tray of what appeared to be kitchen scraps. With a thankful smile, Goldoor ate the entire trayful without a second thought as to their origin. In all probability he would have eaten the tray as well had Mr Fred not whipped it away immediately.

At about midnight, when the second candle had guttered out and he could find no more, he decided to get some sleep. Curling himself up on a heap of rags and tarpaulins piled in a corner of the shed, he pulled a small picture frame from his knapsack and gazed lovingly at the tiny meticulously painted image that had cost him so dear.

'Goodnight, my darling,' he said aloud. 'Soon we will be together.'

With a sigh he put the portrait against the wall, close to his head and passed into a deep, peaceful sleep. As he did so, the small face of the Princess Andromeda Vulpecula of Camelopardis smiled down at him.

★

Goldoor had always been an early riser. Standing in the early dawn with the axe in his hand made him think once more of home. At home in Picton he had worked with his father as a woodsman. It had been a very quiet, idyllic lifestyle, he realised, now that he had been out in the big wide world for two whole weeks. The voice of Mr Fred the landlord broke into his reverie.

'What the fook do you think you're playing at, mekkin' all that racket first thing in the mornin'?' he shouted, with the pale green look of the terminally hungover.

'Good morning, Mr Fred. Nearly done now,' said Goldoor. 'What time is breakfast?'

'Breakfast? What do you think this is? A bloody doss house or summat?'

Mr Fred's voice trailed off as his bloodshot eyes caught sight of the huge pile of neatly stacked cords of firewood.

'You've done all that by yourself?' he asked in disbelief.

'Nobody else Mr Fred.'

'Bloody 'ell. Sorry, I mean I'll go tell the wife to get the eggs on.'

As he turned and shambled off towards the inn, a faint 'Bloody 'ell!' from Mr Fred floated back to Goldoor, and he picked up the axe once more, smiling gently.

At seven thirty, when Fred called him in for breakfast, Goldoor was just stacking the last of the kindling in the shed. Arriving at the kitchen door he was ushered in by the round, red-faced and portly figure of a woman. There he found a large wooden table with a sumptuous feast laid out on it that covered the bare boards.

'There you go lovey, get stuck in. I'm the fat little git's wife for me sins,' the portly woman said and cackled hideously. 'But *you* can call me Deidre,' with a sly wink.

'Oh, great, food! I say, this is grand,' he said rubbing his hands together and completely missing the point of her words. Sitting down, he grabbed a plate and started to fill it with great mounds of bacon and eggs, covered with dollops of butter and hunks of bread. Clutching a cup of coffee in his two hands, the seriously unwell Fred looked awestruck as the pile of food began to disappear.

'Bloody hell!' he said softly.

'You not eating, Mr Fred?' asked Goldoor solicitously.

'Later. Not just now,' said Mr Fred, a little green around the gills.

'You shouldn't drink so much, Mr Fred. My mother says that

alcohol is the evil of the working classes. She says it shouldn't be allowed. It disrupts your ability to work and ruins your liver. She says that the best cure is pig's blood. Raw pig's blood mixed with raw egg yolks and lemon… Mr Fred? Are you all right over there, Mr Fred?'

Deidre snorted over the washing up as Mr Fred made a dash for the door. Goldoor turned back to his food shaking his head gently. The sounds of the overweight, not so florid now, innkeeper being violently ill in the flowerbeds outside caused him to smile smugly.

'Serves you right!' he said in a self-satisfied tone.

'Your mother sounds like a sensible woman, lovey,' said Mrs Fred.

By lunchtime, Goldoor had completely whitewashed the entire shed, inside and out. He was just washing the brushes when Fred came out of the inn with a large jug of ale and an empty tankard. 'I just brought you a some…' he stopped in his tracks when he saw Goldoor and the gleaming white paintwork. 'Bloody hell!'

'Thank you, Mr Fred,' boomed Goldoor, 'just what I needed.' He drained the jug in one smooth swallow, not bothering to touch the tankard.

'Bloody hell!' said Fred. 'I thought your mother was against drinking?'

'Only to excess, Mr Fred, only to excess.'

'Bloody hell!'

'Do you have to keep saying that? It's not very nice you know. My mother says…'

'Sorry. Bad habit. It just sort of slips out, like.'

'That's all right,' smiled the irrepressible youth. 'I thought I might take a stroll round the village this afternoon if that's all right with you, Mr Fred?'

'Yes, yes of course. As you please. I only came out here to get a keg of Best.'

Mr Fred gingerly stepped through the painted doorway. After a short stunned silence an unintelligible scream of dismay came from the obviously distressed Mr Fred, until finding more suitable words he shouted, 'Why the hell have you painted all the bloody beer barrels, you useless great moron? I'll have your guts for garters you imbecilic great oaf!'

By the time he reached the door, Goldoor had already crept quietly away.

'I'll kill him,' muttered Fred, 'I swear I'll kill the stupid bugger!'

★

Goldoor neared the Gatehouse of Castle Camelopardis with a fair degree of apprehension. Maybe he should wait until he had been in the village for a few days before trying the direct approach. Once or twice he had stopped, turned as if to return to the inn, thought of Mr Fred and the beer barrels and had turned to face the Gatehouse once more. Inside the building, Private Second Class Crux was watching this display of hopeless indecision with an air of disbelief.

'Nutter on the starboard bow, Corporal,' he said over his shoulder. In an instant the slight figure of Corporal Serpens in the bright red cap with the shiny black peak was at his side.

'Where away?'

'Yonder, under the crooked elm,' said Crux pointing.

'What's he doing?'

'Dancing. I think.'

'Dancing? Here? Very suspicious. Call Private Second Class Gramm, we may need him.'

Poking his head out of the window, he shouted, 'You. I say, you there. What do you think you are doing? This is private property y'know.'

Goldoor turned again at the sound of the voice, smiled his most winning smile at the nice man in the shiny peaked cap and walked forward.

'Hello,' he said cheerfully, 'I wonder could you help me. Only I need to get to the castle you see. I have an – what do you call those things now?' He creased his brow and searched for the right word. 'Ah yes, an appointment.'

'Who with?'

'Uum, with er, with the Princess Andromeda if you must know.'

'Her Royal Highness is expecting *you*?' asked Serpens incredulously.

'Well, she doesn't actually know that I'm coming yet but she will be ever so pleased to see me.'

'You're right,' murmured Corporal Serpens over his shoulder, 'he is a nutter. Get Private Second Class Gramm here double quick. A big one this. He could be trouble.' And then to Goldoor, 'And why do you suppose that is Mr, erm, Mr?'

'Goldoor. Izzy Goldoor. From Picton,' he said with a wave towards the forestless mountains, and once again gave the smile full of teeth. 'She will want to meet the man she is going to marry, I would have thought.'

A badly suppressed snort of laughter escaped the Corporal.

'Look, if you are not going to take me seriously I shall demand to see your superior and…'

'Sorry,' a snigger, 'but I thought you said,' a giggle, 'that you was going to,' another snort, 'to marry the Princess?' A loud guffaw.

'If you are going to take that tone my man…'

Corporal Serpens's head disappeared backwards into the room as he spoke and the sounds of uncontrollable laughter from deep inside could be heard quite clearly by the confounded Goldoor. He had expected some kind of response, but not this.

'I say there,' he called, 'I don't think you are taking this seriously enough. I must get into the castle today. Only…' A fresh burst of laughter, this time from several different voices, incensed Goldoor into action. He was going to have to report this stupid little man to the Princess. Get him sacked or fired or whatever it is they did with soldiers. He turned on his heel and strode off down the path.

'You'll regret this!' he shouted back over his shoulder, only to be answered with another even louder peal of laughter.

Red-faced with shame he made his way, deep in thought about what to do next, back to The Artisan's Arms. As deep in thought as he ever managed to get that is.

★

34

The very same midday sunlight that witnessed the embarrassment of our hero by the Gatehouse was by now streaming in through the windows of Castle Camelopardis itself. The Princess Andromeda stretched herself and yawned widely. Never renowned as an early riser she was actually conscious before midday today.

'Who have we got today I wonder?' she mused, pouting into the large, oval dressing table mirror and applying some rouge in the approximate region of what could have been high, delicately chiselled cheekbones but weren't.

'I'm sure I don't know, Your Highness,' said the maid softly.

'Who was talking to you? Get on with your cleaning, girl. And don't slouch.'

'Yes Ma'am,' whispered the maid, dejectedly.

It has been mentioned vaguely in passing that the Princess Andromeda was ugly. The truth of the matter is that she was hideous. This was a fact known to all in the kingdom with the possible exception of two. One of them being herself.

Her lack of even a trace of prettiness, combined with not a vestige of feminine charm or grace, was legendary. The fate of the prospective suitor who had compared her face to an elephant's backside served as a warning to all who followed. Two years later he still walked with a limp, wore a leather truss and spoke with a harsh lisp. The elephant was rumoured to have been pretty upset when he heard about the remark as well, it is said.

Looking across at the large-breasted maid brushing down the long, richly embroidered, pristine white, wedding dress hanging in a place of honour on the far wall the Princess Andromeda of Camelopardis suddenly bellowed, 'Stop that you stupid girl! I'm not going to need that thing today. Some days I think you do that just to upset me. Get my shawl and slippers and be quick about it. And don't slouch.'

Lyra, the pretty, young, large-breasted maid, nervously dropped the clothes brush as the loud coarse voice echoed around the room.

'Yes Your Highness,' she whispered.

'And pick up that bloody brush!' bawled the Princess, causing the glass in the window frames to rattle. If there was one thing she really hated first thing in the morning it was pretty, young, large-

breasted maids tarting around with her dress.
  'And *don't* slouch!'

Three

In his small, private office adjacent to the Throne Room, King Vulpecula of Camelopardis sat at his vast hand-carved desk. Ostentatiously ornate it was an object, a relic, from the days when wood was plentiful and labour was cheap.

'So what exactly did this man do that aroused your suspicions?' asked the King.

Corporal Serpens shifted uneasily from one foot to the other and looked nervously about him.

'Tell his Majesty what the man said to arouse your suspicions, Corporal, and tell him now. The King hates to be kept waiting you know,' purred the cultured voice of Captain Parsus of the Royal Guard. Cold, pin-sharp eyes belied the amused smile on his face.

'Erm. Well,' Serpens swallowed hard, 'Private Second Class Crux informed me that there was an unusual *personage* dancing.' He swallowed hard again. 'Dancing under the elm.'

'And did you ask this *personage* what he wanted?' oozed the voice of Captain Parsus.

'Yes sir. He said he wanted to, to… wanted to meet the Princess Andromeda, sir,' he blurted suddenly.

'Now that is bloody suspicious!' said the King. 'What is the point of all this, Parsus? Why are you wasting my time with nutters?'

'Why don't you tell His Majesty what else the nutter said?' The face still smiled but the oily voice was full of dire threat.

'He said,' gulp, 'he said that,' his eyes shot from expectantly waiting face to expectantly waiting face, 'he said that he wanted to marry the Princess Andromeda, Sire!' blurted the terror stricken Corporal.

The King's eyes widened and his jaw dropped several feet towards the desk, 'And you let him go?' he whispered. 'He *wanted* to marry her and you let him go?'

'Well, you see, he looked so down at heel and not the sort of material that would fit with the Royal image and I thought... I thought...'

The thin voice trailed off pathetically under the vicious glare of the King.

'Do you know the odds I could have got on even a *proposal* of marriage from the Duke of Leophus alone?' he said coldly. 'If I could have got the bloody millstone actually married off, I would have been able to refloat the entire bloody economy.'

'But Sire, I thought that, you know, a Princess and all that—'

'You are not *supposed* to think, Private Serpens. That is for your elders and betters! Now, I would strongly suggest that you go and find this nutter and see if he is still interested. If he is, I may reinstate your stripe. If he isn't...'

The King's voice trembled with barely suppressed rage, but the voice tailed off, the threat unspoken.

'Yes sir. Thank you sir. I shall go now shall I, sir?'

'*Get out!*'

'On the double, Private!' said the suave tones of Captain Parsus, adding quite unnecessarily, 'And be quick about it.'

'Yes sir, sorry sir,' muttered the pitiful, newly created, Private Serpens backing ungracefully out of the door.

It was only a knock on the door that connected directly with the bursar's office that stopped the King from shouting rude remarks unfitting of a royal personage after the retreating back.

'Damn. See what the little bugger of a penny-pincher wants now, Parsus,' he said abruptly to the Captain.

Striding to the door, Captain Parsus yanked it open, causing the insignificant shape of Chancellor Antila to fall forwards into the room.

'S-S-Sorry, I couldn't help but overhear...' stuttered the nervous, mousey little chancellor.

'What is it now, Bursar?' asked the King wearily.

'She's called them out again, Your Highness. Leopardis Organ Replacement and Repair Service. Another eighty ducat bill that we can't afford!'

The King hid his head in his hands and mumbled to himself quietly about the trials and tribulations of being a poor king in a rich man's castle.

'All right, Antila,' he said quietly, raising his face, 'I'll have a word with her.'

'Thank you, Your Majesty. Thank you so very much.'

Chancellor Antila backed out obsequiously, thankful that he hadn't been blamed for anything this time and closed the door softly behind him.

'I know!' said the King suddenly with a manic smile on his face, his eyes round and shining. 'I'll shoot the lot of 'em. I'll start with the obnoxious Ortolan Apus and work my way up.'

'Nice idea, Sire,' said Captain Parsus with his oily smile slicked greasily into place.

In the darkness of his hiding place within the King's private spiral staircase, Lacertus also smiled. An idea of stupendous proportions was beginning to form in his mind. The lynchpin would be the nutter.

He, Lacertus, would have to locate him before the unfortunate Private Serpens did. Then he could persuade the poor unfortunate person to try and get into Camelopardis, into the Princess's private chambers and he, Lacertus, could then rush in and save her from his clutches. The prestige would be enormous if he could pull it off. Quietly he crept down the steeply winding stairs to the Servants' Hall to prepare for a foray into Leopardis. He was also in quiet agreement with the King's plans for his family, but in most cases, especially that of the obnoxious Ortolan, shooting would be too good for them.

*

Goldoor sat heavily on a barstool in The Artisan's Arms and reflected on the cruelties of life, as he stared into the depths of his beer tankard. Mr Fred had bawled and ranted about those stupid beer barrels for close on an hour after he had returned from the embarrassment of the Guardhouse experience. And then the fat little man had laughed like a loon when the poor lovelorn Goldoor had described the events to him by way of partial explanation. He had said some very hurtful things about his lady love. If he hadn't been so depressed he would have punched the fat slob in the face.

Goldoor was plunged so deep in his own grief and despair that he did not notice the dark-haired young man pull up a stool beside him and order two beers.

'Excuse me,' said the young man with a polite cough, 'but you're new around here aren't you?'

Goldoor turned his glazed expression to face the stranger.

'What?'

'I said you're new around here aren't you?'

Goldoor's eyes drifted into focus and looked directly at the young man. If he so much as brushes my knee with his fingers, I'll definitely punch him, thought Goldoor.

'What's that to you?' he asked suspiciously.

'I've heard that you were interested in gaining access', the low voice dropped almost to a whisper, 'to a certain not-to-be-named building.'

'What? The castle?'

'Shh. I said don't name it.'

'Name what?' frowned Goldoor.

'The castle!' hissed the dark-haired young man.

'You just said don't…' said Goldoor loudly.

'Shhhhhh,' hissed Lacertus.

'Oh. Sorry.'

'That's all right. Now I have friends. I may be able to help you.'

'Why should you want to help me?'

'Let's just say I have a vested interest in the ah, the outcome.'

Goldoor looked around the bar warily but nobody appeared to be listening,

'Tell me more,' he whispered conspiratorially.

*

Up at the castle, Glimmergoyne's day was not progressing very well. The family lunch had been as farcical as the staff bash had been. The wimp Pyxis had moaned throughout about his stupid head and painful feet and the old bag of a Duchess had complained five times about her egg being overcooked which eventually turned out to be a rubber substitute put on her plate by the insufferable little creep Ortolan. Later still, His Majesty had refused the subtle red and mauve striped suit against Glimmergoyne's manifest protests and insisted on the yellow and lime green tweeds that made him look so obese. The meeting with the Duke of Leophus had gone badly. The man was insisting on his hapless son, Corporal Tucana of the Royal Guard, getting a promotion before he would cough up the donation to the Royal coffers for this quarter. The King had to agree of course. Money was tight enough as it was. Then to cap it all, the messenger had arrived to say that the coach carrying the next of the prospective 'husbands' – the 'Teaboy' – had lost a wheel and would be unavoidably detained for up to two days.

Glimmergoyne could not understand the reluctance of the young men of the realm to come forward. They did not have to actually *like* the Princess, nor even be seen in close proximity to her afterwards. All they had to do was hand over the money, sign the papers and live on the prestige happily ever after. Maybe the King had set the dowry too high? A shameful state of affairs at the best of times but, when all was said and done, it did take a lot of money to run a castle this size.

In the midst of these dismal thoughts there came a thunderous knocking at the door on the level above. Glimmergoyne listened for a few moments to hear who it might be. After a few moments, when nothing happened, he heard the thunderous knocking again. Where's Viktor got to now? he thought making his stately progress up the staircase from the Hall of Fire.

'Viktor?' he called aloud, 'Viktor, there's someone at the door. Where are you?'

'Here I am, Mr Glimmergoyne.' The voice of Viktor floated across from the depths of the high-backed, green leather hall porter's chair in the far corner,

'I am taking my official tea break, as outlined in the Footmen, Doormen and Ancillary Staff Union handbook (FDASU). It quite clearly states that the employee, i.e. myself, is entitled to fifteen minutes for necessary refreshment every three hours. I still have four and a half minutes left. Get it yourself.'

The loud hammering was more impatient this time, insistent. Fuming at the horrible little doorman and muttering oaths under his breath, Glimmergoyne opened the heavy wooden doors to reveal the dirty figure of Hugo Lepus, the organ repair operative from Leopardis Organ Replacement and Repair Services.

'Oh. It's only you.'

'Who were you expecting? The Queen of bloody Sheba?' said the surly little man. '*She* needs a fixer *again*. Got the call just now.'

'Well, you know the way. You should do by now. Take off that ridiculous cap and get going.'

'Yes *sir*,' said the Fixer and shot him an evil look as he made his way past.

Closing the huge doors with some effort, Glimmergoyne reflected once more on the vagaries of life; on the fact that a man in his position and at his time of life still had to open doors for grotty little tradespeople.

Turning on his heel to go back down the stairs he found that Viktor, the diminutive doorman, had appeared at his side.

'All done. The rule book is satisfied, as indeed I am. Thank you, Mr Glimmergoyne.'

Viktor did not even see the heavy roundhouse blow coming and the force of it lifted him from his feet and sent him sprawling on his back across the polished marble floor.

'Stick that in your rule book and eat it. Useless bloody clock-watcher!' said Glimmergoyne, pulling down his immaculate sleeves and dusting them off with his hands as he stalked off.

Viktor from his prone position on the floor just rubbed his chin with his hand and glared at the smartly attired back of the butler as it descended the stairs to the Hall of Fire.

*

'All I did was to press the key, that one there, the white one, and I broke a nail. Can you believe it? I want it replaced now. Today. Horrible thing!' whined the voice of Queen Berenice.

'No problem, your Ladyship,' replied the servile tones of the Fixer from the depths of the ripped out keyboards of the huge great Wurlitzer Organ, 'no problem at all.'

'I just don't understand it,' whined the tall, white-clad Queen from her large heavy parlour chair, 'it was no trouble yesterday. Do *you* understand it, Pettigrew?'

The ladies' maid tying a neat bow on a crepe bandage around

the damaged digit replied,

'No, your Ladyship, I don't understand it at all.' Ten years of nursing the Queen Berenice through broken nails and bruised thumbs had all but left her immune to understanding anything the stupid woman did or said.

'I'm sure the nice man will be able to fix it for you. Then you can carry on with your practise. Won't that be nice?'

'Yes. Yes it will. I really do think I'm starting to get the hang of it you know.'

Pettigrew stood up as she finished and said, 'I'll bring you a nice cup of tea while you're waiting, shall I?'

'Yes, thank you Pettigrew. It's the shock that gets to one you know.'

'I know, I know,' said Pettigrew as she dropped a curtsey and left the room.

★

The clatter of hooves and the creak of overstressed timber announced the imminent arrival of the stately, but severely dilapidated, royal carriage to the watchers in the Guardhouse. Only the heavy iron bars bolted to the window and door frames had any feel of permanence in the trembling mess. As the carriage drew to a juddering halt in front of the massive gates the much-stressed horses coughed and steamed in the cool of the afternoon. The red uniformed guard on the box seat at the back had the look of a man in severe shock. His hands gripped the support bar in front of him, white knuckled, while the look in his eyes suggested sheer, unadulterated terror.

A chubby little man in the blue and gold livery of Castle Camelopardis climbed drunkenly down from the box and staggered over to the doors. Lifting his fist he hammered at the solid wood.

'Gues' for the Cas'le. Open up theer. The Prince Cirsic... Cirsic... Circinus of Corna... Cornia... Cornucopia for the Pri'cess An'romeda,' he slurred.

A small hatch swung open in the top of the door and the face of Private Second Class Gramm appeared, his jaws chewing on an unmentionably large amount of something or other, popped out.

'Wot?' spluttered the face. 'Not now. I'm 'avin' me tea!' and the hatch slammed shut.

Incensed, the coachman lurched forward and hammered once more: 'I 'ave himpor'ant business wi' tha Pri'cess An'romeda. I 'as a guest for 'er!' he shouted. 'Now open this bleedin' door afore I puts you on report. I'm already owerdue by... by...!' He pulled a large gold pocket watch from his waistcoat and tried unsuccessfully to open it. 'Oh sod that,' he said stuffing it back in his pocket. 'I'm already late. Now jus' open this bleedin' door you igno... igno... you dolt.'

Finally managing to disengage his fists, the trembling body and staring eyes of Corporal Corvus came up behind the coachman.

'Open up Gramm,' he said trying to put some kind of authority into his terror-stricken voice, 'unless you want to be cleaning the stables for the next month.'

After a brief silence, the bolts were heard being drawn back very slowly. As the two huge doors were pulled slowly open a small voice said, 'Sorry sir,' obsequiously.

An enormous shape, wrapped rather than dressed in the Red Guard livery, stood in their place.

'I was 'avin' me tea,' he said, by way of explanation.

'It's not good enough, Gramm,' said Corporal Corvus, regaining his composure somewhat. 'Is there nobody else here? Where's your second? Sleeping I suppose.'

'No sir. Honest. Private Volans has gone with Private Serpens on a nutter hunt, sir.'

'*Private* Serpens? A *nutter* hunt?' incredulously. 'You are talking in riddles, Gramm. I shall sort this out with Captain Parsus.'

'Yes sir,' muttered Gramm.

'Righ' the' sur. Shall us be off?' slurred the coachman, swaying gently at his side.

'Ah, no,' said Corvus looking up the sloping carriageway with its steep drop on one side, 'No. I think I shall walk if you don't mind.'

'As yo' like sur,' said the coachman clambering clumsily back onto the box and picking up the reins. With a crack of his whip at the still steaming horses the coach lurched forward ungracefully. Watching the carriage pass through the tunnel, Corporal Corvus felt a certain degree of relief at still being on solid ground.

As the coach passed the stone pillars on the other side, already going at a fair lick despite the knackered horses, it lurched once more, hit the far pillar and seemed to disintegrate in slow motion. The horses, released from their burden, leapt forward joyously, pulling the blue-coated coachman still clutching the long reins in his fists, with them. The battered young man who leapt from the wreckage smiled maniacally, shouted, 'Free, ha ha, *Free!*' and dashed off towards the village, the chains on his wrists jangling as he picked up speed.

Quickly, but not quickly enough, Corporal Corvus tried to set off in hot pursuit. His legs, still trembling with the terror of the high-speed coach ride, would not function in proper order and after only a few steps he fell face down into the dusty road.

'Damn, damn, *damn!*' he muttered. Private Second Class Gramm gazed down at him for a moment and then ambled across to where he lay and asked dutifully,

'Are you all right, sir?'

'Report to Corporal Equuleus in the stables, Private Second Class Gramm. Immediately!' said Corporal Corvus to the road under his face.

*

In the early evening sunlight, The Dowager Duchess Harmonia sat in the huge embroidered armchair in the Tower Room of Queen Berenice Vulpecula. The rest of the room was filled with the huge, voluminous, tuneless rumbling of the multi-keyboard Wurlitzer organ being hammered to death by the Queen herself.

The old lady felt the tears rolling down her cheek, only the left one since the right eye was a glass one, and smiled happily. Being completely tone deaf was an asset when one's daughter-in-law, after ten years of diligent practise, only managed to hit one good note in ten. Even the Queen's beloved spaniel would leave the room with his stump of a tail between his legs when his mistress started to play. As the final notes of a particularly horrendous, barely recognisable rendition of 'Danny Boy' died away the elderly Duchess applauded enthusiastically and said, 'Lovely dear, very beautiful. Almost a good as my dear old mum used to play it.'

The Queen simpering under the adulation was about to ask if an encore would be appreciated, when the doors were flung open and King Vulpecula stormed in.

'Right. Shut that racket up. Now!' he said loudly. So far he too had not had a very good day and things looked like going downhill very rapidly.

'What the hell do you mean by calling out that outrageously expensive repair man again?' he fumed. 'Didn't I spend *four hours* yesterday explaining to you the financial state this castle is in? Are you just trying to upset me?'

'But dearest, the horrid key broke my nail. I had to have it changed. Otherwise my playing would have been disturbed.'

'I think you must be disturbed.'

'Peccy. Just hold with that kind of talk. Honestly, since you became King your manners have deteriorated very badly.'

King Vulpecula cringed. How he hated that stupid nursery name, 'Oh, Mumsy. Sorry Mumsy. I didn't know you were there,' he said abjectly.

'Well I am. Do you think your poor dear father would have talked to *me* like that?'

'Look Mumsy, the thing is we just don't have the money any more and then that accident this afternoon with the carriage there may not be any more coming in for a while…'

'Excuses, excuses. You're King aren't you? Go and institute a new tax or something. That's what your poor dear father always used to do.'

'Things have changed, Mumsy dear, the populace don't like all these taxes we have now. If I—'

'Piffle!' exclaimed the old lady, 'The populace love their Royal Family, they loved your poor dear old dad and they still love me. Just because you're soft, overweight and unpopular doesn't mean your family should do without.'

'But eighty ducats a time is daylight robbery!'

'The Queen Berenice needs to practise and that means proper equipment,' said the Duchess sharply.

The Queen simpered again more volubly at this welcome burst of support and enjoyed the look of discomfort on the Royal visage.

'But Mumsy I—'

'No buts. Just go and organise your finances in a proper Kingly fashion and everything will be all right again. And don't let me hear that you've been persecuting the poor dear Queen Berenice for your own shortcomings.'

She switched her attention back to the Queen and said sweetly, 'Right my dear, where were we? 'Danny Boy' I think wasn't it?'

'Again Duchess?' simpered the Queen.

'Yes dear, it's such a lovely tune.'

'I'll go and see the bursar then, shall I?' said the King but the two women simply ignored him.

As the awesome swelling sound of the mighty organ hit a string of duff notes under the leaden fingers of Queen Berenice, he cringed.

'Yes, that's what I shall do. I'll go and see the chancellor,' he repeated softly, but he had the distinct impression that he had already been dismissed.

*

'What do you mean the carriage has not arrived yet?' demanded Glimmergoyne of the grinning doorman.

'I mean that it has not arrived yet,' replied Viktor, relishing the stiff, old butler's dismay.

'But I've just seen the coachman staggering across the courtyard. The coach must be here too. And what's he done with today's applicant? That Circinus fellow.'

'Coachman and horses are back true enough, but the coach is still down by the Gatehouse. In about ten thousand pieces by all accounts. Dunno where the poor devil of a candidate got to either. If he's got any sense he's legged it.'

'Ye Gods!' swore Glimmergoyne vehemently. 'What has the drunken bastard done this time? I'll have his hide for this.'

'I should like to take this opportunity to remind you, Mr Glimmergoyne, that under rule twenty seven of the current edition of the FDASU handbook members are to be treated with due respect at all times. Physical violence performed on a member will be very heavily frowned upon and, and…' his voice tailed off under the cold, hard gaze of the solemn-faced butler.

'You stupid little man!' he said in the cold, hard, clearly enunciated tone that went with the look. 'Sod the bloody handbook. I'll skin him and you as well if I have a mind. Now just get out of my way.'

He stalked out of the door shaking his head. Viktor gazed after him with hate-filled eyes.

'Bloody fascist dictator,' he muttered under his breath.

'I heard that,' called Glimmergoyne without looking back. Viktor slammed the heavy door violently in his wake.

Four

Private Serpens approached the last house in the main street of Leopardis with a fair amount of trepidation. Every house so far had been the same. First there was the argument with the resident about the Private's right to bring his hobnailed boots into *their* house, then the threats about what would happen to the said house if they did not comply, followed by Private Volans drawing his sword to back up the threats. Private Volans, a clumsy oaf at the best of times, was, with a sword in his hands, positively lethal. Nothing and nobody was safe.

The small, unassuming, rose-covered cottage looked delightful, noted Serpens, as he walked along the path to the pink door. Before his upraised fist could make contact with it, it swung silently open.

A bent little old woman stood before them, staring up at him from somewhere around waist level,

'I knew you would be coming,' she said auspiciously.

'What?' asked Serpens, puzzled. 'Oh. You saw us coming down the road?'

'No,' quavered the voice of the old woman. 'No, I saw a red coated man in my dreams last night. I have been expecting you.'

'Are you a witch then?' he asked abruptly, staring down at her.

'Me? *Me*? A witch? No, no definitely not. No, no, no. Almost certainly not. Well maybe just a little bit, on my mother's side, but nothing was ever proved either way if you know what I mean.'

'You either are or you aren't,' said Serpens totally confused by now. 'Do you, for example, have a black cat?' Exasperation was creeping into his voice.

'No, no. No definitely not. Never had a cat, can't stand the things, they bring on me asthma something chronic. No, never. Never ever. I much prefer dogs. No definitely not a cat.'

Suddenly a black furry ball leapt down from an exposed rafter, hissed loudly and scraped its exposed claws across Private Volans's face before shooting out of the door. In the course of sweeping his arm up to defend himself, Private Volans's hand swung wide and smashed into a large, glass-covered portrait of a bent, grey-haired, old woman which in turn loosened large hunks of plaster from the wall and ripped the supporting brackets out of their fixings, causing the whole thing to come crashing down noisily.

'Oh. You mean *that* cat? No. That's not mine. Belongs to my daughter Ethel. I'm only cat-sitting for the weekend. Honest.' Her eyes squinted down at the picture on the floor and the scraps of plaster and broken glass scattered around it. As the dust settled, she shook her head slowly. 'Mummy won't like that you know,' she said simply.

'Mummy?' echoed Private Serpens. 'Mummy still around is she?'

'Sort of. In a way. So to speak,' she said evasively.

'Look, I'm sorry about the mess,' said Volans. 'Um, have you got a broom or something?'

'And just what are you implying?' asked the old woman coldly.

'Right, um, look here, let's forget about the witch bit shall we?' said Serpens unhappily. The situation was definitely getting out of control. 'I'm sorry I ever mentioned it really.'

He was beginning to feel that he was wasting his time here too. 'Now we need to know if you have seen, anywhere in the vicinity, a nutter? We believe him to be in the village somewhere.'

'You mean him?' she asked, and pointed at Private Volans who was tenderly probing the scratch marks on his cheek with his fingers.

'No, not him. I know where he is. No, this is another one. Tall, blonde, incredibly handsome, a touch stupid. Well, pretty gormless actually.'

'Him,' she said nodding her head and pointing at Private Volans again, 'most definitely him.'

'No, not him. Oh never mind. Sorry to have troubled you.'

'It was no trouble. I was expecting you anyway,' she said ushering them quickly out of the door.

'I did tell you Mummy wouldn't like that, didn't I?' she called after them mysteriously, as the door slammed shut.

Lost in thought as he walked down the path, Private Serpens

did not notice that his ears had turned a curious lime green colour, as had the tip of his nose.

'Sir?' said Private Volans from behind him.

'Yes, what now?' snapped Serpens.

'She lied, sir.'

'What on earth are you talking about now, Private?'

'It's only Wednesday, sir. She lied about the weekend bit, sir.'

'Shut up, pillock!' said Private Serpens. 'Imbecile!' he added with feeling.

★

Still sitting at the bar in The Artisan's Arms, Goldoor was mulling over the content of his conversation with the young, dark-haired stranger. He seemed to have been on the level. He knew all about the West Tower and the South Tower and the bits in between. Or rather he had *sounded* convincing. Tomorrow night he had said. At eleven thirty, under the Main Keep, there would be a rope ladder waiting. Looking up at the clock on the wall behind the bar to try and work out how far away tomorrow night was, Goldoor caught sight of the two men in bright red uniforms with shiny peaked caps entering the bar. The sight put him in such a panic that he did not notice the curious green colour of the smaller one's face. He stood up suddenly, spilling beer all over the floor and the surrounding customers. The bar stool fell with a clatter into the path of a passing busboy who, in turn, drenched the remaining customers with the flagons and the tankards he was carrying, whilst on his way to a painful meeting with the floor.

'Look sir!' shouted Private Volans. 'It's the nutter.'

'Where?' croaked Serpens.

Private Volans looked at him quizzically for a moment. 'Are you feeling all right, sir?'

A tremendous crash and clouds of plaster dust announced the departure of Goldoor through the rickety back door.

'Why do you ask?' croaked Serpens. 'Oh, never mind that,' sharply, 'just get after him man. Now!'

'Yes sir!' said the Private and plunged into the mêlée of beer-soaked customers.

Wrenching open the door through which Goldoor had fled,

Private Volans successfully managed to rip the entire thing off by its hinges, causing yet more plaster to fall and the door frame to buckle. Mr Fred could only stand and stare.

'What the...' he said, slowly.

The angry shouts and complaints going on around him brought him to his senses and he yelled to the busboy, 'Get up from there you lazy git and fetch some fresh beer.' Feeling the hard stares of the annoyed drinkers boring into his soul, he added, 'That will be free beer of course, no charge,' smiling with some difficulty, as if the words were new to him. He looked angrily down at the crumpled red jacket on the floor with a small, green, shiny amphibian on it and shouted, 'And get that bloody frog out of my bar while you're about it!'

*

King Vulpecula cringed into the wall of the wall of the Royal Bedchamber, eyes closed; 'Not here? What do you mean not here? Am I dressed up like a dog's dinner for nothing again? Ye Gods, what kind of organisation goes into these farcical meetings?' bawled the ten-megawatt voice of the Princess Andromeda.

'Here, you, gormless. Get me out of this bloody whalebone corset before it strangles me, d'you hear?'

'Yes Princess,' mumbled Lyra, the pretty little ladies' maid, not looking at the fearsome expression. 'At once Princess.'

'But Daddy!' boomed the Princess Andromeda across the Tower Room, throwing out her arms in supplication, 'you promised he would be here today.'

The attempt at a little girl's cajoling tone made the King wince inwardly. She had a deeper voice and was more masculine than most of the men he knew.

'But dearest heart, there was an accident you see and, the Prince Circinus was hurt and... and...'

How could he possibly explain to his dear, sweet little girl that the spineless wimp had buggered off at the first available opportunity?

'We'll find... I mean as soon as he recovers we'll reschedule the meeting.'

'But Daddy!' she boomed again.

'Sorry dearest. I must go now. I must speak with the chancellor about...'

'Stop that, you stupid girl!' shouted Andromeda. 'Undo the bloody thing, don't tighten it. Ye Gods, are you stupid or what?'

King Vulpecula retreated while the Princess's attention was distracted and dashed down the stairs. His foot landed squarely on the roller skate carefully placed on the bottom step in readiness for just such an occasion and the corpulent frame of the King shot out into the hall, waving his arms and wobbling on only one leg.

'Help!' he yelped as he saw the large padded guest sofa loom up in front of him. Approaching it at speed, his knee hit the padded arm and he shot, momentarily airborne, straight towards the opposite arm. Landing amidst a cacophony of creaking wood and ruptured springs he bounced twice before lying still. 'Ortolan!' he screamed into the upholstery. 'Just you wait until I get my hands on you, you...' Words failed him as the sound of boyish laughter echoed down the corridor from a distance. 'He'll definitely have to go,' whispered the King vehemently to the cushions.

*

Prince Pyxis Vulpecula, the son and heir, had the same thought on many occasions. The Witch in Hansel and Gretel had the right idea. All nasty little children should be kept in cages until they grew up.

Creeping down the stairs that led to the Servants' Hall on heavily bandaged feet was one such occasion. His limited imagination being matched only by his limited intelligence, it came about that whenever he felt down because of the abominable Ortolan, his idea of cheering himself up was to go and abuse a servant or two. Painfully reaching the stone flags of the dining area he found the place deserted. At a loss for what to do next, he made himself a cup of tea and sat at the table to brood. When I am King they will all be sorry, he thought to cheer himself up. All of them.

From the cubbyhole of the boot room, Lacertus watched the thin, gangling figure of the heavily bandaged Prince with a grin on his face. There were occasions, not many admittedly but some, when he positively liked Ortolan. Watching the solitary boy, an idea occurred to him. The trapdoor to the cellar was standing open, which meant that either Glimmergoyne or the pompous great oaf Bootes would be down there. Creeping out of the cramped space without being seen was not easy, but Lacertus managed it and squeezed himself underneath the tall standing china cabinets. With a great deal of difficulty he pulled from his pocket a catapult and three stones. With an ease synonymous with long hours of practise, Lacertus slotted the first stone and took careful aim. The small, polished ball left the leather cup at speed to smash the mug in Prince Pyxis hand splattering hot tea all over the table.

'What the...' he spluttered, standing sharply. 'Who's there? Show yourself, you swine.'

When there was no reply Pyxis glared about him, as if daring the assailant to show himself. Cautiously, on tender feet, he moved towards the boot room end of the hall.

'Is that you Orty?' he asked of the emptiness. 'Show yourself you little bugger!' But there was only silence.

Spotting the open trapdoor, his mind put two and two together and came up with five and a half. He bared his teeth in a grin that was about as close to a smile as an apple is to a horse.

'There you are,' he whispered.

The second stone struck him squarely in the chest and the pain of it made him scream in agony. Lacertus grinned as the expression on the vacant face took on a savage, demented aspect.

'You little bugger. I'll get you for that you bastard!' screamed the Prince and hobbled as fast as he could towards the open trapdoors. As he stood holding the heavy upright door and stared down into the blackness a wave of uncertainty hit him. Maybe the little sod was *not* actually down there at all, maybe he was...

The thought got no further as the third and final stone smacked loudly into his exposed buttock and with a forward lurch and a piercing scream he dropped like a stone into the gaping blackness of the cellar. Lacertus relished the sounds of whining and blubbering as he squeezed himself carefully from beneath the china cabinet and hurried across to close the doors.

'Your Highness!' came the distressed voice of Glimmergoyne

from the shadowy depths. 'Are you all right?'

The son of the Duke of Venatici carefully lowered the heavy doors and left the two idiots to themselves.

★

Prince Ortolan Apus, strolling around the darkened Castle Armoury, was on the lookout for more mischief when he first saw the shadowy figure. He had stopped to take a look out of the huge leaded window just as the shadow flitted across the white road beneath the Main Keep. His curiosity roused, he had watched the furtive, black clad man, a dark shape against a darker background, fumble for something near the wall. Ortolan's spotty, adolescent face broke into a wide grin as the man found the end of a rope which he obviously knew would be there, and began gingerly to ascend. Quickly he left his place by the window and ran towards the doors. Racing up the spiral staircase to his room he ran first down one corridor then along another until arriving at his destination he flung open the door and rummaged in the dilapidated, outgrown toy cupboard for a moment. With a cry of triumph he located the gleaming instrument he was looking for and was off again at a run. It would seem the ugly one had a visitor. As he took the steps up to the top of the East Tower two at a time, his imagination was working overtime. Who could possibly want to visit Her Ugliness alone? And at this time of night? Pushing open the small trapdoor that led to the roof of the tower he was panting heavily from exertion. He spotted the end of the rope almost at once. It was double looped and tied firmly around one of the stone parapets on the west side. Leaning precariously over the edge, he stared down into the gloom to see if he could see the man, obviously a certifiable lame-brain, climbing up.

Lacertus was also thinking about lame-brains from his hiding place behind the portrait of Queen Xenophobe, (for some obscure reason there were a lot of them scattered about the castle) that hung in the Tower Room of Princess Andromeda. Looking through the cut-out eye slits of the dowdy old Queen of yesteryear, he could see almost the entire room. The Princess was sitting at her large dressing table, brushing her hair and tying it into large, night-time rollers in the mirror. Even from twenty feet away she was stunningly hideous. Lacertus groaned inwardly at the sight. Marrying that took on a whole new dimension when confronted with reality of the proposition. Suddenly the piggy little eyes of the Princess swept to the window. The brush hand stopped moving. Shifting slightly, in readiness for his heroic leap to her defence, Lacertus waited patiently.

Not for the first time tonight, Goldoor wished that he were still safe at home in his bed. Hanging on to a slender rope suspended beneath the East Tower of Castle Camelopardis in the blackness of the night, the idea of confronting at long last his beloved was the only morsel of comfort he could find.

A rope ladder, the young man had said. No problem, he had said. Hah. Climbing hand over hand very slowly, as each hand located one of the regularly spaced knots, Goldoor was beginning to get worried. Looking up towards the top of the tower, an infinitely less heart-stopping view than the downward one, he could see up ahead the glimmer of light from the high windows. She was waiting for him. Up there. Nevertheless he was getting worried. It all seemed too easy.

Just as he came within reach of the window and he could almost sense the glow of achievement, a final upward glance made him stare. He caught sight of something that justified all the worry and it made him scream. There was a face up there. A spotty, white face set against the dark velvet blue of the night sky. And the spotty white face was grinning horribly. A window suddenly flung open directly above his head, obscured momentarily the white face, and made contact with the rope causing it to swing violently. Goldoor found himself staring up at the ugliest sight he had ever seen – and that included the back end of Uncle Dingles's pair of dray horses as they pulled the double furrowed plough in the top meadow back home in Picton. But it was not the monstrous vision of the gaping mouth, flared nostrils, piggy eyes and thin ratty hair, surmounted by heavy wooden curlers that comprised the face of the Princess Andromeda that caused him to scream for the second time. It was the flash of moonlight on the secateurs whose sharp blades were closing on the rope high above his head. The secateurs that were clutched in the hands of the spotty, white-faced, grinning youth. A sudden and, unusually for

56

Goldoor, crystal clear realisation of what was about to happen occurred to him.

'Who's there?' bellowed the foghorn voice of Princess Andromeda, glaring out of the window at the defenceless night. But Goldoor had no time to find a suitable reply. He was too busy plummeting towards the roadway below.

'What the hell is going on here?' roared the Princess several decibels louder, causing even the blameless darkness to cringe. Still there was no reply.

The heavily laden cart that passed slowly down the carriageway could not have appeared at a more fortuitous time for the terror-stricken Goldoor. Landing flat on his back squarely in the middle of the wooden wagon he had barely over come his surprise at still being alive before his body began slowly to sink in the heap of still steaming horse manure it contained. Scrambling manfully to the side and gripping the wooden slats, Goldoor had the thought that maybe the hard road would have been preferable to the evil-smelling dung in which he now found himself partially immersed. Coughing and retching in the back of the slow moving cart, Goldoor did not hear the voice of Andromeda screaming for the guards nor see the window of his lady love slam shut in disgust at the interruption.

Nobody saw the spotty, white-faced youth as he danced a solitary jig of victory, high up on the roof of the tower.

Lacertus squeezed through the narrow passage that led to the spiral staircase. Foiled at the last by that ignoramus Ortolan! He did not need to see the little monster to know that it was he who had buggered up the beautiful plan and his thoughts tended toward the murderous. He would definitely have to reschedule the 'accident' planned for him to an earlier date.

*

At the approach of the dung cart, signalled by the horrendous stench, the response of Private Second Class Pavo on night duty at the Gatehouse was to run quickly out of the Guardroom and swing the gates open before dashing back inside. The cart rumbled slowly through the huge stone arches, the short, fat man on the box whistling merrily. Having been a dung carrier for some twenty years the man was well used to the loneliness of his profession and could amuse himself with ease. He waved cheerily to Private Second Class Pavo as he passed the tightly closed windows. Private Second Class Pavo waved back, his face a sickly green colour that clashed badly with the bright orange handkerchief clutched to his nose and mouth.

Once the cart had safely passed the outer archway, he ran once more to the gates and swiftly slammed and bolted them, a look of intense relief on his face. By the time the kettle had boiled and he had made himself a nice cup of tea, Private Second Class Pavo was feeling a little better. Putting his feet up on the small leather footstool he relaxed in the heavily carved nightwatchman's chair.

The sounds of running feet as they clomped down the hill woke him from a happy reverie in the depths of the deep chair. With an eyebrow raised look which said 'Here we go again', he hauled himself to his feet once more. Corporal (soon to be Sergeant, as soon as the cheque cleared anyway!) Tucana arrived at a run with Private Second Class Gramm puffing along behind just as he opened the doors.

'Sir!' shouted Private Second Class Pavo. 'All quiet here, sir!' as he snapped to rigid attention.

'Where's the dung wagon?' demanded Corporal (soon to be Sergeant, etc.) Tucana quickly, 'We must faind hit.'

'It's gone, sir. Just now. I was—'

'Well we must get hit back 'ere. Niaow!' bellowed Corporal (soon to be Sergeant, etc.) Tucana.

'But sir, it's gone, sir!'

'Then go and get hit and bring hit and hit's load back 'ere. *Now*, Private.'

'But sir, I…'

'*Now* I said, buffoon!' screamed Tucana.

'Yes sir,' muttered Private Second Class Pavo, leaving the room slumped forward and dejected.

Corporal Tucana shouted again, 'Run man. We must search it for a hintruder. Double quick march, you slovenly little man.'

'Yes sir,' muttered Private Pavo.

Search it, he thought with disgust. Bloody hell.

Goldoor, coughing and spluttering, had finally managed to

ease himself over the side of the wagon and disassociate himself from its obnoxious load. He had part fallen, part rolled into the ditch that ran from the Gatehouse. Flat on his back and gazing up at the night sky he calmed as his breathing became easier. The terror of his plummet from the tower and the horror of the awful vision imprinted on his memory did not stop him from passing at once into a deep, black, dreamless sleep. He did not hear the running feet that passed along the road soon after, much less the agonised creaking of the wagon as it made its slow trek back to the Gatehouse. It was the sleep of the bedpost, the unconsciousness of the log.

Prince Ortolan Apus having finished his lonely victory jig made his way back to his room with a toothy grin spread all over his nasty little face. All in all it had been a good day. The prat Pyxis had spent three hours in the wine cellar with boring old sod Glimmergoyne tending his broken leg and concussed head before someone had found them. The grin widened when he thought that it would only have been twenty minutes if he had reported it at once. Three hours alone with the boring old butler would pay the rat Pyxis back for many a nasty turn. Turning in for the night, well pleased at the success of the rooftop excursion, he too soon dropped into a deep, dreamless sleep. It was the sleep of the unconscionably wicked.

Lacertus did not sleep well. Barely at all in fact. Once too often that slimy creep Ortolan Apus had thwarted his ambitions. Direct action was now a necessity. Sleep, when he did find, it was filled with lances and foils, mashie-niblicks and lots and lots of blood.

Private Volans was far from sleep, though having spent two days chasing across fields and hedgerows in search of the elusive nutter he was pretty close to exhaustion. He had gone back to the inn yesterday, when the initial search had proved fruitless but he had been unable to find Private Serpens. The nasty, fat, little barman had dumped the red jacket, black trousers and shiny peaked cap Serpens had been wearing into his arms and said some very nasty things. He had called him all sorts of names in connection with the damage to the door. He had braved the tirade stoically and without orders to the contrary, Private Volans being very proud of his reputation as a man devoted to his duty, he had carried on the search alone. Alone that is apart from a cute little frog that had somehow found its way into the pocket of Serpens's red jacket. It kept him company as he searched high and low. Finally, defeated, exhausted and hungry, he turned towards the castle and home.

The sight that greeted him when he reached the Gatehouse was one of such blatant, childish absurdity that it caused even the tired and hungry Private to laugh aloud. The fat, little dung cart man was sitting on a small stool whistling softly to himself as the unfortunate Privates Gramm and Pavo waded knee-deep in the thick, black muck in the back of his cart, probing it with pointed sticks. Private Second Class Pavo shot him a look so filled with disgust and loathing that had glares been daggers he would have been impaled on an extremely large and very sharp fence post.

Private Volans couldn't help but laugh again. The green colour of the little Private's face put him in mind of his friend the little frog, except that the frog didn't have a clothes peg on its nose. In what he believed to be a kindly gesture he casually lobbed the small creature into the back of the cart as he passed, thinking its loud croaking sounds an expression of happiness. Still laughing he carried on alone, up the winding road to Castle Camelopardis.

Five

The Witch of Leopardis was not a particularly good witch; good that is, in the sense of capable as opposed to non-wicked.

Mona-Cygnus, as she had been named by her mother, had her dreams of being a mighty sorceress thwarted at an early age when her total inability to control even the most basic of spells had her laughed out of the Wizard Wango School of Demonic Sorcery. In an attempt at a rather complicated spell to preserve her youthful charm and good looks she had fouled up badly, with the result that at the age of only thirty two she had the grey hair and bent old body of an eighty year old hag, warts and all. Nevertheless, she had persevered against all the odds. Unable to reverse the age spell, she had studied a small blue book on lateral thinking by a very clever man with all sorts of letters after his name, but whose actual name she could never *quite* remember, and come up with the concept of bewitching some poor fool of a man into *thinking* she was young and beautiful instead. Success in this had also eluded her, so far.

Thus it came about that Goldoor woke from his sleep in a cold and damp ditch to the strong smell of sulphur mixed with cordite, in the small cellar of a certain rose-covered cottage. When his eyes met those of the simpering, grey-haired witch, he screamed loud and long.

'Damn,' muttered Mona-Cygnus. 'Not again.'

She wrinkled her nose in disgust at the terrible smell that was quickly replacing the brimstone.

'Horse manure? But I never use horse manure in my recipes. Where's that bloody spell book?'

'Who are you?' asked Goldoor, his fear subsiding a little.

'Don't worry yourself about that for the moment, dearie. Everything will become clear when I can find that damn book.'

'Look, I don't know who you are but I've had a rather nasty time of it lately, what with the fall from the tower and that pile of horsy-poohs in the back of that dirty old cart and…'

'Ah. So it's you? What do you mean by coming into my nice, cosy, little rose-covered cottage smelling like that?'

'But I—'

'Honestly, the manners of young people these days.'

'But I didn't—'

'You just have no respect for a poor, grey-haired, old lady, throwing stones at her when she goes for her bits and pieces at the corner shop, painting rude words on her windows at night when she's sleeping.'

'But I never threw anything—'

'And then coming in here smelling like that. It's disgusting.'

'Look, shut up for a minute will you.' Bluff it out, he thought, having mislaid his initial fears. 'I didn't *come in here* smelling like this. One moment I was lying quite comfortably in this cold and damp ditch smelling like this and the next I was here staring up at you.'

'You don't remember coming in? Damn. You should remember that. Must amend that bit of the incantation when I can find that bloody book,' muttered Mona-Cygnus to herself.

Totally confused by now, and not having an incredibly long attention span at the best of times, Goldoor said, 'Look, I don't know who you are but all I was trying to do was to get to meet my lady love in the castle and then some stupid bugger cuts the thing I was climbing – what do you call those long stringy things with knots in them? Anyway no matter, someone cuts this thingy and I fall off and end up in this cartload of nasty, smelly horsey-poohs. *Then* when I manage to get out of that I suddenly find myself here. If you could just tell me how I get back to The Artisan's Arms from here I should be most—'

'Lady love?' asked Mona-Cygnus suspiciously. The boy was confused, maybe that part of the spell had worked after all. 'And who might that be?' she asked sweetly, lifting her chin with her fingers and fluttering her eyelashes alluringly.

'Why, the Princess Andromeda of course!'

Mona-Cygnus peered closely into his eyes for a moment and shook her head sadly. 'Oh boy. And I thought *I* had problems,' she muttered gently as she settled herself heavily down on the

Persian rug beside him.

★

Lacertus stood in the long corridor of the armoury and waited patiently. His face behind the crossed wiring of the oval fencing mask was impassive as he contemplated the far doors. It had been so easy to cancel the appointment of M. Belvoire, the fencing master. The man was a fool, he had not even been suspicious when he, Lacertus, heavily disguised as a Castle Messenger, had personally delivered the note saying that the poor Prince Ortolan was sick and would be unfit to take his lesson today. In fact he would have said that M. Belvoire had looked positively relieved at the release. A masterful piece of forgery that note had been, complete with the King's signature. He swished the shining steel of the thin-bladed epée with casual ease and flexed his muscles. His eyes swept the walls covered with the pennoncels and banners of long ago battles, the shining helms and foils. It made a very apposite setting for the first stage of his plan.

Pushing open the great wooden doors with all the arrogance of his youth, Ortolan Apus strode in attired in the white, protective canvas of the fencer. From his position at the end of the hall, the similarly clad Lacertus bowed low and on rising lifted the handle of the epée to his chin in salute.

As the son of a Duke, albeit a minor one and in spite the lack of proven legitimacy, Lacertus had schooled himself in the finer skills required of a gentleman, namely the etiquette of the court and the use of the finer weapons such as the fencing blades. Ortolan Apus bounced up to him.

'Bon joor Monsewer Belvoire,' he said cheerfully. 'How are you this fine morning?'

Without a word Lacertus slipped into the watchful, feet apart, knees bent stance of the swordsman and waited.

'Very quiet I see,' said Ortolan jovially but stopped suddenly as the slight figure took two paces forward and poked him in the chest with the sharp blade, watching it bend as the tip met the resistance of the protective jacket. The expression on the spotty face behind the wire mesh mask changed to one of seriousness, as with casual, arrogant ease he parried the blade with his own.

Sweeping it away easily he said, 'En garde,' and smiled again behind the gauze.

★

Sergeant (the cheque finally cleared) Tucana strode into the office of King Vulpecula and saluted crisply.

'Dung cart searched an' cleared, sah!' he shouted.

'Dung cart? What dung cart, Captain?'

'The one that the intruder escaped in last night, Sire,' oozed Captain Parsus at his side.

'Yes sah! The hintruder what tried to henter the room of the Princess, sah!' shouted Sergeant (the cheque etc.) Tucana.

'Must be the nutter, Captain,' said the King with an optimistic smile. 'At least he's not buggered off completely. Has that prat Serpens reported back yet?'

'Not yet, sire. But I believe Private Volans has returned. Find out would you, Sergeant.'

It was not easy to make a simple rank sound abusive but Captain Parsus managed it.

'Yes sah! Right away sah! On the double sah!' shouted Sergeant Tucana, and spun on his heel.

'And Sergeant,' said Captain Parsus.

'Yes sah!' bawled Sergeant Tucana, spinning back to face him. 'You don't have to be *quite* so loud about it.'

The sarcasm passed right over Sergeant Tucana's head. 'Not so loud, sah! Right sah! Quiet and hefficient it is, sah!' bawled Sergeant Tucana, turning on his heel once more and marching noisily out.

'Was it worth it for 20,000 ducats, Parsus? The man is a complete moron,' said the King as the footsteps died away.

'We must do what we must, Sire,' smiled Captain Parsus. 'Until Her Highness is safely hitched at least,' through shining white teeth.

The King nodded morosely.

★

Glimmergoyne was not a happy man. He had been unable to find out what the obese little coachman had done with the Prince Circinus, and now the oaf had passed out under the table in the Servants' Hall and was snoring loudly.

'Drunken bastard,' muttered Glimmergoyne under his breath. 'What is zee matter, M. Glimmergoynes?' sneered the voice of Chef Bootes from the kitchen doorway. 'Lost anuzzer wun as we?'

'Nibbles for the King ready yet, Cookie?' snapped Glimmergoyne needled more than usual by the fat slob's comments in that ridiculous fake accent of his.

'*Ze Canapés* arr compléte, Monsieur. I 'av garnitured zem myself!' said the chef, smugly twirling his long, dark moustaches.

'Oh God. Not covered with bloody fish eggs again are they? That's all I need.'

'I 'av used ze best caviare, yez. Only ze best for theer 'ighnesses.'

'Well don't go giving any to the obnoxious Ortolan. He was sick as a pig all over floor of the State Bathroom the last time you gave him that rubbish.'

'Hi do not serve hrubbish from mai kitchen, you decrepit old plate carrier,' answered Bootes, haughtily.

'No? What about that game pie you slopped together last week? The rabbit was so high it almost had airsickness.'

'Hi can honly use wot hi gets. The gamekeeper guaranteed moi—'

'Listen, the only game that drunken bum knows is shove ha'penny in the bar of the Dog and Ferret. He buys all that garbage from Perseus Timms. Old Percy the Poacher as he's known locally.' Fornax sitting in his chair by the fire glowered at this exchange but said nothing. His head still hurt quite badly from last night. The vast, white bulk of Chef Bootes quivered and his face reddened, but he suppressed his anger.

'At least I manage to stay inside my budget by buying wisely,' he snarled, the cultured accent slipping in his anger.

'Only by half-starving your staff and buying crap!' retorted the butler.

'Now then boys, enough of the abuse please,' boomed the voice of Ethelreda, the pastry cook, 'it does nobody any good.'

Recovering his composure through sheer effort of will Chef Bootes stopped himself, open-mouthed, from replying to this. With a loud harrumph of disdain, he stalked off towards the kitchens, muttering something indistinct about interfering women.

'There now,' she said sweetly: 'Isn't that better?'

The large, unshapely figure of the woman crossed to the table and flopped down on a chair, sending a cloud of flour dust into the air. Fornax glowered at the fire nursing his mulled wine with raw egg yolk; yet another unsuccessful attempt at a hangover cure.

★

Viktor passed the door to the armoury on his way to the 'Comfort Room', as prescribed by the FDASU handbook as being essential to the welfare of the workers whilst on duty, when he heard the loud crashing and clash of metal on metal from within. It sounded like there was a pitched battle going on in there. He glanced at his watch, noted that he still had seven and a half minutes to go before his return to duty, shrugged his shoulders and strolled on.

★

Mona-Cygnus was almost in tears sitting on the huge Persian rug by the fire of her cauldron pit. She was not normally soft-hearted, it didn't quite fit with the image, but Goldoor's tale of woe had affected her deeply.

Goldoor himself sat and gazed blankly into the flames, frowning. Since the frown required a good deal of mental effort to maintain, there was not much of anything else going on. Suddenly Mona-Cygnus sat up and declared,

'My boy, I am going to help you. I don't normally do requests but just this once, by my dear old mummy's bones, I shall help you!'

The window frames rattled and the fire sputtered briefly as a cold breeze swept through the room.

'Sorry, Mummy. No offence,' she whispered meekly.

'You will?' said Goldoor slowly, the changeover from a frown to a smile took quite a lot of effort, but he managed it eventually.

'Thank you,' he said, 'that would be wonderful.'

He threw his arms around her and hugged her and the young, little, old hag wondered if she were doing the right thing. Suddenly there was a loud bang, followed by a whiff of sulphur and Goldoor evaporated from her arms.

'Damn, damn, damn!' swore the wizened old lady vehemently. 'Just when I thought I'd got that bloody boomerang effect ironed out too. Where the hell is that damned spell book?'

Mr Fred stood alone behind the bar, whistling cheerfully to himself. Maybe the cost of that free beer would be worth it if the smiling moron had gone. He was a nice boy and all that but a real pain. Still, he hadn't been back for nearly twenty four hours now. All the signs were good. He stopped whistling abruptly, wrinkled his nose distastefully and sniffed.

'If that bloody dung cart driver thinks he going to get served in here he's got another thing coming,' muttered the little man running around to the back bar in search of the noisome smell and ready to swear at somebody. Suddenly he bumped up against the manure stained Goldoor.

'Sorry I'm so late, Mr Fred, but I had a little accident and—'

'*Get out of my bloody bar*! You moronic swine, coming in here smelling like that. *Get out.*'

'Sorry, Mr Fred. I'll just go and—'

'*Get out!*' shouted Mr Fred, his face reddening with near apoplexy.

Goldoor ducked out from behind the bar and ran out of the hastily repaired back door.

'And don't slam that…' as the door slammed in his wake.

Mr Fred watched the newly repaired door slowly come away from the frame and fall squarely across a wooden bench. He rubbed the bridge of his nose between finger and thumb until it hurt.

'Why me?' he mumbled, 'Why *me*! What did I ever do to deserve *him*?'

Oblivious to the destruction he had just caused, Goldoor was busy hanging the bucket with the holes drilled in the bottom that was loosely termed a shower unit, from a beam in the roof of the shed when Mrs Fred poked her head round the door, a faint whiff of 'Midnight Mist' following her.

'Hello dear,' she called, and stopped short at the sight of Goldoor, naked to the waist, bucket in hand.

'Well, hello dear,' she breathed softly, gazing at him, 'I just brought you some nice hot water. Lovely,' she said, meaningfully.

'Thanks, Mrs Fred, just what I needed. I say, have you been eating plums or something? Only the juice is smeared all over your lips.'

'Plums?' echoed Mrs Fred carefully, her lower lip starting to tremble.

'Yes. When Mummy eats too many of the plum harvest as she's picking them she looks like that. I call her Plummy Mummy,' he answered, chuckling cheerfully.

'You think I look like your mother?' The lower lip quivered violently.

'Yes as a matter of fact you do look a little bit…'

He turned at the sound of the bucket of water being thrown to the ground and the patter of footsteps, as Mrs Fred ran back to the inn as fast as she could go. Goldoor pondered the significance of this for a moment, came up with no reasonable explanation for such strange behaviour, shrugged his shoulders and carried on with his bucket hanging.

*

On his return from the 'Comfort Room', much comforted, Viktor paused outside the Armoury. The sounds of clashing metal and grunting were still going on. Viktor grabbed at the door handle and paused. He bit his lip pensively as he tried to decide whether the rule book covered situations like this, but being an inquisitive man he decided to take a look anyway. If there were any comeback the Union would sort it out for him.

Swinging the door wide he had little time to know whether there would be any comeback or not as the thin-bladed, ultra-sharp pointed epée pierced his jacket, his breast and then his heart. In that order.

Prince Ortolan Apus, who had been standing in line with the blade when the heavy door had swung open and pushed him bodily aside, pulled off his gauze mask and looked down at the crumpled body with a curious smile. Turning to Lacertus he said in a jovial tone, still panting heavily from the exertion of the unaccustomed exercise, 'Oh dear M. Belvoire. I do believe you have done for the doorman.'

Lacertus, also breathing heavily, lowered his arm but said nothing.

'I would suggest Monsieur, that we leg it. Mais oui?'

For once Lacertus was in complete agreement with the little monster. It was time to go. There was a pool of bright red blood spreading from under the body onto the carpet and the still open eyes looked distinctly surprised.

Without a word Lacertus leapt over the body of the little doorman and headed for the nearest exit only steps behind the little Prince.

Ortolan Apus was grinning cheerfully as he ran up the stairs towards the Royal Apartments. It was a shame, but he had never really liked the horrible little doorman anyway. The battle had been great fun. M. Belvoire had never fought him like that before, it was much more fun than those stupid 'doublez, redoublez' manoeuvres he normally insisted on.

Lacertus did not think it had been fun. The little bastard was very fast. Even so, once or twice he had almost had him. He had almost nailed the little bugger at the end there, he would have done if that stupid prat of a doorman hadn't interfered. Running as fast as was possible in the confines of the wall tunnel that led from the portrait of Queen Xenophobe on the Armoury level to the portrait of Queen Xenophobe on the Servants' Hall level his mind went back over the vital points. He had a cut on his arm that he would have to disguise and he would have to get to his alibi position within fifteen minutes or so. The tablet he had put in Matron Beamish's tea would be wearing off soon, and he had to be there when she woke up if she was to be his alibi. Reaching his small box of a bedroom he hastily tied a bandage to his forearm to stop the bleeding, changed in record time back into his kitchen boy's uniform, and dashed off down the corridor to the matron's office. Once safely back in his chair by the desk, he studied the old woman's sleeping face. She was still out. Good. As silently as possible he refreshed the teapot and, crossing to the matron again shook her by the shoulder asking gently, 'More tea, Matron?'

'What? Oh. More tea. Sorry, I must have dozed off for a moment there. Yes please my boy. Oh dear me. Was I asleep long? What was I saying?'

'No, not that long. You were just going to tell me about Queen Velma and the chancellor,' prompted Lacertus indulgently.

'Oh yes, now she really was a one, I remember when she and the late Chancellor Triculum... I'm not boring you am I, young man?'

'Not at all, Matron, I could listen to you all day,' smiled Lacertus innocently.

★

Scrubbed and thoroughly washed, Goldoor returned to the bar to find Mr Fred.

'Mr Fred,' he bellowed, 'are you there?'

'I'm here,' came the weary voice of the much-troubled innkeeper.

'Oh, good. There you are. Now what do you want me to do next?'

'Go away?' said Mr Fred hopefully.

'Come on now. Be serious,' said Goldoor with a smile.

'All right then, go and get me some crates of—'

The bright orange flash with silvery tinges accompanied by loud swooshing sounds momentarily blinded Mr Fred and singed his eyebrows. Opening his eyes gingerly he looked at the space that had been occupied by Goldoor. The huge boat-like boots were smouldering around the tops, but of Goldoor there was no other sign. Stunned into silence, Mr Fred wrinkled his nose and sniffed.

'Sulphur? I never use sulphur,' he said inconsequentially, then he laughed, maniacally. 'He's gone, gone. The stupid bugger's gone up in a puff of smoke. Ha ha. He's gone, he's gone.'

★

Glimmergoyne had been up and down the stairs so many times in the last two hours that he was beginning to feel dizzy. The Prince

Pyxis had only been conscious for a short while but his insistent demands were enough to limit his life expectancy quite dramatically. Clasping the back of a chair with his hands and resting heavily, the disturbing vision of a little seaside cottage popped into his mind yet again.

'Not yet, not yet,' he muttered to himself.

'Mr Glimmergoyne? Matron Beamish? Mr Glimmergoyne? Are you there? Is there *anybody* there?' bellowed the voice of Ethelreda, the pastry cook.

'Here Ethel,' he called wearily. 'I'm in here.'

'Oh Mr Glimmergoyne. You must come quick. There's been an accident!'

'Don't tell me the adorable Pyxis has decapitated himself shaving?' he said in mock horror. 'Personally I blame the idiot who gave him that cut-throat razor in the first place.'

He smiled wickedly to himself as he remembered his birthday present for the boy last year.

'No, no. This is serious. Come quick, quick now. Viktor has been stabbed and—'

'And he's bleeding all over the oriental rugs? Dear God the man has no sense of values.'

'No, no. It's worse than that. He's—'

'Demanding compensation for wounds sustained in the course of duty? That won't wash either.'

'He's *dead*, you stupid, old man!' screamed the flour-dusted, white clad shape of the cook.

'Now that is different. I wonder what the FDASU handbook will have to say about that?'

'You must come at once. This is serious.'

'Well if you put it like that.'

'What's all the shouting about?' called the matron from her office door. 'Can't a person enjoy a quiet cup of tea and a chat in this castle any more?'

'Oh Matron, come quick. Viktor's dead. Stabbed. It's horrible.'

The matron's head disappeared momentarily from view then returned, accompanied by the rest of her huge bulk with her small medical bag clutched in her hand.

'Follow me! To the Armoury!' shouted Ethelreda dashing off

up the stairs. The vast blue cloud of the matron crossed the hall and began to climb after her.

'Being a bit optimistic with the bag aren't you, Matron? I mean if the sod is actually dead there is nothing in there that will help him,' said Glimmergoyne with a smirk.

She glared at him over he shoulder and said levelly, 'Just shut up, you old fool, and come on!'

Lacertus peered around the door of Matron's room just in time to see the butler's coat-tails disappearing towards the upper floors. He smiled to himself. It was the self-satisfied smile of the crocodile that has just eaten the baby. Full of teeth and completely guiltless.

★

The enormous miasma of acrid yellow smoke filled the small room in the rose-covered cottage as Goldoor once more materialised beside Mona-Cygnus. Sparks crackled and spat all around him and there was a glazed look in his eyes.

'A little bit too much juice,' muttered the little witch as she peered at the singed eyebrows and smouldering clothing of the stunned Goldoor. Picking up a bucket of water she threw the contents over him, putting out the embers and reviving him at one and the same time. Spluttering and blinking rapidly, he shook his head, looked her straight in the eyes and said, 'I wish you would stop doing that. It's playing hell with my sense of reality. Not to mention my digestion.'

'Do you want me to help you or not? Ungrateful little…'

'No, I don't mean… What do I mean…?'

He thought for a moment, frowned, thought a bit longer and said, 'It's just that, well, it's just that it's teatime at The Artisan's Arms and first I was there and now I'm here and, and all this hopping around is making me very hungry.'

'Is that all?' she said, 'I can soon fix that.'

'Oh goody!' said Goldoor with a smile. 'Food!'

Six

M. Francis Belvoire, Fencing Master to the Sons of Gentlefolk, was sitting peacefully in the parlour of his little cottage and about to take a nice sip of freshly brewed tea when the loud hammering at the door disrupted him, causing him to spill the scalding hot liquid down his trousers.

'Ahhhgh!' he screamed loudly dancing up and down to cool off. 'Damned idiots,' he muttered and crossed to open the door in a foul temper.

'Might we come in?' said the smooth, cultured voice of Captain Parsus, in full dress uniform put on for the occasion, glittering with thick gold braid as he brushed past the startled fencing master without waiting for a reply.

'But I was just about to… look is this important, only I have to be—?'

'Oh yes,' said Captain Parsus curtly to the little man, 'it is important. You see, the King does not like his staff bleeding all over the carpets.'

He nodded to Private Second Class Gramm who had moved in behind M. Belvoire.

'Right then, Private, shall we go?'

'Sir!' said Private Second Class Gramm picking up the wildly protesting M. Belvoire as easily as if he were a pillow and stuffing him under one arm.

'Good. Let's go then,' said Captain Parsus conversationally.

'I am going to speak to the King personally about your appalling treatment of my good self. Get your hands off me, you great oaf!' shouted M. Belvoire from the level of Private Gramm's waist.

'I'm sure his Highness will take great pleasure in that,' oiled Captain Parsus with a smile full of teeth. 'Now shut up. Please.'

'But I must protest. What is the charge? What am I supposed to have done? Put me down or I'll…'

'Private Gramm?' said Captain Parsus.

'Yes sir!' said Private Second Class Gramm as he clamped a huge meaty paw over the mouth of the unfortunate M. Belvoire.

'Thank you Private, that's much better. Off we go then.'

'Sir!'

★

'And where is the body now?' asked King Vulpecula of the assembled group that conspired to make his small, private office look even smaller and a lot less private.

'In the meat chiller, Sire,' answered Captain Parsus smoothly.

'The *meat* chiller. Dear God is that the best you could do?'

'Under the circumstances, Sire, yes.'

'And the idiot of a fencing master?'

'Cell number two in the dungeons, Sire.'

'But nobody has been down there in years,' spluttered the King.

'It is a bit drastic one must admit, Sire, but he could be dangerous. He *is* a killer.'

'The carpets are being cleaned even now, your Highness,' cut in Glimmergoyne conversationally. 'Mr Hydrus seems to think they will come up nicely...'

'Mr Hydrus?' squeaked the King.

'Yes Sire. The laundryman. He seems to think that cold water and salt will do the trick.'

'Cold water and salt?' squawked the Royal voice once more. 'A man is dead and all you can think about is the bloody *carpets*?'

'They are very rare carpets Sire, quite unique and priceless,' came the nervous twitter of Antila the Chancellor.

'Sod the carpets, you moronic little clown. What are we going to do with the body? And what are we going to do with the bloody fencing chappie?'

'Well Viktor had no living relatives that we are aware of.' The King glared hard at Matron Beamish.

'And M. Belvoire won't be missed for a few weeks. He goes away a lot,' chimed in Glimmergoyne.

'And since we don't need any bad publicity at this moment,' oozed the voice of Captain Parsus, 'the wisest course would appear to be to just let things slide for a little while.'

'Let things *slide*? You mean cover it up?' said the King, horrified.

'It would be safest in the long run, Sire,' said Captain Parsus.

King Vulpecula of Camelopardis buried his face in his hands and counted to a hundred. Ten did not seem quite adequate to cover a situation like this.

'We could bury the body in the rose beds, Sire,' boomed Ethelreda, 'No one need ever really know.'

'But we can't just forget the whole thing.'

'Why not, Sire. It need only be between us. Then in a few weeks we can give the fencing master a nice little gratuity, send him off to some far-flung corner of the realm and that will be the end of that!' said Glimmergoyne. 'Do we really want to go through the fiasco of an investigation at this time?'

'No. No I suppose not,' muttered the King in a defeated tone.

'This is to be between us and us alone. Any one of you who so much as breathes a word of this outside of this room will be dead meat,' oozed Captain Parsus, an edge of iron in the oiliness. The assembly nodded as one, and the King's mind caught a glimpse of the cold, dank meat chiller and he shuddered.

'Just us then,' he added quietly.

Behind the face of Queen Xenophobe, the same face just a different pose, Lacertus smiled.

'And me,' he said softly, 'don't forget me!'

With a chuckle he closed the 'eyes' of the ubiquitous Queen, stepped down into the passageway and set off back to his own room. Things were definitely getting more interesting.

*

'Now you are *sure* it's the Princess Andromeda you want? I mean you couldn't be mistaken?' asked Mona-Cygnus.

'That's what the old gypsy woman said. That's the name she gave me. The picture is in my backpack at The Artisan's Arms so I can't show you. She is lovely, flaxen haired, so sweet and pure and… you know…'

His voice petered out and a glazed look came into his already glazed eyes.

'It takes all sorts I suppose,' said Mona-Cygnus peering into the double glazing with a shrug of her bent old shoulders.

'This is this going to work, isn't it?' asked Goldoor nervously, as he watched the little witch stirring her cauldron. 'I mean you're sure you've got the mixture right this time?'

'Piffle boy. Never fear. I just overdid the bats' wings a bit, that's all. Trust me,' she said confidently.

Goldoor smiled weakly.

Muttering unintelligibly, Mona-Cygnus stirred the bubbling cauldron until a loud ear-splitting crash followed by multi-coloured sparks and an intense blue vapour announced the departure of Goldoor.

'Well,' said Mona-Cygnus to herself, 'he's gone. Let's just hope I got the right address.'

★

Closely followed by a loud thunderclap and a cloud of blue smog, Goldoor appeared swathed in sparks and bright argent flashes in the middle of the large expanse of carpet that covered the floor in the bedroom of the Princess Andromeda. Turning swiftly on her boudoir chair she screamed in horror at the sight of the soot-blackened face of our hero. As his eyes focused on the stark white blob of a face, the large, red painted lips and piggy eyes surmounted by large wooden curlers, Goldoor opened his mouth and began to scream along with her. The combined volume was sufficient to rattle the very glass in the window frames. A second loud thunderclap followed by a hiss of air as it hurried to occupy the space left vacant by the departing Goldoor filled the room. He was still screaming when he reappeared, momentarily, in the crowded public bar of The Artisan's Arms, causing the unfortunate busboy to soak a few more harmless drinkers with a tray full of beer and almost giving one old man a heart attack.

'Oh,' he said suddenly, his brows furrowing. 'Where am I? Where is she? Hello, Mr Fred. Sorry about this but—'

With another flash and the smell of scorched metal he once more disappeared from sight, leaving only the fug of sulphur and a bemused Mr Fred watching his customers fighting to get out of the doors.

'I'll kill 'im!' whispered Mr Fred. 'If he shows his gormless smiling face in here one more time I am going to kill him.'

★

Suddenly Goldoor came face to face with Mona-Cygnus and the shock caused him to start to scream once more.

'You were quick,' she said when the garbled noise had dropped a few decibels. 'You found her then?'

Looking deep into his confused, blurred eyes she nodded and said, 'I thought so. You got the wrong one didn't you, lovey?'

His mouth continued to open and close long after the screaming had stopped. 'Yes. I believe that's the effect she has on most people,' said Mona-Cygnus with a nod, but Goldoor was too deep in shock to reply.

★

Lacertus decided to lay low for a while. He stayed down on the kitchen level for nearly three full days after the contretemps with Ortolan Apus. He had to admit to feeling a small twinge of remorse when he thought of the fencing master stuck in a six foot by six foot cell, a hundred and fifty feet below ground but it *was* only a small twinge and it didn't last long. When it came down to brass bedposts, all was fair in love, war and burning ambition. After all the fuss died down he had decided that maybe the Prince Pyxis, candyfloss-brain himself, deserved a turn.

It might be easier to get to the still bed-ridden son and heir. To that end he had been working away in his small room late into the night, messing around with a discarded Junior Chemistry Set from the Royal toy collection. There were a few indelible stains on the bedclothes that would take some explaining away, but that could be worried about later. He had four formulas worked out that looked promising. The first three he had written out carefully in a disguised hand on a plain unassuming piece of paper while the fourth he would keep in reserve for the Prince Pyxis. Lacertus had a vague idea of what it should do but before taking any drastic steps he needed to find a suitable guinea pig to test the concoction on. Having rearranged the contents of the box to his own satisfaction and slipped in the three 'useful' formulas with the innocent phrase 'stink bomb mixtures' scribbled on the top of the page he set out to return the Junior Chemistry Set to a prominent position in the Royal toy cupboard.

With luck the obnoxious Ortolan would do the rest.

*

The Dowager Duchess Harmonia was on a mission of mercy. She was making a desperate attempt to cheer up her favourite grandson, the Heir Apparent, who had been having such a lousy time of things lately. Propped up in his bed with his heavily plastered leg, his sore feet still tightly wrapped and a long white bandage entwined around his head, the Prince Pyxis made a pitiful sight. The fact that the dreadful old one-eyed woman sitting dutifully beside the bed was another part of the reason for his pitiful expression was not a thought that had occurred to her.

'Your father is on one of his money-saving binges again,' she was saying. 'Why he can't just implement a new tax is beyond me. After all it's what your dear old Grand-Daddy would have done.'

Having been subjected to this single-track harangue for the past three hours Pyxis was getting decidedly suicidal. That the unwelcome appearance of the old hag had interrupted a far more interesting mission of mercy being performed by his sister's young, pretty, large-breasted ladies' maid Lyra, was something that only increased the sense of frustration he felt.

'...and now he is complaining about your poor dear mother and her organ. Just because the man from the repair service had to come out again. I really don't know *where* it will all end.'

With closed eyes Pyxis listened to the droning voice, and was just considering the best line of sarcastic abuse to use to get rid of the old lady when he heard her say, 'Ah, he's gone to sleep bless him.' And then to herself, 'Must be near teatime anyway.' And she stood up with a creaking in the joints. Pyxis tried very hard not to smile and let the old bag think he was asleep. The old lady was still muttering about tight-fisted old men as she softly closed the door behind herself. With a deep sigh of relief, Pyxis had to stop himself from cheering out loud. Lying back he let the quiet of the room seep into his bones. The creak of the large, wooden wardrobe door caused his eyes to flicker open.

'Has she gone?' whispered a sweet, gentle voice.

'Yes. The old bag has finally gone,' answered Pyxis with a smile. The blonde head and ravishing body of Lyra slipped lithely out of the cupboard. Pyxis watched her slip silently over to the door and turn the large brass key in the lock. With a knowing smile she slipped the key into the cleft of her breasts and sauntered lazily over to the bed, 'I thought she would never go. I was almost going to sleep in there myself,' purred Lyra. Slowly, she untied the laces on the front of her tight, straining bodice until the key dropped onto the bed. The gormless face and vacant eyes of the Heir Apparent lit up with lustful greed as the large, white breasts fell into his outstretched hands.

*

Returning to his own quarters via the nefarious routes he preferred, having replaced the Junior Chemistry Set in a prominent position in the Royal toy cupboard, Lacertus decided to see what the pea-brained Prince was up to. From behind the portrait of Queen Xenophobe he watched open-mouthed and gaped enviously at the sight of Lyra slowly rolling up the hem of Prince Pyxis's dreadful striped nightgown, while her firm breasts were being mercilessly massaged.

'The lucky son of a...' he whispered to himself with feeling, his eyes glued to the ancient Queen's open eye-slits. 'The bloody lucky son of a...'

It was nearly half an hour before he could tear himself away from the extraordinary vision and carry on back to his own quarters, limping with frustration.

*

Glimmergoyne was standing on the top step of the massive stone staircase, leaning with one hand against an enormous stone lion when the thunder of hooves announced the imminent arrival of the second royal coach, the only one left since the disaster at the Gatehouse the other day. He had quite enjoyed being back on the doors for the past few days since the unfortunate departure of

Viktor. It brought back memories of the old days. The wild-eyed horses careered around the corner, the wildly swinging coach just clearing the stone pillars of the Gatehouse and racing around the huge circular driveway. They needed three complete revolutions of the central statue of the late King Monoceros before they could slow to a halt. The blue clad coachman half-dismounted, half-fell from the front box seat. He staggered up to Glimmergoyne and stood swaying at the foot of the steps.

'Got 'im sur! Fineley got the lil' bugger.' At which he attempted a swinging salute, missed his forehead by a good six inches and carried on by the momentum swung through a hundred and eighty degrees to collapse unconscious on the cobbles.

Glimmergoyne paced the measured pace of the efficient butler down the stone steps, carefully stepping over the prone figure of the coachman and approached the barred windows of the coach.

'Good morning, sir. It is my pleasure to welcome you to Castle Camelopardis.' At which he bowed low.

'Look, if you let me out now,' whined the terrified looking young man behind the bars, 'I could sneak off down the hill and then when I get home I could have a word with Daddy about sending you a nice fat...'

The young man's voice tailed off as he caught sight of the smile on Glimmergoyne's face and his slowly shaking head. '...A nice fat cheque?' more faintly, then, 'Just for you. Please?' with a hint of desperation creeping in. The smiling face just turned slowly from side to side.

'I believe it was your father that sent you in the first place, sir,' answered Glimmergoyne, 'something to do with your unpaid *gambling debts* I believe,' speaking with obvious distaste.

'Look, can't we sort this out like gentlemen, I mean things don't need to go too far...'

'I shall go and announce your arrival to His Majesty at once,' said Glimmergoyne firmly and turned on his heel.

'Go on then, you cranky old git. Sod the money. You can die a poor man, you crabby fart. Go and tell your precious Majesty.'

Glimmergoyne did not rise to bait, he merely smiled sweetly at the stone lion as he passed through the doors.

★

'What I need is a picture or description of the young lady,' said Mona-Cygnus to Goldoor.

'She is the most beautiful of creatures, flaxen-haired with the palest blue eyes and the most marvellous, large and shapely—' Mona-Cygnus slapped her hand over his mouth to shut him up.

'No, no. Not that one. I've heard that one. Dear *God* have I heard that one,' she said with feeling. 'You mentioned a picture. Do you have it with you?'

'Mmmmph, ahhummph.'

'Where?'

'Mmmmphh mmmphamm phummph.'

'The shed at The Artisan's Arms hey? Right, if I take away my hand will you promise to keep your mouth shut?'

Goldoor nodded quickly.

'You'd better. The first mention of flaxen hair and you're on your own, sonny. Got that?'

He nodded again.

'Right, well, I know where the shed is. The bag is in there, is it?'

Goldoor nodded again.

'Right, here we go then.'

Standing up as straight as her wizened old body would allow, she began to chant a series of unintelligible words. Goldoor watched, bemused by the whole process. Suddenly there was a loud roar and a flash of orange lightning in the small room. As the golden blue fug cleared, Goldoor turned to see the figure of Mr Fred with the large, flaccid backpack in his hands.

'I say, that's mine,' he shouted and grabbed the bag from the startled innkeeper just before he vanished again in another cloud of blue smoke.

'I really do think I'm starting to getting the hang of this,' said Mona-Cygnus to Goldoor as he waved the bag in triumph.

'I think Mr Fred was a bit surprised too,' said Goldoor. 'Did he get back all right?'

'No idea,' said Mona-Cygnus with a non-committal shrug. 'Now, where's this picture?'

'Here we are,' said Goldoor proudly, 'See that gorgeous flaxen—'

'I'm warning you!' she said coldly. 'Now shut it.'

'Sorry.'

★

King Vulpecula of Camelopardis was feeling a great deal more cheerful. Prince Circinus of Cornucopia had been found and was safely ensconced in one of the more secure 'guest rooms'. Friday night's dinner for the Duke of Philbert would be the ideal opportunity to announce the nuptials if it could be arranged and the Princess was happy with the idea. Bounding up the stairs of the tower two at a time, he smiled happily to himself.

'Dearest? Are you there dearest?' he called as he reached the top landing, 'It is only I. Your Daddy.'

'Oh Daddy,' boomed Andromeda throwing open the doors, 'I have the most wonderful news!'

'Oh? So have I. He's arrived, darling, the Prince from Cornucopia, the one I told you about. Remember?'

'Sod him,' said the Princess gruffly, 'I don't want him. I want the one who was here the other night. The blond, muscular one.'

'But dearest heart, Prince Circinus is a really nice chap, young, pleasant, nice to his mother. The dinner is all set for the night after tomorrow, the chef has been working—'

'Is he blond with strong, muscular arms? Does he have just the cutest biceps you've ever seen? Are his shoulders broad and powerful?'

'Who? The *chef*?'

'No stupid, not that hulking great barrel of dough. The other one.'

'Well no, not quite, but…'

'Then I don't want him. I want the one who was here the other night,' she said firmly, 'Not some noisome little oik who is paying for the privilege.'

'But dearest…'

'He flashed in here, all blond hair and powerful muscles, then flashed out again at will. He's the one I want. My hero. The one I love!' she said wistfully gazing at the ceiling, smiling her gap-toothed smile.

'Look, I don't even know who he was dearest. The guard couldn't find a trace of him anywhere, remember?'

'He even managed to get past those morons. Isn't he *wonderful*, Daddy?'

King Vulpecula stared at her incredulously. This was not going quite the way he had planned. She was obviously distressed. The waiting was beginning to tell on her.

'Look, darling, I'm sure he was a nice boy and all that but—'

'I said he was *wonderful*, Daddy. Don't you listen?' snarled Andromeda. 'He's the one I want. Find him for me. Now!' she snapped.

'But dearest—'

'Just find him. You promised me a husband by Christmas. He is the one I want.'

'But dearest, I don't know who—'

'Then send your stupid guards out to look for him. I mean how many tall, blond, muscular heroes can there possibly be in the Kingdom?'

'All right dear,' said the King, capitulating gracelessly, 'I'll see what I can do.'

'Thank you Daddy,' she bawled, rushing up to him and throwing her arms around his neck, 'I *knew* you would see reason.'

Trudging slowly down the stairs, his good temper completely evaporated, the King tried to think of what he was going to say to the King of Cornucopia. After all, the man had already sent a down payment. In all probability it had been spent as well. He was so deep in thought that he did not hear the minute crack as he stepped heavily on the small glass vial laying in wait for him. He did however notice the sudden waft of a foul, fetid odour that quickly spread across the room.

'*Ortolan!*' he screamed, 'Just you wait until I get my hands on you, you little…' he choked off as the stench became unbearable and ran for the open doors. Coughing and retching the King dashed out into the open air and leaned against the stone lion.

'He will definitely have to go,' he muttered to the perpetually silent, petrified feline.

Seven

Down in the depths of the castle the fencing master was beginning to get worried. Three days he had been here now and nothing had happened. His requests to see the King had been ignored by the surly watchman who brought him his food. This horrible mess would have to be sorted out soon. After all, how long could they possibly keep him here?

A sudden flash and cloud of acrid smoke filled the tiny space as M. Belvoire shrank back against the hard stone wall in terror.

'Um, hello? Is there anybody there?' called the voice of Mr Fred from the cloud. 'Er, excuse me. Hello?'

'Who whh-wh-who are you?' quivered the voice of M. Belvoire.

'Fred Dobbs. Artisan's Arms,' said Mr Fred. 'Now if you could just tell me how to get out of here I have a pub to run.'

The voice sounded a trifle unnatural, as if the mind were trying desperately to understand what was happening against a background of minimal information. Hysteria was very close to the surface.

'Sorry,' said M. Belvoire with a shrug, eyeing the fat man warily, 'I'd love to go down the pub too but I'm stuck here myself.'

'Where the hell are we then?' asked Mr Fred, the tones of his voice rising noticeably.

'The dungeons of Castle Camelopardis, of course. So what did you do?'

'Nothing. Nothing at all. One minute I was in my beer cellar changing a barrel of best, the next in a strange room with a smiling blond-haired, blue-eyed prat in it, and then the next? Well, the next I was here.'

M. Belvoire looked carefully at the confused publican and tried to draw himself even closer to the wall. As far away as possible from the fat, red-faced madman.

'So who was this prat then?' he asked cautiously,

'Calls himself Gold Door. Tall lad, blond hair, very big. Left his smouldering boots in my bar when he went up in a flash of bright yellow smoke the other day. Took hours to get rid of the smell of the sulphur too.'

'I see,' said M. Belvoire cautiously. 'And you say he was in this strange room?'

'Yes. I mean no. I mean… What the hell do I mean?'

'Tell me about it,' said the confused little fencing master soothingly, playing for time. The man was obviously so far out of his own tree that, in all probability he was halfway out of somebody else's as well.

'Well it was like this you see. I was searching in this Gold Door's travelling bag, looking for a forwarding address, you know like you do, when suddenly there was this big flash and lots of smoke and I'm in this small room with a black cauldron in it with all sorts of strange objects flying about and other funny things hanging from the ceiling and then, and then the big lad, he says to me "I say, that's mine" and grabs this bag out of my hands and with another flash and a bang suddenly I'm here with you.'

'I see,' said M. Belvoire, nodding his head sagely. 'And then?'

A sudden blinding flash and a scream from Mr Fred that was suddenly cut short announced that the Mona-Cygnus Rubber-Band Effect was still in operation. As the smog cleared revealing that the tiny cell was once more strictly single accommodation, M. Belvoire sighed with relief and laid out on his small cot.

'I suppose I should go round the twist as well. Then maybe I could get out of here in a flash of green smoke,' he muttered to himself and giggled.

*

'Vot do you mean cancelled?' bellowed the voice of Chef Bootes across the fume-filled kitchen. 'Ve haf been preparink for zis shite for zree days now. No, no. You cannot canzel. I forboden it!'

'Sorry Chef,' said Glimmergoyne gaily, 'it seems the Princess has decided she doesn't want this one. Pity really.' He smiled sweetly at the bright red face of the chef as it emerged from a cloud of steam. 'Just when things were looking like coming right too.'

'But Ve mussen get all zis food and sinks eaten.'

'Terribly sorry, Chef,' replied Glimmergoyne, enjoying every moment of the great fat dollop's discomfort.

'I vill go und speak viz der King about ziz, personliche,' boomed the white linen mountain. 'Zis ist my reputation at stake hier.' Chef Bootes drew himself up to his full height, twirled his magnificent moustaches, puffed out his chest and marched out of the kitchen.

'That's the way the cookie crumbles, Cookie,' called Glimmergoyne after him.

'Bog off plate carrier,' floated back the rough farmyard accent.

'He seems a bit miffed don't you think?' said Glimmergoyne loudly to the smirking faces around the kitchen. Ethelreda appeared at his side in a floury white cloud.

'Come with me,' she whispered to the bemused butler, 'I've got a little something you might like to sample.'

The huskiness in her voice was suggestive of deeply sprung mattresses and black silk sheets. Slipping her hand confidentially into his, she led him to the small pastry kitchen and closed the door softly behind them. Once inside she put a finger to her lips indicating silence and led him to the small sweets cupboard in the corner.

'Here,' she breathed sensually, pressing an apricot Madeleine into his hand. 'I made these *special*,' she said, watching him stuff the sticky confection into his mouth.

'Very nice,' mumbled Glimmergoyne. 'Very nice indeed, Ethel,' he said through a mouthful of moist sponge.

'Mind the coconut,' she said coyly, 'it can get caught in your teeth, and all *sorts* of funny places if you're not careful.'

Glimmergoyne smiled sweetly at her. She was a dear thing really, always letting him in on the nice little dainties. Mumbling his thanks as she pushed a small pile of iced cookies into his hand he made his way to the door.

'I really must be about my business, Ethel, lots to do you know, now that we don't have a doorman and all that.'

'The poor man,' she breathed. 'Such a shame really,' as she gazed deeply into his eyes.

'These things happen,' he said nonchalantly. 'Well, I really must be off. I will see you later then.'

'Any time Mr Glimmergoyne. I'm always here. Or somewhere,' she said meaningfully with the faintest flicker of her eyelashes. The gesture went completely unnoticed.

Opening the door Glimmergoyne did not notice the smirking faces under the tall white hats that were bobbing around the kitchen either, nor hear the hissed comments that went with them.

Ethelreda watched his pristine tailcoat gliding up the stairs wistfully and sighed as he vanished from sight. Ever since that Christmas party five years ago when he had become a little more tipsy than was usual for such a conscientious head butler and things had become quite amorous beneath the Ballroom table, the redoubtable Ethelreda had had her sights set on the erstwhile Mr Glimmergoyne; Mr Glimmergoyne and a small cottage by the sea. Coming back down to earth suddenly on hearing the badly muffled giggles, she hardened her momentarily softened features and bawled, 'What the hell do you lot think you are looking at? Get on with your work unless you want my rolling pin across your knuckles!' Silence fell on the vast, high-ceilinged kitchen. She glared at the down-turned faces, snorted once and slammed the door to the tiny pastry kitchen noisily behind her.

*

Behind the portrait of Queen Xenophobe in the King's private office, Lacertus listened to the whining voice of Chef Bootes. The great lard-ball himself was not a happy man.

'…ze canapés alone are costin' youse a good few ducats, Your 'ighness. To cancel now is madness. My boys 'ave been workin' overtime which ai cannot afford to pay on mai budget for this month.'

'Do they want a job next month or not?' oozed the voice of Captain Parsus.

'His Highness cannot extend your budget *again*,' said Antila the Chancellor nervously. 'You overran by three point two per cent last month as it is, costs appear to be rising by an average two point nine per cent per month and have been for the past six—'

'Yes, Yes. We've bin frough all that, you penny-pinching wee tartar, all ah'm fookin' askin is…'

The cultured accent disintegrated into the rural patois of his native village as his anger increased.

'…and there is just no more leeway for extravagances!' continued the chancellor doggedly. 'Now please, let's hear no more about it.'

'Sod the bleedin' figures. Wot am ah gonna do wi' all this grub? You tell me.'

'No need for abuse,' cautioned Captain Parsus. 'His Majesty does not like to have his meetings turning into verbal mud slinging. I suggest that you return to the kitchen and sort out the staff, the food and the budget and compile an abuse-free report for his Highness before morning.'

The coldness in the voice had all the depth of an Icelandic iceberg. 'Run along now,' he said with a frosty smile.

Chef Bootes opened his mouth to speak, thought better of it, looked from face to face one last time searching for some glimmer of support and finding none, stormed out. The reverberations of the slamming door faded away to leave a deathly quiet on the room.

'Well,' said the King eyebrows raised, 'all that for a cancelled party. I don't suppose there's any doubt about the figures?'

'Sire,' said the chancellor in hurt tones, 'as if I would make up something like that. The very suggestion…'

'All right, all right. Run along now. See me in the morning and we'll see what we can do about the books.'

'Yes Sire,' said the chancellor faintly with all the petulance of a wrongly accused and scolded child, 'as you wish.'

The King watched the chancellor's back disappear through the door and turned to his Captain.

'Is there no good news about these days, Parsus?' he asked wearily. 'All I seem to get these days is petty little grievances about money. Money, money, money.'

'You could always ask me why there is a slimy green frog sitting on the middle of your desk, Sire,' said the Captain with a toothful smile.

'A *what*? Bloody hell. There's a frog on my desk. What is a slimy green frog doing on my desk, Parsus?'

'I have absolutely no idea, Sire,' grinned Parsus.

'Well get shot of it, man. Out the window with it!'

'No!' croaked the frog, 'Not again. I must speak with you, Sire.'

'Do that again, Parsus,' said the King in astonishment.

'Do what again, Sire?'

'Make the frog talk without moving your lips.'

'Nothing to do with me, Sire.'

'Look, are you going to listen to me or not? I need to find some water soon or my skin goes all dry and itchy. It's bloody murder, I can tell you.'

'What the…'

'Never mind that, dear God this is hard work. I've had a frog in the throat before but I never thought I'd have to use a frog's bloody throat.'

'Serpens?' queried Captain Parsus with furrowed brow.

'Yes sir. It is I. I have returned, sir.'

'You *know* this frog, Captain?'

'Yes Sire. Corporal Serpens, reduced to Private by your good self, sent on nutter hunt, failed to return to duty, thought to have legged it to the residence of a certain Mrs Frobisher in Barton Regis,' reeled off Parsus in his best 'Captain of the King's Guard' manner.

'How do you know about Mrs Frobisher in Barton Regis?' demanded the frog in a wheezing croak.

Captain Parsus just smiled sweetly and said nothing.

'Forget that for the moment,' said the King hastily. 'I mean dear God. What on earth happened to you man? Er, frog? Er man? Whatever you are.'

'Well, you see Private Volans upset this witch, well this witch's dead mother to be more precise and she put this spell on me and I turned into this horrible little thing you see before you and I've had a very, very bad week. It took me five bleedin' days to get the vocal cords in some sort of order.' The croaking became less lucid with every word spoken.

'And did you find the nutter?' asked the King with a smile. 'Where is he? She has decided she wants him after all, you see.

For this you could get your stripe back. Then I could call in a few rather large bets, tie that bastard Duke of Leophus's sarcastic comments into a lead sack and drop them on his head, the castle would be saved and... and... I... I could go on holiday!'

He smiled and his eyes glazed over dreamily.

'I couldn't find him, Sire,' said the frog bluntly. 'He ran off when we spotted him and, hey wait, no, hey, no please, not again, I aaaaaghhhh...' croaked the frog as Captain Parsus casually tossed the unfortunate amphibian out of the window.

'He, ah, he said something about needing some water, Sire,' said the Captain with a leonine grin as a distant splash in the moat announced the arrival of the frog.

'Oh dear,' said the King in an unconvincing tone of care and concern. 'Serves him right. Should keep the stupid bugger happy anyway. Right. What's next on the agenda, Captain?'

Still behind the portrait Lacertus grinned and jumped down from the alcove. He had seen and heard enough. So, there was a witch in Leopardis, was there? She could be very useful indeed. Hurrying with careless ease, down the labyrinthine routes carefully mapped out in his head through long years of patient searching, he set off downwards and outwards towards the moat, in search of a certain frog known as Serpens.

*

Ortolan Apus had spread the contents of the Junior Chemistry Set across the large wooden table in his room. Having improvised a few pieces of equipment with bits of rubbish from the kitchens, and having found a very useful book on alchemy in the castle library he had advanced far beyond the quaint little formulas on the piece of paper. Lacertus would have been hard-pressed to recognise the current complex scribbles and symbols on stained pieces of paper littering the open spaces of the table. Contrary to popular belief, Ortolan Apus was not stupid. Quite the opposite, the stupidity could almost have been said to have been a display of cleverness. He was simply lazy; too lazy to apply himself to his studies or follow the more standard forms of learning. Both he and Lacertus had more in common than either would have admitted to or liked. Both wanted to be King at all costs. Lacertus through a sense of injustice at his humble position in life, Ortolan Apus just to spite big brother Pyxis. As he was carefully measuring a particularly powerful acid into a test-tube of tiny yellow crystals there came a soft knocking at the door.

'Come in,' he called absently, not looking up from the delicate operation. The door swung wide and Matron Beamish floated in.

'Hullo Orty,' she said sweetly. 'How are you today? Oh, playing with your chemistry set. You haven't had that out for years. What are you making? Some perfumes for your dear Mamma perhaps?'

'Not quite,' said the spotty youth distractedly.

'Oooh let me see if I can guess. I know, you are trying to discover a new medicine that will cure all the ills of the world and make you rich and famous,' she said triumphantly.

'Not quite,' he repeated, gingerly putting the acid bottle into its stand and removing the stopper from a small green bottle.

'Well is it a pesticide then, to kill off all the nasty little bugs on the farmers crops and make them grow big and strong?' His sidelong glance at her that said in no uncertain terms 'Where's the fun in that you stupid old bat' went unnoticed as she continued to smile sweetly at him, at her little Orty.

'Not quite,' he said again, turning back to his bottles.

'I really came to see if you would like some tea and a game of crib? You know, it's so long since we had a nice quiet game and a cup of tea. What do you say?'

The nanny to sweet little boy tone in her voice made him cringe inwardly and he was about to refuse politely when an idea struck him. It was all very well theorising about these things, but he did need to find a test subject for some of the more interesting concoctions.

He turned to face her and said in his very best mannered voice, 'That would be very nice, Nanny.'

'Oh good. I'll see you in the playroom in ten minutes then?'

'I'll just clear up here, shall I?'

'Lovely,' she said happily and floated out of the door. 'Ten minutes then.' And she was gone.

The moment Matron had disappeared, Ortolan hurried to the door, closed and bolted it and returned to the table. Quickly he assembled all the more noxious substances and returned them to their box. Then he picked out a small yellow bottle, checked the stopper, and slipped it into his pocket. He failed to notice the smell, something akin to burning copper wire, that was beginning to emanate from the box on the tabletop as he walked, grinning cheerfully, up the circular staircase to the playroom, on his way to tea and crib with Nanny.

★

'Now as I see it, the problem has been in getting the right amount of bat's wing and toad's liver. This page of the book is a little blurred you see, it looks suspiciously like the cat's peed on it. What that does you see is make the retroactive element uncertain – the Mona-Cygnus Rubber-Band Effect as I have tentatively called it… Are you listening to me?' demanded Mona-Cygnus of the blank-faced Goldoor.

'What?' he asked. 'Sorry I was off in a, in a, what do you call it now? Well I was off somewhere anyway. I think.'

'Do me a favour,' she said wearily, 'let me do the thinking. All right?'

'Sure, no problem.' He smiled back at her.

'Now, what we have to do is to mix this here, with this here, like this…

She stopped talking as she worked. After a while her tongue poked itself out of her mouth in the manner of a schoolboy puzzling over a rather difficult maths problem. Goldoor's eyes glazed over after a short while and the smile went on to automatic pilot.

★

Back in the playroom of Camelopardis, Ortolan Apus and Nanny were having tea. They had played a few games of crib and chatted about minor goings-on in the castle for a while. Having had but a brief moment to perform the deed, Ortolan could only manage to slip a couple of drops of the 'formula' into Nanny's tea. As time went on and nothing seemed to be happening, Ortolan was getting bored. He had just starting to think about getting away from the boring old woman when she suddenly declared, 'Boy, oh boy, is it hot in here.' At which she removed her uniform belt and starched white cap. Deciding to stay and see the experiment through, he suggested another game of crib. He was not disappointed by his decision. By the end of two more games the matron was looking decidedly warm. Her face had reddened and her eyes were glazing over.

'Gosh! It is so hot in here. Can't you feel it, Orty?' He shook his head and smiled at her.

'Well I certainly can.'

She removed her jacket and shoes, rolled down her stockings and took them off before undoing all the buttons down the front of her uniform.

'That's better,' she said and giggled, a pure girlish giggle. 'I do feel strange though,' she said and giggled again.

'Would you like some more tea, Nanny?' asked Ortolan sweetly, as if there was nothing out of the ordinary going on.

'Not for the moment, dear. I feel, I feel, I feel more like *dancing!*'

Ortolan grinned as she stood and began to twist and twirl around the room to some imaginary music. As she swung her arms the opening of the uniform would part revealing to his gaze the large, lace-covered bosom and fleshy thighs of stuffy old Matron Beamish. To his never-ending delight she suddenly declared, 'This room is far too stuffy. I need more *freedom!*'

In throwing off the blue uniform and pulling the voluminous underskirts high over her head she also threw off the last vestiges of the staid and sober children's nanny. She danced around the outskirts of the room, uncaring in her nakedness. Ortolan could only marvel at the way in which her sagging breasts and fleshy thighs jiggled up and down as she moved. He was speechless.

'Let's go into the garden,' she said joyfully, 'it will be cooler there.'

So saying she danced her way to the door, opened it wide and waltzed out onto the landing. Ortolan Apus followed quickly to the doorway of the playroom and watched, grinning with amazement. He would never, ever be able to see Matron in quite the same light again. He fingered the glass vial in his pocket carefully. Though he had only managed to get a few small drops of the stuff into her tea the results were stupendous. This stuff was dynamite.

As the wrinkled, white figure twisted and twirled her way around the landing there was a look of pure exhilaration on her face. Dancing and singing she began a slow descent of the broad staircase. Ortolan followed her as far as the banister rail and watched as she reached the marble floor of the Reception Hall.

'Matron Beamish!' bellowed the voice of Glimmergoyne. 'Cover yourself up woman, it's obscene!'

'Mr Glimmergoyne!' she called. 'Come and dance with me. It's a beautiful day and—'

'Just go and get some clothes on before the King sees you. Ye Gods woman, have you been drinking?'

'Only tea, Mr Glimmergoyne, only tea, tea, tea. Do reh me fah so la tea...'

Glimmergoyne appeared from his post by the door with a horse blanket in his hands. Throwing the cover over the prancing woman he hustled her towards the servants' stairs.

Ortolan rubbed his hands in glee. This was better than he could ever have hoped.

'Oh Mr Glimmergoyne! Where are you taking me, you naughty man?' came the muffled voice of Matron Beamish.

'Just shut up and get down those stairs,' came the reply followed by dull silence. Still grinning, Ortolan made his way thoughtfully back to the playroom.

Eight

After nearly four hours of fruitless searching Lacertus returned to the castle, dirty, wet and foul-tempered. He had scrubbed around the fringes of the moat and interrogated every frog he could find, without success. Private Serpens was not amongst them. Lying back on his cot with his hands clasped behind his head, he concentrated his thoughts on finding the witch. If she did exist, as seemed all too likely seeing that a frog had said so, then she would be able to assist him. Now what was the name of the other Private involved in the nutter hunt? He would know where she lived. He racked his brain in search of the name. The frog had said it in the King's office. Vogle? Yodel? Vocal?

It was just a matter of concentration. He had read a small blue book once on lateral thinking, written by a very clever man with all sorts of letters after his name. Had he but known it, it was the same little blue book that Mona-Cygnus had read in her search for a cure for her loneliness, but be that as it may. Start from what you know, it had said, and then work out from it. You can then look back and view the situation from a different angle.

Frog speaking. Frog talking. Frog on the desk of the King. Voice of the frog. The lonely frog. The voice of the lonely frog. Volans! That was it! Private Volans. Quickly, Lacertus leapt up from the bed, started to shout Eureka, then thought better of it. It was hardly original after all.

Pulling on his best kitchen boy's jacket, the smart Sunday one that looked pretty near official, he ran off down the corridor towards the Guardhouse.

*

The vast expanse of Private Second Class Gramm sat at the small table in the little office of the Gatehouse stuffing sandwiches into his mouth.

'Private Volans!' shouted Lacertus pushing open the door swiftly. Private Second Class Gramm spluttered at the sudden interruption and standing awkwardly sent both table and sandwiches flying, 'Bloody 'ell!' he said petulantly when he caught sight of the young Lacertus. 'That was me elevenses, that was!'

'I need to find Private Volans, Private!' shouted Lacertus in an attempt to catch the big man off guard.

'I dunno about that, sir,' muttered Private Gramm uncertainly, 'Who are you, sir?'

'Never mind that now,' snapped Lacertus. 'Captain Parsus needs to see Private Volans right now.'

'Well if it's for the Captain then I suppose…'

'Hurry up, man, I haven't got all day!'

'Well if you're sure it's for the Captain…'

'Look, do you want me to tell the Captain that you were evasive and unhelpful?'

'No sir!' muttered Gramm hastily, snapping to his own sloppy version of a salute. 'In the back there, in his room, sir, second on the left down the corridor, sir. It's just that…'

'I'll find it,' snapped back Lacertus. 'Finish your elevenses, Private.'

Lacertus made off towards the back door before the idiot could think too much about what was going on. The fact that he could have gone for a ten-mile walk, had a good night's sleep, laid in until well after sunrise and had a sumptuous breakfast before Private Gramm could have formulated a thoughtful question was not something that occurred to him, even though it was pretty close to the truth.

Finding the right door and deciding to carry on the direct action he had begun, he turned the handle, pushed it open and bawled, 'Private Volans? Are you there? I need…'

He stopped in mid-sentence not quite sure what to make of the sight that greeted him. Private Volans, sitting on the edge of the narrow cot dressed only in brightly coloured undershorts and knee-length, highly polished cavalry boots stared back at him, horror written deep in his eyes. The man's lips were still enclosed around the inflating tube of the partially filled, pink plastic doll that lolled in his lap.

The pair of them stared at one another for a long moment, until regaining his composure, Lacertus once again assumed the authoritative tone.

'Volans, I need to speak with you. Privately.'

Glancing conspiratorially over his shoulder, Lacertus pushed the door closed behind himself and approached the man on the bed. Spurred into action, Private Volans released the inflator from his mouth and tried to stuff the pink plastic doll under the bed. When he realised that it showed off his naked legs and the tops of his shiny boots he swiftly put it back again in confused embarrassment.

'What do you want? Now this is not what it may appear to be. It is a private room after all. I'm looking after this, ahh this, um, for a friend...' The unpleasantly high-pitched voice tailed off slowly.

'I'm not interested in any of that,' snapped Lacertus with a casual wave of his hand, enjoying the feeling of complete control over the situation.

'What I need from you is some information. Some information concerning a certain witch?'

'Look, there's no need to tell the Captain about this... is there? I mean, he doesn't need to know, does he?'

'As I said, all I need is some information. Then you can forget that I was ever here and I shall do my best to forget...' Unable to find the right form of words Lacertus just jabbed his finger vaguely in the direction of the slowly collapsing pink plastic blob.

'Well,' said Volans, his voice a little firmer, 'if I forget *you* and you forget *me* there will be no harm done will there, I mean...

'Where does she live?'

'Promise first?'

'We'll see. Where does she live?' repeated Lacertus coldly, a thin-lipped smile on his face. He found himself greatly enjoying the man's discomfort.

Private Volans rubbed his face in his hands and told the kitchen boy what he knew of the witch of Leopardis.

★

'Quick, wake up!' called Mona-Cygnus, 'Quick now. This

mixture is a bit unstable.'

Opening his eyes, Goldoor took one look at the excitement on the face of the little witch and leapt to his feet.

'You've got it?'

'I think so. Just stand there a minute.'

'Oh I say. At last.'

'Right, here we go.' Mona-Cygnus began to chant rapidly.

The small, square room blazed suddenly with yellow and silver light and sulphurous fumes filled the air and then just as suddenly it became a different room. Lyra, woken from a very pleasant dream about blond-haired, blue-eyed, heavily muscled athletes, tried to shriek but the acrid fumes grabbed at her vocal cords and she began coughing and spluttering.

'I say!' said the voice of Goldoor. 'I think it might actually have worked this time!' from the midst of the smoke cloud, 'Damn, my shirt got singed. Help, the bloody thing's on fire!' He dragged off his shirt and jumped up and down on it several times to put out the flames. Finding her voice after much choking and gagging, Lyra began an awful high-pitched scream.

'No. No don't. Sorry and all that but it is only I. Your beloved.'

The screaming stopped suddenly.

'What did you say?' she asked cautiously.

'I said it is only I!'

'No, no. The next bit. What was that next bit?'

'Um. What did I say?' His brow furrowed as he thought. 'Um, I said um what did I say? Dum-di-dum, I said, um. Ah yes, I've got it, I said "Sorry and all that but it is only I".'

'No, no. The next bit, the bit after that. What was that *last* bit?'

The yellow mist suddenly cleared and Goldoor found himself face to face with the girl of his dreams. The long blonde hair, the cool, ice blue eyes, the deep cleft in the huge bosom that was putting untold stress on the flimsy material of her nightdress. It was her; the girl from the miniature.

'My beloved!' he whispered.

'That's it!' she cried, leaping from the bed. 'That's what I thought you said.'

'Oh, I say,' said Goldoor as she threw her arms around him

and pressed herself close to him. He sniffed cautiously. Above the soft, sweet scent of her hair, he could smell burning.

'I say, can you smell burning?' he asked of the blonde head resting on his broad chest. 'Only I'm sure… It's me! Quick, help. My trousers are on fire.'

Hurriedly he removed the smouldering wreckage that had once been his best trousers and threw them onto the floor. He jumped up and down on them a few times until the smoke stopped rising.

'There now, that's put a stop to that. Oh, I say.'

Lyra's steady gaze swept the large muscled torso and thighs, until it came to rest on the cartoon-festooned boxer shorts. She giggled throatily and said, 'I don't know what you are doing to Minnie Mouse but she looks very happy. Let's hope Mickey never finds out.'

'I say,' said Goldoor again and swallowed hard.

He stared at the petite figure with the huge breasts and the nightdress that barely covered the essentials. Without taking her eyes from Minnie's smiling face, Lyra lazily untied the satin bows at her shoulders and let the gauzy confection of a nightdress slide gently to the floor.

'I say!' whispered Goldoor, taking in the full extent of the huge breasts, the pearl white skin, the voluptuous curve of the thighs.

'Now then, big boy,' purred Lyra, 'let's find out why Minnie is looking so happy.'

'I say,' whispered Goldoor.

'Shut up,' said Lyra.

★

In line with popular belief, Prince Pyxis Vulpecula *was* as stupid as he appeared. After nearly a week of lying in his bed and generally upsetting everybody that came into contact with him he was beginning to get bored. That it had taken an entire week for him to become bored was a good indication of the rate at which his mind worked. Ringing the bell for Glimmergoyne, he angrily swore to himself and repeated his self-comforting litany about what he would do to them all when he was King while he waited. When after about twenty minutes nobody appeared to answer his summons he decided to try and go and *find* someone to abuse instead. The old wicker bath chair was just out of reach. Swearing profusely he swung his stiffly-plastered leg to the floor, stood up much in the manner of a totally demented stiltwalker, wobbled a little then fell flat on his face.

'Damn, damn, damn!' he muttered to the rug under his nose. Just then the door swung open and Columba, the under-maid, slouched heavily into the room.

'Wha' ya want now?' she said languidly.

'I want to go down stairs. Is that too much to ask?' said Pyxis to the rug.

'If you fink I'm gonna do my back in liftin' your carcass off the floor you got anuver fink comin'!' answered the slovenly wench.

'I could speak with Father about a small *promotion*,' said Pyxis in a flash of inspired mental effort.

'Promotion,' breathed the under-maid, her eyes lighting up. 'You'd do vat?'

'Of course,' continued Pyxis, knowing he had found her soft spot. 'I'm sure he would be happy to agree, I mean how long is it now you have been here at the castle now?'

'Twenty eight years,' she said coldly. 'Twenty eight bleedin' years. But if you could hav' a word, like I'd be ever so grateful, like.'

The coldness melted into excitement in mid-sentence.

'Leave it with me,' lied Pyxis fluently, 'I'm sure he will see reason.'

'Well, awright ven,' she said finally. 'Where's you wantin' to go?'

'To the chair. That one there with the wheels. If you could just...'

It took more than half an hour for the short, overweight and ageing under-maid to get Pyxis fixed into the chair, half an hour of swearing, grunting and shoving. Once done, she tied the straps around his waist and adjusted the rest under his stiffly forward-jutting leg. She wiped the back of her hand across her reddened forehead and said, 'Fank Gawd fur vat. Na, we goin' dahn them steps?'

'Yes please,' said Pyxis pleasantly.

'An' you will 'ave a word wiv' 'is 'ighness.'

'Trust me,' said Pyxis with a smile that no one with a single brain cell in operation would have trusted. It was the smile of the Egyptian 'Genuine Oriental Rug' salesman as he tucks a wad of genuine crisp banknotes into his wallet.

Pushing the unwieldy chair to the door was a job in itself. Actually getting it through and pointed in the right direction was another matter. It was just as Columba got the front wheels freed from the rug that Glimmergoyne made his stately appearance.

'You rang, sir?' he said with a deferential smile.

'Where the hell have you been?' bawled the young Prince. 'I've had one hell of a horrible experience with this stupid bint humping me up off the floor just because you couldn't get your fat arse out of its chair…'

'Oh sir,' whimpered Columba, 'I did me best, sir. But I woz all on me lonesome like an'—'

'It's all right, Columba,' said the butler calmly, 'I shall take His Highness from here.'

'Fank yu, sir,' she whimpered again.

'I'm sorry I'm late in attending to you, Your Highness, but there was an urgent staff matter that required my immediate attention.'

'Well, all right,' muttered the Prince with bad grace, 'just don't let it happen again, that's all.'

'No, Your Highness,' said Glimmergoyne calmly.

At that precise moment a number of the more noxious substances in the Junior Chemistry Set laid out so carefully on the Prince Ortolan's table decided to make their presence felt. The exact formula for the event was lost in the ensuing conflagration, but the momentous explosion that rocked the East Wing of the castle was a beautiful example of how to explode in sumptuous style. The blast swept the heavy wooden door off its hinges and straight across the corridor towards the opposite wall, towards the exact spot occupied by the unfortunate Columba. Her shriek of terror was cut short as the impact squeezed her hefty frame into the equivalent of a gigantic steak sandwich. Turning quickly, Glimmergoyne was just in time to have his eyebrows and most of his moustache singed completely away by a sudden flash of yellow flame that issued from the doorway.

'*Get me out of here you moron!*' screamed Pyxis in absolute terror, but Glimmergoyne was too stunned to hear him. His wordless gibbering went completely unheeded. The sound of running feet announced the arrival of Captain Parsus and some red-jacketed minions, armed with fire buckets.

'What seems to be the problem?' asked the Captain smoothly.

'The, the, the maid, see there, the maid, what's her name, her there,' babbled Glimmergoyne in confusion.

'*Get me out of here!*' screamed Pyxis once more, hysteria making his voice squeak appallingly.

'Just one moment if you please, Your Highness,' oozed the Captain. 'Let's first get some facts straight here shall we?' he said calmly as the smoke billowed around them and the sounds of flames being beaten out with expensive Persian rugs resounded from the decimated room.

'The um, the, what is she called? Ah yes, the maid,' stammered Glimmergoyne, and pointed at the ghastly mess on the wall.

'A subversive element you think, sir?' asked the Captain, but Glimmergoyne felt his knees go weak and he subsided unconsciously to the floor with a distinct lack of grace or precision.

'*Get me out of here!*' screamed Pyxis again.

'Shut up you mindless wimp,' muttered the officious little Captain.

*

'So, let me get this straight, said the King wearily, 'Prince Ortolan's bedroom explodes, for no apparent reason whatsoever, plastering the poor unfortunate maid, whatever her name was, all over the wall with a *door* of all things, while the matron here was cavorting around the castle stark naked, singing obscene nursery rhymes, and there is a suspected anti-monarchist subversive element amongst the staff of the castle. Is that correct so far?'

'Not quite, Sire, but it seems to cover the main points well enough,' oiled Captain Parsus.

Behind his vast carven desk the King glowered around the

assembled group crowded into the small office.

'I think we had better start again from the beginning, don't you?'

Glimmergoyne cleared his throat noisily and began.

'There seems to have been some kind of misunderstanding about the chain of events here, Your Highness…'

'You're not wrong there,' said the King sarcastically.

'Well, I was down in the kitchen, getting the matron to her room since she was feeling a little bit "unwell"…' began the butler.

'Pissed as a fart you mean,' muttered Ethelreda bitchily. Glimmergoyne shot her a withering look, somewhat lacking in intensity due to the missing eyebrows and singed moustache.

'"Unwell",' emphasised the butler carefully, 'when I heard the bell from the Prince Pyxis's room. I dispatched the under-maid Columba to attend to his needs as soon as—'

'While you were tarting about with the old bag of a matron. Very cosy!' blurted out the flour-dusted pastry cook.

'I was only helping the lady out of an embarrassing situation,' said Glimmergoyne icily.

'Oh, sure,' replied Ethelreda scornfully.

'People, people,' oozed Captain Parsus. 'Let's not start bickering now. The King doesn't like bickering.'

'Where is the Prince Pyxis now?' asked the King suddenly. 'He wasn't hurt was he?'

'Unfortunately not, Sire,' said Parsus bluntly. 'He is under sedation in the apartments of the Dowager Duchess.'

'I suppose that's something,' muttered the King. 'And the other little bugger?'

'He was in the playroom I understand, Sire. Most unusual place for him to be, but still. He claims not to have seen anything.'

'We were playing crib in the playroom when…' began the matron. She stopped when she noticed the assembled faces suddenly staring at her. 'Look there was nothing in it, only tea and crib. He's only a little boy, after all,' she wailed unhappily.

'Claims to have seen nothing? That is where your clothes were found, is it not Matron?' said Glimmergoyne nastily.

'Yes but, but…'

'And he's not that little any more.'

'Now look, this verbal sniping is getting us nowhere,' said the King. 'The most important thing has got to be, what do we do with this body?' He shivered as he said the words.

'And where exactly is it at the moment? No don't tell me, it's in the meat chiller. Yes?'

'Yes Sire,' said Captain Parsus.

'Dear God what a mess.'

'Now as I see it, the best way out of this is to just ignore it,' continued the Captain.

'No, no, no. Definitely not. Not this time,' blurted the King.

Captain Parsus ignored the comment and carried on.

'*Because*,' he paused to emphasise the word, 'because if there *is* a subversive element at work here then we need the time to isolate it, or him, or her. I believe we should carry on just as normal and clean up the mess and I will make my own *private* investigation into the matter. A public scandal now, particularly since the 'other matter' was covered up, could cause untold damage to the realm, Sire.'

King Vulpecula of Camelopardis buried his face in his hands and let the wave of despair sink in. If only there was the money. If he could just get the millstone married off, there would be enough funds to ride out any scandal. He looked up tiredly and scanned the faces of the gathering in the room.

'Does anybody have anything to add?' he asked.

'I never touched him, Sire,' blurted out the matron, her lower lip quivering. 'I don't know what came over me.'

Glimmergoyne snorted.

'What?' said the King, confused.

'The boy. I never touched him,' she repeated tearfully.

'Who?'

'Ortolan, Sire.'

'Ortolan? Sod Ortolan. I'll touch the little bugger until he screams one of these days. No, I mean about the need to hold only a... a...' He licked his lips distastefully at the words, "private investigation" as the Captain so articulately puts it.'

The assembled staff looked guiltily at one another, then at the King, finally at the floor.

'So that's it then. We keep it in-house. Captain Parsus, I leave the matter in your hands. Keep me informed of developments. Now, go away the lot of you. I need some time to think.'

'Thank you, Sire,' said the Captain with real feeling, 'Now then people, I'm sure we all have work to do. Run along now.' The eloquence of the bared-toothed smile was very persuasive.

'Oh, by the way, Parsus,' the King asked when the room had emptied.

'Yes Sire?'

'What about the other matter? The fencing chappie? We shall have to get him out of the castle soon. It worries me, him being shut up down there.'

'It will not be a problem, Sire, trust me. I am giving the matter some thought.'

'Tell me, why don't I like the sound of that, Parsus?'

'He will not be a problem, Sire, trust me.'

'*That's* it, that's the bit I don't like the sound of,' muttered the King.

Captain Parsus smiled to himself as he left the room.

★

Early the next morning, as he was on his long cold trek to the bathhouse, Glimmergoyne reflected on the events of the past few days. Things just seemed to be going from bad to worse. Corpses scattered all over the castle, that bloody tyrant Captain Parsus poking around in the ashes before the maid's body was even cold. That maniac was definitely a man to watch. A power hungry lunatic if ever there was one. A sound caught his attention. It was coming from one of the maid's rooms. It was a funny, regular knocking sound. He slowly walked down the line of doors to locate the source. Ah, there it was. Room six. That would be the large-breasted one that looked after Her Ugliness.

Glimmergoyne pressed his ear to the wooden panel to see if he could make out what was going on. The regular thumping became louder. That's the sound of the headboard banging against the wall. She's got a man in there, the tart! In a fit of sudden, outraged indignation he reached out and grabbed hold of the doorknob. The brazenness of the girl. The castle turned upside down by fire and mayhem and there she was humping away like there was no tomorrow. It was just not right. But hold on now. Who is it inside there with her? Fornax? No, he would be incapable at this time of day, as would the enormous oaf Bootes. Crater, the pantry boy? Highly unlikely, if not impossible. Hydrus? No he would be working by now anyway. So who did that leave?

Glimmergoyne stood in the deathly cold passageway and wracked his brains. Pyxis then? No, he was out of his tree at the moment, well, most of the time actually. Ortolan? No, no self-respecting tart, however desperate, would even look at that pimply yob. So who then? The grunting and groaning behind the door intensified as he listened, the hammering of the bedstead against the wall upped its rhythm. Lucky sod, smiled Glimmergoyne. Memories of past conquests in these very rooms flooded his mind. That's it! It had to be Lacertus. The dog. Glimmergoyne took his hand from the doorknob and stood up straight. That was all right then, let the kids have their fun. She was a very nice girl that one. Ah. If I were only ten years younger. With a grimace and a sigh the ageing butler turned away from the thumping, moaning sounds behind the door and carried on towards the Laundry.

Nine

In the same early morning light, Lacertus knocked loudly at the pink door of the rose-covered cottage. When there was no answer he knocked louder.

'All right, all right, keep your hair on. Give a poor old lady time to get to the bleedin' door!' she shouted.

Lacertus stepped back and assumed the watchful pose of the patiently polite young man.

'Well, what do you want?' demanded Mona-Cygnus rudely as she swung the door open, stopped, looked up at the fresh faced boy standing there and smiled sweetly.

'Well, well. Don't just stand there young man, come in, come in,' she said with a sudden gleam in her eyes. Prepared for the necessary negotiations to obtain the items he was in need of, Lacertus stepped confidently over the threshold.

'I need to speak with you on a matter of business,' he said as the door swung closed silently behind him.

★

Ortolan Apus woke to find himself in strange surroundings. This was certainly not his own room. The different furnishings, the chintzy curtains, all was vaguely familiar but not quite the same. It took him a while to remember where he was. These were his mother's rooms. That was it. Since his own room was now no more than a burned out shell he had been moved in here temporarily. He lay back and smiled. That must have been quite some explosion. And he had missed it. Such a shame. Still, Matron Beamish dancing around the Reception Hall in her badly wrinkled birthday suit had gone quite a long way towards making up for it.

The loud humming and whistling of the Mighty Wurlitzer starting up caused him to leap out of bed with a startled scream and dress hurriedly. He had got as far as the door before the first string of duff notes broke the stillness of the morning. He dashed down the spiral stairs of the East Tower two at a time, the awful sounds resounding down the narrow column faster than he could run. Reaching the upper corridor of the East Wing he slammed the heavy wooden door behind himself and leaned back breathlessly against it. That had been a close run thing. If he had slept on for just a few more minutes the horrendous sounds would have woken him up, a prospect more terrifying than a thousand alarm clocks. He glanced at the ancient grandfather clock standing against the opposite wall. Damn. Only seven fifteen. Who the hell gets up at this time of day, he muttered. He stood for a while, undecided about what he should do next. Coming up with no viable idea for mischief, he decided to go and have a look at what was left of his room. The Junior Chemistry Set was long gone but there may be something worth salvaging from the wreckage.

The cold morning breeze that blew through the glassless window frames made the smoke-blackened room feel cold and uninviting. Of the large table there was no sign. The remains had probably been removed by the guardsmen yesterday during the fire damping operation. There were a few shards of glass that looked as if they could possibly have been test-tubes at one time but that was about it. All the notes and formulas were gone. The fire-blackened doors of the Royal toy cupboard were still tight shut. Ortolan grinned. Possibly the things inside were still intact. With a great deal of pulling and levering he managed to get them partially open. Inside, apart from an awful smell of burning wood and some stray soot, everything was much as he had last seen it. If that were so, then in the pocket of that jacket there would be two small glass vials. Gingerly Ortolan put his hand into the pocket and felt around with his fingers. No, there was no broken glass. There, there they were, in that corner. The last two of the three stink bombs he had made that first day from the recipes he had found in the box. The evil smile that spread across his pimply features was not a pleasant sight at such an early hour of the morning. Carefully wrapping the two in his handkerchief, he slipped them into his pocket, closed the cupboard and left the remains of his once comfortable bedroom in search of mischief.

★

Lacertus left the small rose-covered cottage after a rather informative and interesting conversation with Mona-Cygnus, and set off on his trek back to the castle. He had found out a few things he did not know in the course of the morning, consulting Mona-Cygnus's spell books. Safely tucked in his pocket was a sheaf of notes, painfully transcribed in minute detail by dim candlelight. The sun glinted on the acres of tiny windows in the façade of Castle Camelopardis causing Lacertus to look up and smile. If things went to plan it would soon be his, all the jumbled turrets and scarred battlements. Lacertus was so lost in thought of the great things that were to be, that the challenge of, 'Who goes there?' from Private Second Class Pavo went unnoticed.

Brought up sharply by a long-bladed sword pointed directly at his chest Lacertus hissed sharply.

'Who goes there I said!' repeated the little man.

'Don't be silly, Ernie, it's only me. You know me,' replied Lacertus uncertainly.

'I got to ask. New orders. Who goes there?'

'All right, Ernie, it is I, Lacertus the kitchen boy. I give in. I'll come quietly.'

'Let me see your pass.'

'What pass?'

'Your entry pass.'

'But I don't have a pass. I have never had a pass. There has never *been* a pass. What is all this nonsense?'

'New orders. All persons wishing to enter the castle must have the relevant pass with the Captain's signature an' all on it.'

'But you know me. Ernie, it's me, Lacertus, remember?'

'I don't know nobody,' said Private Second Class Pavo bluntly.

Lacertus considered for a moment. Ernie Pavo was not the brightest of men. If he was demanding a pass then somebody had put the fear of God into him to do so. Knowing that Ernie Pavo could neither read nor write, the simplest thing to do would be to give him a pass. He smiled at the little man who smiled in return.

'All right, Ernie. I give up. You're too clever for me,' he said cheerfully. 'Here you are.'

The handwritten receipt from the local butcher did look pretty official as he handed it over.

'Where's the Captain's signature?' demanded the Private, intent on carrying out his orders to the letter.

'There look, scrawled on the bottom. Next to the little picture of the red bull. See it?'

'Oh right. Well, that appears to be in order. Sorry and all that, Mr Lacertus, but orders is orders.'

'I shall be sure and tell Captain Parsus how conscientious you are being, Ernie. When I see him.'

'Oh, thank you, Mr Lacer – sir,' said the little man gratefully. 'I'll maybe see you later for a game of crib then?'

'That would be fun,' answered Lacertus with a grin.

Treading carefully, Lacertus edged his way around the still upraised sword and began to walk quickly up the driveway. This was a new development that would require some thought. Why should the guard start to impose such things now? Had somebody spilt the beans about the doorman? Had the fencing master found a listening ear? The stiff climb up the winding road had him breathing heavily by the time he reached the upper Guardhouse, but there was no challenge here. Corporal Second Class Gramm just waved him through with a sandwich-filled hand.

'Good morning, my boy,' called the immaculate figure of Glimmergoyne from the top of the stairs.

'Morning, Mr Glimmergoyne,' breezed Lacertus cheerfully, 'How are you this fine morning?'

'Oh, as well as can be expected, you know. Been for a walk have you?' inquisitively.

'What? Oh, yes, just to the village shop, you know. Get some sweets and things,' he lied fluently.

'Ah. I see,' said Glimmergoyne with a casual leer. 'Got to keep your strength up what? Chocolate is very good for restoring lost energy,' he said and winked slowly.

Lacertus smiled at him, not quite sure what he was referring to but not in the mood to ask the old coot.

'See you at lunch then, Mr Glimmergoyne.'

'Most certainly, my boy, most certainly.'

Mona-Cygnus sat thinking to herself as daylight dawned quickly outside the windows of the rose-covered cottage. The young man had been very good company, but he was very young. He was not the sort of thing she was looking for anyway, even if she had got a spell that would have worked on him. He was very strong-minded. The way he had talked, the way he had listened even, showed a great force of personal will. With a start she realised that the gormless blond one had not come back. Had he found her, his Princess? Maybe the Mona-Cygnus Rubber-Band Effect was a thing of the past? On the other hand though, he could have found the wrong one again. He could be languishing in one of the dungeons of Castle Camelopardis even now. The thought of those guileless blue eyes and shining white teeth trapped behind strong iron bars made her wince inwardly. He was mind-numbingly stupid, but, when all was said and done, he was a nice boy for all that. So what to do? The sun rose higher and higher outside the pretty rose-covered cottage as she wrestled with her conscience. She lost by two falls out of three.

I'll bring him back just in case.

With a flash of unusual inspiration she amended that thought. She would not bring him back willy-nilly. She would scan the basement levels for a body, down near the dungeons, and bring out whoever was there. Having made up her mind at last, Mona-Cygnus set to work with a will.

The fine-tuning of the search spell took rather longer than she had anticipated. Before she finally managed to get the hang of it there were a number of fairly large rats running loose around the little cottage and a bleached white skeleton, complete with its own oak cupboard, standing silently in the corner of the room.

Finally everything was ready. If the poor boy *was* confined down there she felt it her duty to bring him out. Mixing the unmentionable contents of the black cauldron slowly, she began to chant the words of the spell, her eyes squinting at the stained page of the spell book. The flash of blue light was quite pretty and the green gas was flecked with some rather tasteful glittering bursts of colour this time, the awful smell of sulphur was all but gone too. Mona-Cygnus nodded her head in satisfaction. Very nice.

'Well, hello there gorgeous,' said a rich cultured voice from within the cloud. 'And what's a nice girl like you doing in a nasty little place like this?'

Mona-Cygnus quickly swivelled her head around to see who had come into the room behind her, but there was no one there. Returning her attention to the smoke cloud, she came face to face with the adoring eyes of M. Belvoire gazing at her. Wordlessly she pointed to herself and mouthed 'me' at him.

'There's no need to be bashful, darling. We were meant for each other!' he said, taking a step towards her. 'Give us a kiss, you gorgeous creature you.'

Clasping her hands in an attitude of devout supplication, Mona-Cygnus looked skywards and muttered, 'It worked. By Satan's left titty, it worked! Thank you, oh thank you, Mummy. It worked!' before flinging herself wantonly into the outstretched arms of her Prince Charming.

★

Captain Parsus had spent the morning dictating laborious notes to First Secretary Puppis. The little man had spread out on the desk before him the personnel files of the castle's thirty seven staff. Some of them made for quite interesting reading. The Captain was not a particularly ambitious man, he was quite happy with the degree of power he held at the present time, but he was also not stupid. It was obvious that the old King would not last for ever and a man had to look after his own future.

If, as he suspected, there were a subversive element at work in the castle then it would be in his best interests to know who was at the bottom of it. The idea of being Captain of the Guard to either of the little Royal bastards did not appeal to his sense of justice either, nor did the prospect of being an underling to the bought and paid for husband of Her Ugliness, should such a mythical creature ever be found. Captain Parsus felt a desperate need to maintain the status quo that provided his cushy little job here in Camelopardis. He had divided the files into three main categories. First, those who could possibly be responsible. Second, those who could not by any stretch of the imagination be held responsible. And third, those he would *like* to see held responsible. There was a fourth file, a file he privately referred to as the garbage file, which covered the Royal siblings, everybody else not covered by the first three and the bodies already accounted for. Ambition was the key.

Somebody wanted the keys to the Throne Room and he, Parsus, had to find out who that was for his own peace of mind, if not his own job security.

'Sir?' squeaked Secretary Puppis nervously.

'Yes, what is it now?' snapped Parsus.

'Mr Fornax, sir. You were saying, "…drunken bum. Rarely sober, no threat to anybody except himself" and then you stopped, sir.'

'Did I?' said the Captain glaring at him.

'Yes sir. You did. Only it's nearly lunchtime and I'm getting a mite peckish.'

'A mite peckish,' echoed Parsus quizzically. The man was a complete prat. 'All right then, make a note to check out the cronies of the aforesaid Mr Fornax at the Dog and Ferret, particularly a person who goes by the name of Perseus Timms, aka Percy the Poacher, and then bugger off,' he said wearily. 'We'll resume at two thirty.'

'Thank you sir, thank you!' squeaked the little man and minced off towards the door. The file on Secretary Puppis had been one of the very first to be consigned to the garbage file.

★

Lacertus arrived back at his little cubbyhole of a room in a bemused frame of mind. It seemed that he had missed quite a party last night. His covert questions below stairs had revealed the extent of the confusion within the castle. Still, a little confusion never hurt anybody. It might even make his job that little bit easier. Changing into his kitchen boy's uniform and hating the feeling of servility it conferred on him, he was thinking deeply about his next move. The notes from the witch would need some careful reading first. Tucking the sheaf of papers under a loose floorboard, he was suddenly brought up short by a loud croak.

'Oi you!' it said.

Turning swiftly Lacertus was confronted by the sight of a small green frog sitting on the middle of his bed.

'I understand you were looking for me,' croaked the frog.

'Ahhhh!' said Lacertus happily. 'A small green, talking amphibian. Corporal Serpens, I presume?' he said with a broad smile.

★

King Vulpecula trudged wearily up the spiral staircase of the East Tower in a state of mild depression. He would make one last attempt to see if he could persuade the Princess to at least meet Prince Circinus, though he held out no great hopes of success. She was too much like his mother. Once she made up her mind that was it, it was set in perpetual amber. The Guard had been unable to find the tall, blond stranger, which was no surprise really. They were a gormless bunch of wombats at the best of times. In these times of severe cash flow problems though, one could only afford to employ those nobody else wanted. If you paid peanuts you got monkeys as the saying had it. The only glimmer of hope had been the landlord of The Artisan's Arms who had reported employing a stranger by the name of Gold-something-or-other but the man had babbled quite a lot and seemed quite unhinged. Mind you, a couple of nights in the dungeons here would do that to anybody. Sergeant (the cheque etc.) Tucana had brought the man in on some vague charge of harbouring a known criminal and he was at this moment languishing in the lower cells awaiting Captain Parsus's interview.

'Dearest, it is I, your Daddy,' he called softly.

'Oh Daddy,' bellowed the Princess, 'have they found him yet?'

'Not yet dear but we do have some clues—'

'Bugger the clues. I want my hero and I want him *now*!'

'But dearest, these things take time…' he mumbled.

'I'm twenty five years old, Daddy, just how much time do think I've got before my allure starts to fade? Hmm? Hmmmm?'

The King's gaze took in the piggy eyes, the widely spaced teeth and the bearded chin and he shook his head slowly. About five seconds would be pushing your luck, he thought nastily.

'We are doing all we can, dearest. There are men hunting high and low—'

'Men? Is that what you call them. They're supposed to be soldiers aren't they? The useless bunch of old women!' bellowed the Princess. 'And that's another thing, that tart of a maid has been slacking again. All day yesterday she looked half asleep. She hasn't reported for duty yet today. I don't know where you get these people from, Daddy. If she doesn't buck up her ideas I shall want you to find me a new one.'

'I shall look into it dearest,' he muttered with a sigh. 'But look, won't you even consider meeting Prince Circinus? Otherwise I've got to send him back…'

'I don't really care what you do with him. I want my hero!'

'Will you be down for lunch dear?' asked the King, desperately trying to change the subject.

'Bugger lunch. I'm not leaving this room until you find him for me!'

'All right, dear. I'll see what I can do.'

'And send that big-breasted tart up if you can find her,' said the Princess with an air of dismissal.

'Yes dear.'

King Vulpecula trod warily down the last two dozen steps of the tower, looking for hidden nasties, but he found none. Hah! The little sod must still be asleep. Pushing open the lower door, the bucket of fetid moat water came as a complete surprise as it emptied its contents over the Royal cranium.

Closing his eyes, the King felt the anger rise and his face reddened dangerously under its small cap of stinking river weed.

'Ortolan!' he screamed. 'You abominable little monster.'

The waft of childish laughter from the floor above did little or nothing to cheer his mood.

★

Glimmergoyne had quite enjoyed serving lunch in the Hall of Fire on this particular day. He and Lacertus had made a fine show between them. Since His Royal Pain In The Neck Pyxis was still indisposed, Her Ugliness was refusing to leave her room and the obnoxious Ortolan was in hiding somewhere, it had been more of the quiet dignified occasion it had always been when King Monoceros was still alive. Even the old bag of a Dowager Duchess had found nothing to complain about. Once or twice he had glanced at the youthful Lacertus and felt a twinge of pseudo-paternal pride in the bright eyes and smiling face. The dirty dog, he thought jealously.

'Glimmergoyne!' boomed the King as the immaculately groomed butler obsequiously poured beer into the Royal mug, 'Her Highness the Princess has complained about her maid. You know, the one with the large... umm, sorry Mumsy. Well anyway, it seems she's been slacking these past few days. Talk to her would you.'

'Of course, Sire,' purred Glimmergoyne. 'This very morning, Sire.' He glanced across at Lacertus but the boy showed no sign of response. A chip off the old block, he thought happily. Once the family had dispersed and gone about their business, the table cleared and laid for dinner, Glimmergoyne strode purposefully down the stairs to the Servants' Hall.

'Crater?'

'Yes sir, Mr Glimmergoyne, sir!' answered the little boot boy eagerly.

'Make sure we have a good fire, boy. I shall want to burnish the King's new riding boots this afternoon.'

'Yes sir, of course sir, my pleasure sir.'

'Have you seen Mr Lacertus anywhere, boy? He would have come down with the lunch things.'

'Mr Lacertus, sir? Chef has asked him to go to the village for some nice ripe plums, he said, sir. Her Ladyship the Queen asked for some specially, he said, sir.'

'Very good Crater. I shall speak with him later.' Glimmergoyne started down the corridor towards the maids' quarters slowly. He didn't much like chastising the female staff. It always made him feel so cheap and mean. He was stopped by the deep voice of the pastry cook calling from the kitchen.

'Mr Glimmergoyne? A moment of your time if you please.'

'Of course, Ethel,' he said, grateful for any delay in seeking out the sweet young Lyra.

Closing the doors of the small sweets pantry behind them, the red face of the portly woman turned to him and said quietly, 'I really must apologise for my remarks in front of His Highness like that.'

'No need to apologise, Ethel. It's been a bad time for everybody.'

'Oh, Mr Glimmergoyne. You are so understanding. As if a gentleman of your class would take advantage of a lady. I'm sure Matron Beamish is very grateful to you. I know I would be.'

'Nice of you to say so, Ethel.'

'I just didn't want there to be any *misunderstanding* between us,' she said, gazing into his eyes. 'Here, I have a little something for you,' she whispered. 'A few chocolate covered fruits. I know how much you like them.'

'Well thank you, Ethel. That's very kind of you.'

'My *pleasure* Mr Glimmergoyne.'

*

Glimmergoyne strode towards the line of maids' rooms for the second time that morning. Standing in front of the door of number six he straightened his already immaculate tie and cleared his throat before raising his hand to knock. Dull thumping sounds came to his ears as he stood there. Dear God, they're at it again. Like bloody rabbits. Gone to the village for some ripe plums, the boot boy said. Hah! Sounds like he got that nearly right anyway!

Straightening up he readjusted his tie and strode off up the corridor. He would speak to the girl later. There was no rush. Digging into the paper bag in his pocket he drew out a small chocolate-covered oval and looked at it.

'A dipped plum! How apt,' he said with a grin, biting into the succulent fruit as he walked on.

Ten

'So there you are!' boomed the terrible voice of the Princess Andromeda. 'And just where do you think you have been?'

'Sorry,' whispered Lyra in a small voice. 'I overslept.'

The snort of disbelief sounded like a foghorn in the confines of the room.

'Well, you're here now. I want you to play for me. Sing a bit too if you like. I want to be entertained. Entertain me. *Now*!' The terrifying body of Princess Andromeda turned back to her dressing table mirror. The little maid sat down at the piano in the corner of the room and began to play. Her sweet, soulful voice filled the room as she began to sing an enchanting Bizet aria.

'And you can shut up with that melancholy garbage!' bellowed the Princess without turning. 'I said entertain me. Stupid girl!' Without a pause, the young maid switched to a lively rendition of one of Matron Beamish's bawdier nursery rhymes.

'Much better,' declared the Princess through a mouthful of hairgrips as she began to tidy up her mop of stringy hair.

★

'Bring me the chef first,' said Captain Parsus commandingly.

'Yes sir!' answered the mincing voice of Secretary Puppis. The great white shape stepped into the room fiddling nervously with the tall, starched white cap in his hands.

'You vonted to seez meez, zur?' he said unhappily.

'Ah. The chef. Tell me Chef, how did you come by that ludicrous accent?'

'Vot? I vill haf you know zat mai manner off speakin' is off no relevance hier,' he said, pride momentarily overcoming his nerves.

'No? On the contrary, Chef. In the search for subversive elements all foreign nationals must be considered suspect,' said the Captain with a smile.

'Forin nationals. Und vy should zat be? Mai papers arr in perfeckt order, I vill haf you know.'

'But who are you *really* working for?' demanded the Captain leaning forward and looking directly into the frightened face with the bristling moustaches.

'Ai dont zee vot—'

'Cut the crap, Bootes. I happen to know that your mother was a maid on the Leophus Estates. There is no record of your father,' he said with a cruel smile.

'Ya fookin' bastard. Just 'cos I comes from 'umble beginnings you lot think you can treat me like dirt. I'll have you know I trained wiv' some 'o the best cooks in… in…' the voice tailed off slowly under the steady gaze of the little Captain.

'You hate those more advantaged than yourself, don't you, Chef?'

'No, no, it's no' like tha' at aw',' answered the large man, fear tinging his voice.

'I would suggest that working in a royal household was a rather strange job for one who hated the, er, the more advantaged shall we say. What would you say, Chef?'

'I don't know what you are suggestin'. I loves my King an' all of them lot upstairs. I do, honest.'

'All of them? Even the obnoxious Ortolan? Now that is *very* suspicious.'

'Well, awight mebbe not all but—'

'Hah. So you admit it. Private Second Class Gramm. Cell number three please.'

'But ye canna do this t' me!' shouted the large, white blob as he was escorted out of the room by the even larger red blob of Private Second Class Gramm.

'Right. Who's next?' asked the Captain cheerfully.

'Git your hands off me ya great oaf!' floated Bootes's voice from the corridor.

'A Mr Hydrus, Captain. The laundryman,' answered Puppis quietly.

'Ah, right. Mr Hydrus.'

The grubby figure of the laundryman sidled into the room clutching his floppy cap in his great ham fists.

'Good morning, Mr Hydrus. I just have a few questions for you,' said the Captain cheerfully.

*

As Lacertus trudged up the hill the afternoon sun was making a desperate, but futile, attempt to catch his attention and shining happily, but he was too lost in thought to notice. The Captain poking and prying around the castle could make things a bit dodgy. The man was a lunatic, capable of anything. But then on the other hand, what better time to strike than when all was confusion and mayhem anyway? Pyxis the Prat could quietly expire in the apartments of the Dowager Duchess just as well as he could anywhere else, and life would just carry on as before. Captain Parsus would run around for a few days like a chicken with its head cut off and then things would settle down again. The trip to the village for some plums for the Queen had provided him with the opportunity to pick up the few necessary additives for his concoctions. The little witch had really been most helpful. He was so deep in thought that he did not know he had reached the castle until the voice of Glimmergoyne from the doorway called,

'We'll have to see what we can do about getting you a horse if you are going to be up and down to the village every few hours.' Lacertus just smiled at him innocently.

'Find some plums did we?' asked Glimmergoyne archly.

'Yes, some real beauties. Got them quite cheap too.'

'I'm sure the chef will appreciate that,' answered the butler affably.

'Yes, and I managed to pick up a couple of nice ripe melons as well, I thought we might... Mr Glimmergoyne?... Are you all right?'

With a great deal of effort the butler managed to stop the fit of coughing that suddenly came over him.

'Are you all right, Mr Glimmergoyne?'

'Yes boy,' wheezed the man, 'just a little catch in the throat there. Sorry, you were saying?'

'I just said I found some nice melons that we could maybe have with dinner. What do you think?'

'Yes, very nice,' said the old man with a sly glint in his eye.

'I'll just get them inside then?'

'Right. Well, I'm on door duty still. Got to stay here for a while,' said the butler enigmatically. 'Stay here. For a little while at least anyway.' and he winked broadly at the youth.

The old man's going potty, thought Lacertus to himself as he made his way down the stairs to the Servants' Hall. He's cracking up under the strain.

★

The King looked down at his dinner plate in disbelief, 'What on earth is *that*, Glimmergoyne?'

'Cheese on toast, Sire.'

'Cheese on bloody toast? What does that blubber mountain of a chef think he is playing at?'

'He is temporarily indisposed, Sire.'

'But there are staff down there who can do better than this. God knows we pay them enough.'

'*Staff*, Sire? There is only the one trainee *left*, Sire.'

'What?' spluttered the King, 'only one trainee?'

'And the boot boy, Sire.'

'So where are they all? Is there a severe dose of lethargy going on down there or something?'

'No, Sire. I thought you knew. Captain Parsus has arrested the chef and five of the assistants as political activists, Sire.'

'He's done what?'

'He's arrested them, Sire.'

'Why for God's sake?'

'Because they all have funny accents, Sire,' answered Glimmergoyne, greatly enjoying the King's indignation. 'Apparently the chef is a well known anti-monarchist subversive and there is a conspiracy going on amongst the kitchen staff that threatens the security of the entire castle.'

'The bloody man has gone round the twist. The power-crazed fanatic has finally snapped!' shouted the King. Throwing his napkin on the table he pushed back his chair and stormed noisily out of the room.

'More toast, Your Highnesses?' asked Glimmergoyne politely

of the two Royal ladies who had watched the outburst of Royal rage in stunned silence.

'Do you notice how he only gets masterful and commanding when his stomach is adversely affected?' said the Dowager Duchess to Queen Berenice conversationally.

The Queen merely nodded her head and smiled weakly.

'Would that his father were still here,' added the Dowager Duchess nastily.

Glimmergoyne applauded the sentiment wholeheartedly, even if it were only silently.

For the rest of that day and most of a sleepless night Lacertus worked on his new formulas. The frog was of very little use as an assistant since he had no hands and had not been spectacularly bright even in human form. Lacertus had sent the little green amphibian to check on the Captain. That man had the potential of becoming a right pain. By dawn he was finished.

As he stretched himself out on his bed for a short hour of rest before breakfast, his thoughts centred on Pyxis the Prat, the ultimate aim of all this effort. But first he really needed a guinea pig to test the mixture on. He had considered the frog briefly but quashed the thought. Frogs were not guinea pigs and the little creature could prove quite useful in other ways.

★

In the little hutch of a room that served as the maid's living quarters Goldoor opened a bleary eye and looked about him. The room was empty. His head fell back against the pillow of the narrow bunk, totally exhausted. It had been a long two days. He smiled happily to himself as vivid images of the luscious Lyra flitted across his mind. And very active days too. He must have shed a good few pounds. Food. That was it. That was why he had woken up. He was hungry. There must be something to eat here somewhere. She *had* told him not to leave the room under threat of dire consequences but he decided to take a chance on it. What could possibly happen? All they could do was to send him packing surely? And he would be very careful. Pulling on the remains of his singed and tattered clothing he thought of Mona-Cygnus and whether he would ever see her again, now that he had his heart's desire.

As if the thought were father to the deed, there was a loud thunderclap and a cloud of sulphurous gas which consumed the startled young hero and took him back to the small rose-covered cottage.

'Help, I'm on fire!' he shouted patting wildly at his patches of clothing,

'Shhhh!' hissed the familiar voice of the little witch as she casually threw a bucket of water over him. 'I thought you were long gone.'

'Yes, phtewie, yes, so did I. Thank you. Seems to have stopped the smouldering. No, it's just that I was feeling a bit peckish and I was going to find some food and...'

'I might have known. We will talk about this later. You know where the kitchen is,' she said with a groan. 'Now I am going back to bed. Disturb me at your peril!'

'Right. I'll see you later then, shall I?'

★

By the time Goldoor had finished there was very little left that was even remotely edible in the little kitchen. With a heavy sigh of contentment he settled himself in a deep chair to wait for Mona-Cygnus to wake up and send him back.

That the little witch was far from sleep and that Goldoor and his petty little problems were the last thing on her mind at that precise moment in time was not a thought that occurred to him. M. Belvoire had not yet suffered the Mona-Cygnus Rubber-Band Effect, and she was taking full advantage of the fact.

★

When things on the culinary front had not improved greatly by breakfast the following day the King's temper became more and more frayed. The Captain had been adamant in his assertions that the chef was a dangerous character and a threat to the security of the castle.

'Why he can't release just one of them to prepare breakfast I shall never know,' he said petulantly.

'Then you must tell him to in no uncertain terms,' said the Dowager Duchess rudely. 'Are you the King here or not?'

'It's more complicated than that, Mumsy.'

'Piffle. He's a Royal servant isn't he? What's so complicated about that? You just send for him and *tell* him.'

The King glowered down at the poached egg on his plate that resembled one of Ortolan's unfunnier jokes and grunted.

'No backbone, that's your trouble,' said the old lady nastily.

King Vulpecula stood up angrily, grunted once more and stormed out of the room.

'He's getting hungrier. We might see some kind of positive action out of him soon,' remarked the Duchess affably to the Queen. The King ignored the comment as he once again headed for the cubbyhole Captain Parsus had appropriated for his own use. King Vulpecula barged into the small room red-faced and shouting,

'Look Parsus, this is getting ludicrous. Am I King here or not? I need my food. Do you hear!'

'I'm only carrying out your own instructions, Sire,' purred the Captain.

'That's all well and good but I need my breakfast!' shouted the King.

'But Sire, what if one of them slips a nasty in your porridge, hmmm? What are you going to do then?'

'Don't be so stupid, man. Most of them have worked for me for years. If they had wanted to bump me off they could have done so on any number of occasions.'

'They could easily be *sleeping* agents, Sire,' answered Parsus smoothly, 'setting up a smokescreen of normality while all the time they were plotting your downfall.'

'Can't I just have one assistant cook? Is that too much to ask? You could put a guard on him and have everything tasted beforehand...'

'That *might* work,' answered the Captain slowly.

'Just do something. Preferably before lunchtime!' barked the King angrily.

'I shall deal with it, Sire. Never fear,' oozed Parsus.

'And be quick about it.'

'Yes Sire.'

As the door slammed behind the angry King, Parsus smiled to himself indulgently. He enjoyed upsetting the old fool.

Lost in thought he was taken by surprise as the door swung wide and Lyra breezed into the office. She sat down daintily in the chair opposite the desk.

'You wanted to see me, Captain?' she said sweetly.

'Well hello there!' he said. 'How very nice to see you. And you are?'

'Lyra. Ladies' maid to the Princess Andromeda,' smiled the girl, flashing pearly white teeth at the captivated Captain.

'Would you like some tea, my dear?'

'That would be lovely,' she purred, gazing into his eyes.

'Puppis! See to it!' ordered the Captain. 'Now then, my dear, how long have you worked here?'

Lyra stood up, put a finger to her lips and crossed silently to the door. Turning the key in the lock, she removed it and slipped it into the cleft of her breasts.

'Now that was very naughty,' admonished the wide-eyed Captain, 'I shall have to have that back you know.'

Lyra sauntered around the desk towards him and slowly unbuttoned the straining lace bodice.

'Well, here it is,' she answered saucily, 'all you have to do is hold out your hands...'

'Like this?'

'Just like that!'

*

Behind the portrait of Queen Xenophobe on the wall beside the desk, Lacertus groaned inwardly. Not again, he thought wearily, this is getting to be a bad habit.

Transfixed he watched the antics of the voluptuous Lyra and the little Captain for quite a long while. Eventually he managed to tear himself away, and limp frustratedly down the passageway towards the kitchen.

The time had come to do something positive. While the Captain was having his attention distracted by the nubile Lyra, Lacertus decided he would attempt his experiment. Stopping by his hutch of a room he picked up a small phial of brown liquid and flipped it up in the air before slipping it into his pocket.

'Going somewhere?' croaked a harsh voice.

'Oh. You're back. Anything to report?'

'Nothing much. The Captain seems set on imprisoning the entire staff. The man's a nutter,' croaked Serpens.

'Yes,' said Lacertus thoughtfully, 'I may have to do something about him before much longer.'

'Let me know if you need any help,' said the little frog with a grin. 'Now I've definitely got to go and find some water. This skin itches like a tart's knickers if it gets too dry.'

'Yes,' said Lacertus coldly not wishing to hear the punchline, 'you hop along now.'

'I suppose you think that's funny, do you?' croaked Serpens nastily to the boy's back as Lacertus quietly left the room.

On the trip from his room via the back recesses of the kitchen to the Servants' Hall, Lacertus found that he had decided on his guinea pig.

Hidden once more behind the portrait of Queen Xenophobe in the Servants' Hall he watched the slight figure of Crater the boot boy as he relaid the fire in the hearth. The problem was how to administer the necessary dose. He could hardly go and offer to make the *boot boy* a cup of tea. Things like that were just not done. Oblivious to the eyes watching him Crater was singing mindlessly to himself as he worked. Coming from a very large family, of which he was one of the smallest and weakest, he was used to getting all the dirty jobs. He had been sent to the castle by his worn-out, tired, old mother to ease some of the burden in her overcrowded boot-shaped house. To Crater, in his overwhelming simplicity, the castle was just an extension of what his life had been at home. Lacertus watched the boy light a match on the brick fire surround, still in a quandary as to how best to carry out his plan. Maybe the straightforward approach would be best after all. Fetch the boy some lemonade or something like that. Nobody need ever know if it worked. Lacertus felt, rather than saw, another person enter the room in front of and below him. Swivelling his eyes awkwardly he caught sight of the unmistakable back of the Prince Ortolan Apus. The Prince stood and watched the young boot boy for a moment.

'Wotcha Crater!' called Ortolan. 'How's tricks?'

The boy looked up and smiled cheerfully. Unlike most people he liked Ortolan Apus, who reminded him of his older brother, Cassius.

'Hi,' he said eagerly. 'Would you like some tea or something? I'm getting to be a dab hand with the teapot.'

'Not just now. Here, I have something for you. Catch.'

Ortolan carelessly lobbed a small glass phial in the direction of Crater.

'Oh God no!' whispered Lacertus, recognising the blue liquid in the glass phial as it flew through the air.

'Not the blue one. Not near the fire, please! Not near the…'

Clumsily Crater fumbled the catch and nudged the small glass container into the waiting flames. The resulting detonation filled the long hall with gouts of flame and thick, black smoke, the force of the blast throwing Ortolan up against the far wall. Lacertus leapt down from his hiding place as soon as the boy had missed the catch and was protected from the force of the explosion by the thick walls.

'Oh God. The stupid prat. The stupid, *stupid* prat!' he muttered to himself as he ran for the sanctuary of his own room.

*

In the Servants' Hall, propped up by the wall at his back, with his legs stretched out in front of him, Prince Ortolan Apus surveyed his handiwork with a bemused expression. As the smoke cleared there was no sign of the boot boy. A large portion of the china cabinet had shattered throwing priceless porcelain and glass in shards across the floor and there were black scorch marks on the walls and ceiling.

'Oh boy!' he whispered in awe. 'Oh boy, oh boy, oh boy!' Glimmergoyne dashed into the room closely followed by Fornax and the matron.

'Ye Gods!' cried the butler. 'What the hell is going on here? Call the Captain of the Guard at once. Search the castle…'

'My Orty. Oh my Orty!' screamed the matron in anguish as she caught sight of the boy against the wall. 'He's hurt. What have they done to you my darling?'

Glimmergoyne covered his face with his hands and swore vehemently.

'Bloody obnoxious Ortolan again. I might have known he was involved in this somewhere,' he said with feeling.

'He's hurt. My baby's hurt!' screamed Matron.

Ortolan smiled at her words. Maybe things would be all right after all. He could load all the blame onto Crater and suck up the sympathy.

Fornax poked about in the ashes of the fire distractedly and finding nothing he shrugged and pulled a hip flask from his pocket. Tossing his head back in a deep swig, his eyes caught sight of something that made him choke and splutter noisily. Gesticulating wordlessly, his bloodshot eyes bulging, he pointed up at the chandelier in numb, stabbing gestures until he caught the attention of the morose butler. Following the pointing hand with his eyes, Glimmergoyne caught sight of the dismembered arm draped across the metal framework – all that remained of the unfortunate little boot boy, still clutching a box of matches in its hand. At that moment Captain Parsus marched into the room buttoning up an uncharacteristically crumpled jacket, closely followed by Private Second Class Gramm and Private Volans.

'And what has been going on here, gentlemen?' he demanded with a long suffering smile. 'Not the mysterious intruder again I trust.' The smile stated quite blatantly that it did not trust anybody.

'It seems there has been an accident, Captain. Apparently the boot boy was lighting the fire and there was this almighty explosion, and well, that seems to be about all,' said Glimmergoyne slowly. 'Bloody odd thing if you ask me.'

'I didn't,' replied the Captain curtly, still smiling, 'I want an account of the movements of everybody in the vicinity of this room for the last three hours. See to it, Volans.'

'What about him, sir?' asked Fornax in a quavering tone, pointing at the lonely limb hanging on the chandelier.

'And who might that be?' asked the smiling face tonelessly.

'The boot boy, sir. The one who was lighting the fire…'

'Another subversive element hmmm? Get it down from there,

Gramm. We'll need it as evidence.'

'But sir I…' blustered Gramm.

'Don't argue.'

'No sir,' answered the fat Private unhappily.

Eleven

Lacertus lay sleeplessly tossing and turning long into the early hours, his mind alive with explosive devices and violent death. Try as he might he could see no pattern in the mysterious chain of events that had so totally disrupted the castle. Ortolan Apus, for all his faults, *all* of them mind you, could not be totally responsible. Not even as a bad joke. There had to be some other explanation. If there were some third party at work it was imperative that he find out who it was if his own plans were not to be buggered up completely. With the chef and half of the below stairs staff locked up in the dungeons the list of suspects was much diminished.

But then there was also the blond idiot from the village. Where was he? No trace of him had been found. Could he be wreaking revenge on the inhabitants of the castle for keeping him from his lady love? But no, that was stupid. After all, he had seen her. Probably he had crept off with his tail between his legs to whatever obscure corner of the realm he had come from, never to be seen again. With his mind in a turmoil Lacertus barely noticed the faint tapping at his door. Swinging his legs gingerly over the side of the cot he approached the door and put his ear up close. Could he have been mistaken? It came again. Very softly. The bloody frog's got himself locked out again, he thought with relief, and swung the door wide.

Standing on the doorstep was the voluptuous figure of luscious Lyra.

'Well hello there!' she said quietly, 'I saw your light on and I was feeling a bit jumpy all alone by myself so I thought that I would... you know...'

Lacertus recovering from his momentary silence smiled wolfishly.

'That's all right,' he said amiably. 'Why don't you come on in?'

Closing and bolting the door behind her he turned to face his unexpected visitor and stopped, open-mouthed as he caught sight of the young girl. Sitting herself on the edge of the bed she had slipped the thick dressing gown over her shoulders to reveal the extent of her distress. Lacertus suddenly began to formulate a plan, a plan of such mind-blowing audacity that he even surprised himself. With his eyes fixed firmly on the voluptuous breasts Lacertus cautiously closed his mouth and strolled as nonchalantly as possible across the tiny space.

'How can I be of assistance?' he asked softly.

'Well, you know how it is, a girl alone and all that. Well, one just never knows,' she purred.

'Well, I would suggest a little nightcap so that we might both sleep the better,' said Lacertus in a voice so calm and oily that had it been an oil slick it would have covered the top third of the North Sea.

'That sounds like a *wonderful* idea!' murmured Lyra, reclining gracefully onto the eiderdown.

She missed the gleam in his eyes, the gleam that meant more than simple carnal desire, the gleam that sank to the depths of his soul and encompassed his entire life and ambition.

The two glasses of ruby claret that Lacertus carried across from the cabinet appeared quite normal, looked in fact rather sophisticated in their tall glass normality. Reality rarely being kosher meant that although the left glass appeared the same as the right, only one contained enough knock-out drops to floor an elephant. This glass Lacertus handed to Lyra with a smile reminiscent of the smile of a fox that has just found the key to the chicken shed lying in the farmyard.

'Very nice,' she breathed through wine reddened lips, then sipped again.

'Why don't you come over here and join me?' she supplicated, patting the quilt at her side. 'I'm sure we could...'

Lacertus's smile broadened as the glass slipped to the floor with a tinkle, spreading its contents in a pool across the carpet. I can clean that up tomorrow, murmured Lacertus, beginning to remove the clothing of the supine girl, the gleam in his eyes more enigmatic than ever.

'Am I disturbing you?' croaked a voice at his feet. With less emotion than it would take to stamp on an ant, Lacertus picked up the frog and very accurately threw him through the narrow window. Ignoring the screams of indignation from the frog, Lacertus carried on with his work.

★

Nobody else in the castle slept well that night either. As Glimmergoyne strolled around the corridors and passageways later in the evening, locking up the windows and checking the doors, he felt a great lethargy that seemed to be settling on his bones. It had been a long hard day and all he really wanted to do was to go to bed. Lights showed under the doors of all the rooms in the Royal Apartments. Their Highnesses were obviously still up and about. As he was pacing down the stairs to the Servants' Hall, Glimmergoyne found his thoughts drawn to the image of the little cottage by the sea and was surprised to find that the idea was not quite so unappealing as he had at first thought.

★

Mr Fred did not sleep well, but for totally different reasons. He lay on his small bunk and pondered life in general. He was not a happy man. For two days now he had been stuck in this awful little cell, the only light available coming through the heavy metal grille in the door. There had been little to eat beyond a pile of toasted nibbles and some funny-tasting stuffed mushrooms. All he had been doing was standing in his own woodshed looking for a forwarding address in the blond idiot's rucksack when the nightmare had started. First there had been the flashing, mind-blowing trip to the little cauldron room, then to another cell here in this very castle with that strange little man with the ludicrous French accent in it and then he had miraculously reappeared in his own bar, clothes on fire and screaming insanely.

Deidre had been very level-headed about the whole thing. He smiled at the memory of her calmly throwing a bucket of water over him, and soothing him with a cup of tea and a sticky bun. Good old Deidre, she took it all in her stride she did. But then the real ignominy had been perpetrated. The gormless blond one must have said to somebody at the castle, that he had been stealing from his belongings or something, because the spidery little man with the shiny peaked cap, half a ton of gold braid and slimy voice had arrived with two enormous henchmen and arrested him. Arrested *him*, Fred Dobbs, landlord of The Artisan's Arms. Right in the middle of his own bar, in the middle of a busy service. Had he *known* that the blond idiot was a radical subversive, anti-monarchist as the slimy Captain had said then he would certainly never have taken him in. It was just that he had seemed so normal. As thick as two short planks undoubtedly, but otherwise quite normal. On the other hand though, maybe the lad hadn't actually *told* these vicious thugs anything. Maybe the information had been obtained through torture. Mr Fred shuddered at the thought of the poor gormless idiot having red hot pokers shoved under his fingernails and those beautiful teeth pulled, one by one, with a pair of rusty pliers.

Racked with doubt and unable to get even the basic information straight in his befuddled mind, the corpulent body of the innkeeper remained stretched out on the little cot and wallowed in misery.

A little while later he was woken from a troubled slumber by loud scuffling out in the darkened corridor of the castle dungeons.

'Ye cannae dae this ta me!' bellowed a very loud voice.

'Why not?' answered the ever reasonable, slimy voice he recognised as that of the heavily gold braided Captain.

'Ah know ma rights, sunshine. Ah demand tae see ma lawyer.'

Mr Fred closed his eyes. He didn't need to see the slimy smile on the Captain's face to know it was there.

'Get yere fookin' hands off me ya bastards,' bellowed the voice.

'You heard the man, Private Second Class Gramm. Take your hands off him.'

A loud thump, like a bag of wet cement being dropped onto concrete from a great height preceded a lurid curse. A heavy metal clang and the sound of strong bolts being slammed into place put a seal on the unseen man's fate.

'Ah demand ta see ma lawyer, ya feisty great wimp.'

'Shut up!' ordered Captain Parsus sharply, then more matter-of-factly, 'Shall we go, Private Second Class Gramm? I believe it must be time for breakfast.'

'Good-o sir!' came the enthusiastic reply.

Two pairs of metal shod boots clattered off into the distance and an uneasy quiet settled on the cells. After a few moments of the deathly silence, Mr Fred pulled himself to his feet and approached the grille.

'Hello there,' he called softly.

'Fook off!'

'Sorry. Wish I could and all that but you see…'

'You in here too then? Wut did yu dae?'

'I really have no idea.'

'Fookin' nutters. Who are ye?'

'Fred Dobbs. Landlord of The Artisan's Arms. Maybe you've heard of me…'

'Nah. Heard of it o' course. Never bin there. Ah'm in the caterin' mesel' ye know.'

'Oh yes? Where?'

'Here in this fookin' nuthouse, would you believe. Ahm am ze great Artemis Bootes. Chef and personliche foods advisor to sum of 'ze finest crowned heads in ze known world',' replied the chef, the cultured accent slipping back into place as his composure reasserted itself.

'I say. That sounds very interesting,' enthused Mr Fred.

'Oh yez. I 'ave cooked for and been toasted bai some of ze most renowned persons in ze hentire realm,' said the voice, all trace of the farmyard accent gone.

'My, my. Well, I know that my Deidre would be ever so pleased to meet you, you know after all this is over. You must come to tea at the Arms and tell us a few stories.'

'It would be mon plaisire.'

*

Mona-Cygnus shook the sleeping Goldoor by the shoulder roughly. Waking blearily, he looked deep into the witch's face and smiled happily.

'Time to go home?'

'If I can remember the directions,' said the little witch cautiously.

'I say. You look very perky this morning. Is that a new shawl?

Makes you look years younger.'

Mona-Cygnus reddened visibly and lowered her eyes. 'It's nothing. Just an old thing of my mothers...' A roll of thunder swept the room and a flash of lightning outlined Goldoor's horrified face in harsh shadow.

'Sorry Mummy. It's very nice, really. I like it,' said the little witch, glancing up at the ceiling demurely.

'Does she do that often?' asked Goldoor.

'Only when I mention her really.'

'Oh, right,' he said, considered this for a moment, then his mind switched tracks once more. 'So, can you put me back do you think?'

'You found her then?'

'Oh yes. I'll say I did,' he answered emphatically.

'And...?' asked Mona-Cygnus innocently.

'She's lovely. Beautiful flaxen hair, calm blue eyes, sweet and charming with the most enormous—'

'Yes, yes,' said the little witch tetchily. 'That's enough of that. So, what was that address now?'

Goldoor sat and watched her flicking through a pile of scrawled notes. She really does look quite a bit younger, thought Goldoor uncharacteristically. Normally it took a the equivalent of a brick wall falling on his head for him to notice anything outside of his own immediate self.

'Ah ha!' she said suddenly, 'here it is.'

'Oh goody!' said Goldoor.

★

Lacertus approached the apartments of the Dowager Duchess with some trepidation. The fact that his chest was weighed down with sixteen pairs of tightly rolled socks and the purple elastic garters were cutting unmercifully into the tops of his thighs had a lot to with his discomfort. As he tapped on the door of the Crown Prince's room his mood changed, the gleam in his eyes flickered in anticipation. Approaching the Prince lying prone on the vast four-poster bed he felt a very significant moment approaching.

'Hello Pyxie,' he whispered softly, sitting on the side of the broad mattress.

'Wha...?' muttered Pyxis, turning awkwardly in his sleep.

'Tis' I, beloved,' murmured Lacertus. 'I thought you would like a small tipple with a lonely young girl.'

Pyxis shot upright, as upright as his heavily plastered leg would allow anyway.

'Drinkies for me? Super!'

'Just for you,' murmured Lacertus trying to hand him the glass of ruby wine whilst avoiding the groping hands.

'Lovely. Just lovely,' he said, reaching for Lacertus.

It took some doing but Lacertus managed to avoid the avaricious hands for the entire four minutes it took for the drug to take effect. Following the plan as closely as possible with the added distraction of a non-participant, Lacertus managed to exchange his, or rather Lyra's, dress with the nightshirt of the mumbling, drugged Prince and left the room to return to his own. Events could now be left to take their own course.

*

'Now that is much better!' exclaimed the King as Glimmergoyne put his breakfast of fresh grilled bacon, tomatoes and beautifully poached eggs in front of him.

'Yes, sir. The Captain has released one of the kitchen assistants under the watchful eye of Sergeant Tucana to prepare the meals, Sire.'

'Well, well. My message must have got through to him at last. These kidneys are delicious!'

Glimmergoyne looked sideways at him but said nothing. The Dowager Duchess just snorted.

'This really is much better, I must say,' repeated the King happily.

Captain Parsus, grim faced and extremely unhappy strode into the room flanked by two red-coated minions and strode boldly to the table.

'Sire,' he said with a curt nod of his head.

'Much better, Parsus,' said the King heartily. 'Thank you. So how are things going with the investigation?'

'I think we have the situation under control, Sire. But there is a small but *very important* matter that I must discuss with you. It concerns the Prince Pyxis. It seems his—'

The burst of blue and yellow sparks that preceded the appearance of the blond bulk of Goldoor at the head of the table stopped him dead.

'Oh, I say. Food!' said the young hero and waved a hand in the general direction of the gathering. 'Hello people. Sorry about this but I seem to be in the wrong...'

The concussion from the mild explosion that preceded the departure of our hero did little or nothing to disturb the frozen tableau of standing and seated occupants of the Dining Hall for several long moments.

'Who on earth was *that*, Parsus?' whispered the King after a long pregnant pause.

'I have no idea, Sire,' muttered the little Captain from the depths of his shock,

'*Then I strongly suggest that you find out, you imbecilic little moron*,' shouted the King. 'I thought you said you had the situation under control. Of all the incompetent... he flashes in here and... and... and all you can do is stand there gaping... get after him, man.'

Captain Parsus snapped to attention.

'Private Second Class Gramm, search the room for clues. Then I want the entire castle searched for that, that *person*. Sire, there is something I *very urgently* need to tell you about the Prince. Something terrible has—'

'Later, Parsus, later,' ordered the King, 'I'm busy.'

'But Sire, this is very, *very* important!' hissed Captain Parsus.

'Nine thirty. My office,' said the King. 'Bring me news of that intruder at the same time. Now go away.'

'Yes Sire!'

'Very masterful, I must say,' muttered the Dowager Duchess to no one in particular before returning her interrupted attention to her food.

Glimmergoyne watched the red-coated figures running around the room hunting for clues with a bemused smile.

'Thick as pig shit,' he growled quietly to himself, 'Thick as pig shit, every last one of them!'

★

Glimmergoyne strode to the heavy doors in answer to the heavy pounding from without. As the door creaked open Deidre Dobbs stormed in, hit the erstwhile butler across the shoulders with her folded umbrella and bawled, 'Where is he? What have you done with my Freddie? How long you going to keep him in this awful place?'

With each question she hit him with the umbrella.

'Madam, please. I have done nothing with your... Ow... stop that... Ow... Freddie.'

The corpulent form of Mrs Dobbs shivered, the umbrella clattered to the floor and her face seemed to fold inward, tears beginning to flow.

'Where is he? Where is my Freddy?' she sobbed, throwing herself into Glimmergoyne's arms and sobbing into his immaculate lapel.

'Calm yourself dear, calm yourself. Let me go and I shall consult with the King on the situation,' he said, smothering his revulsion at the close contact of this awful woman.

'You'd go and see the *King*? Just for *me*? Oh you wonderful man you, *wonderful*!'

Guiding the huge form was not easy, but Glimmergoyne managed to manoeuvre her to a nearby sofa in a cosy niche.

'You just rest there, dear. I'll organise you a nice cup of tea and then see His Majesty.'

'Thank you. I'm terribly sorry. Sorry about hitting you and sorry too about making such a mess of your lovely jacket.'

'Don't you worry about that. Stay here and rest. I'll be back shortly.'

Glimmergoyne strode off to the Servants' Hall stairs thinking that if he never saw the horrible woman again it would be too soon.

'Matron!' he called, as he reached the Servants' Hall.

'In 'er room,' mumbled Fornax from his seat by the fire, bloodshot eyes staring at a mug of questionable liquid.

'Shouldn't you be at work?' snapped the butler.

'Bugger off!' replied the surly gamekeeper glaring with red-rimmed, half-closed eyes at Glimmergoyne.

'Matron!'

'Ow! Not so bleedin' loud,' muttered Fornax with a grimace.

'Yes Mr Glimmergoyne?'

'Ah. Matron. Hysterical woman in the Reception Hall. Take her some tea and comfort would you?'

'Of course, Mr Glimmergoyne.'

Glimmergoyne nodded curtly and strode off to change his jacket before his encounter with the King.

★

Lacertus woke in his cramped cot and tried to stretch, but there was a large bulk lying beside him. He looked down at it, eyes blurred, trying to work out what it was.

'I shouldn't have finished that bottle of red last night, celebration or not.'

Celebration! That was it. He had carried out his little plan so successfully that he had celebrated. So that lump there must be...

Lifting the cover on the bed he revealed the fantastically proportioned body of the young Lyra lying naked beside him. He stroked the smooth skin with his fingers, softly and tenderly. The girl murmured in her sleep and turned towards him. Lacertus smiled the smile of the man who has just found a hundred ducats lying in the street unattended. He looked up at the window at the morning sun filtering in. The sleeping draught would be wearing off soon. Lacertus laid back and folded his arms across his chest. He dozed off anticipating the awakening of his sleeping beauty.

★

Finding himself alone in hutch number six did not worry Goldoor overmuch. That his lady love would return shortly he did not doubt. Maybe she had gone to fetch him some breakfast. That would be it. She would have gone to get him some breakfast. He looked around the small room, glazed eyes not really taking in any detail. It did not occur to him to ask himself who those other people had been. The people at breakfast. Goldoor did not very often ask himself questions, more often than not he would not know the answer anyway. He sighed and pulled the small miniature from his pocket and gazed at it longingly. He dozed off on the bed whilst awaiting his beloved. Hopefully she would be carrying a breakfast tray when she came.

★

'Come in, Parsus,' snapped the King in response to the rap on the office door.

'Terrible news, Sire. I did try to tell you over breakfast but I felt it better that you hear this tragic news personally, Sire. Only, you see it is such tragic news that I felt that, well, that you hmm, you know…'

'Dear God get on with it man. I haven't got all day,' snapped the King. 'You should be trying to find that blond idiot from this morning. The Princess wants him y'know. Be a nice bonus in it for you if you can find him.'

'No Sire, what I mean is, it's not him, it's His Highness, the Prince Pyxis.'

'What's the little bugger done now? Been caught red-handed with one of the chambermaids? I would have thought the chambermaids had more sense. Still, there's no accounting for taste…'

'No Sire, no. Nothing like that. Worse than that. It's, well it's just that he's dead, Sire.'

'Dead you say. What's so tragic about that? Oh I see what you mean. The obnoxious Ortolan will inherit the Kingdom. Now that *is* tragic. Still, since it won't be until I'm dead and gone I can't see any reason to worry.'

'But Sire. It's far worse even than that! He was found by the manure cart driver. On the road. Plummeted from the top tower I would imagine. But worst of all, *he was dressed up as a woman*!'

'Dear God that is tragic. Who knows about this? Besides you and me?'

'Only the manure man, and he is now in the cells. And Private Second Class Gramm, of course. Gramm took the driver to the cells and cleaned up the mess on the road. You see what I mean, Sire?'

'This could be serious. Nobody must know. As a woman you say? With, you know…' His hands indicated a ripe bosom.

'Sixteen pairs of socks, Sire.'

'Dear God. The lad was ambitious, I'll give him that…'

A polite tapping at the door interrupted him and he motioned for Parsus to open it.

'Sire. Pardon the intrusion but there is one Deidre Dobbs here to see you. About her husband,' said Glimmergoyne icily.

'What about her husband?'

'Apparently he's here in the castle dungeons, Sire. The landlord of The Artisan's Arms I believe.'

'Do I have to see her? Can't somebody else deal with it? Parsus, you caused this mess, you sort it out.'

At that moment the door sprang open and the bulky form of Deidre Dobbs stormed into the room, waving her umbrella menacingly.

'Where is he? Where's my Freddie? You can't do this… You, it's you. Kidnapper! Thief! Bastard!' and set about Captain Parsus with her umbrella.

'Guard!' he screamed, 'Guard. To the King!'

Glimmergoyne stood silently, enjoying the Captain's trauma, until the woman was hauled off to the cells by three red-coated soldiers.

'What a mess,' muttered the King into his hands. 'What a bloody awful mess.'

Twelve

It was not quite true that only Captain Parsus, King Vulpecula and Private Second Class Gramm knew of the incident on the tower roof. Ortolan Apus had actually been there. He had spotted and followed darling Pyxis, dancing, hobbling and singing some of Matron Beamish's bawdier nursery rhymes through the corridors and up the long flights of stairs. The plastered leg had been a great hindrance and the tight dress had not been of much help, but sheer, mad determination drove the young Prince and got him as far as the top of the topmost tower of Camelopardis Castle. From the darker shadows Ortolan watched the swirling skirts and ample bosom of the son and heir in awe. Matron Beamish had done very similar things when influenced by his potion. Ortolan Apus, as it has been said, was not stupid. He knew that a dose of a similar substance had been fed to his idiot brother. Once, twice, three times, Pyxis stumbled near the parapet, not quite falling.

'Get on with it!' muttered Ortolan under his breath. 'It's getting bloody cold up here.'

When after another quarter of an hour, Pyxis was still dancing and singing, hobbling and singing rather, Ortolan decided to lend a hand so that he could get to his nice warm bed.

'Hello Pyxie. What are you doing up here?'

''Allo. Wha yoo wan?'

'I've come to take you to your bed. It's very cold up here.'

'Bu' fun all same.?'

Ortolan took his brother by the arm to support the plastered leg and led him towards the stone doorway.

'Than's. Awfu' good of you. Do, reh, me, fah, so, la...'

Ortolan smiled, first he would dispose of Pyxis and then he would set about finding out who had administered the substance. Nearing the doorway they came to a place where the surrounding wall was only a few feet high. With one tremendous shove Ortolan sent Pyxis hurtling out into space, arms and legs wheeling.

'Wheeeee,' called Pyxis.

Ortolan looked over the edge just in time to see his poor darling brother hit the very hard road with a very satisfying thud.

★

Deep in the dungeons of the castle Fred Dobbs and Chef Bootes were deep in conversation concerning the virtues of red wines in cooking. Suddenly Bootes stopped his eloquent discourse on the health benefits of certain types of rough country wines and sniffed at the air.

'Wot ist das for an awful schtink?'

'No idea. But it does smell a bit like…' Suddenly the outer door clanged opened and the stench grew stronger. '…the dung cart man!'

Private Second Class Gramm marched the little man to a cell, slammed and locked the door and clattered away up the stairs as fast as his legs would carry him.

'Oi! You can't leave him here. I demand to see the King! This is an outrage. The smell down here was bad before but this is nasal terrorism!' shouted Dobbs. Gramm didn't hear a word of it. His desire to disengage himself from the awful man overrode everything else.

'Hello boys,' said the dung cart man. 'What are you in for?'

Dobbs and Bootes exchanged awkward glances at each other through two sets of bars and grimaced at one another.

'Mine Gott!' muttered Bootes.

★

Lacertus surfaced from a deep, dreamless sleep to the sound of a loud rapping at his door. Lyra was gone and the small cot felt awfully large and cold without her. With a weariness deep in his bones from late night travels around the castle and mid-morning exercises with the voluptuous Lyra, he was not really in the mood to see anyone.

'All right, all right. I'm coming,' he called. The tapping stopped. Wrapping a towel around his waist, he went to open the door.

'Good morning, my boy. I just came to see if you were, ah, you know, all right? When you did not appear for breakfast this morning I must admit I was a little bit worried. Disastrous goings on, disastrous.'

'Sorry Mr Glimmergoyne, I was feeling a little unwell. But I shall be fine really. I just need to sleep off a slight chill I seem to have picked up.'

'Ah. Right. Well, just so long as you're not sick. Call me if you need anything.'

Lacertus noticed that the old man's eyes were fixed on a point somewhere above his head. Fighting the desire to turn and see what he was looking at, he said, 'I shall be fine. Really. Right as rain by tomorrow. See you bright and early.'

'Fine. I will see you then. I hope you feel better soon, my boy.'

As the door clicked to and the slow measured tread disappeared down the passage Lacertus let out a sigh of relief and turned around, leaning back against the door. He saw what the old butler had been staring at so openly. Hanging from the small, grubby lampshade was a pair of soft, pink, frilly, very feminine panties. The lecherous old sod, thought Lacertus, he didn't believe a word I said. Retrieving the offending flimsy article of underwear he smiled softly to himself before returning to his bed.

★

Ortolan Apus was also up and about early that morning. By now he was used to getting up early, not through an enthusiasm for life or a sense of duty but to avoid the awful dawn chorus of his mother and her terrible playing. This morning, however, he stole quietly along the corridor to his grandmother's apartments.

Opening the door to Pyxis's room he searched it as thoroughly as possible without disturbing anything. The only unusual thing was the two tall stemmed glasses on the cabinet and the absence of the favoured striped nightgown. On a hunch he took the two glasses, hid them in the toy cupboard of his own burnt-out room and went down for breakfast. Afterwards he strolled up to the top tower, to see what could be seen. Ortolan looked over the parapet in the early morning light to see if there was any trace of the incident, but someone had cleared away the mess. Still, it had been fun while it lasted. Now he only needed to find the perpetrator of the deed. It could not be M. Belvoire after all. If indeed it had been his intention to run him through on that day in the Armoury. Since M. Belvoire was out of the picture on this one then he was probably innocent of the other too. Ortolan made his way to the Armoury so that he could give the matter some very serious thought in peace and quiet.

★

'Put me down, you great dollop!' screamed Mrs Dobbs.

'Deidre? Is that you Deidre?'

'I would have thought you would have remembered your own wife's voice, Freddie Dobbs. God, what's that awful smell? Smells like something's died and not yet gone to heaven. Get your hands *off* me, you gormless slob!'

'Ah. Hello. You there. I say. Take your hands off my wife!'

A short scream, followed by a door slamming shut indicated that Private Second Class Gramm had done so and locked the door behind him.

'Hello? Deidre? Are you all right? There's someone here I should like you to meet.'

'Dear God. We're stuck here in this dung pit and you want me to *socialise*?'

'No dear. But it appears we have a world-class chef down here with us. Knowing how much you like the cooking and all I thought you might like to…'

'Bon soir madame. I am ze great Artemis Bootes. I 'ave cooked for a great number off de Konigins der Welt,' said Bootes proudly.

'Is that so. Well, that's different. Who did you have to poison to land up in this pigging place then?'

★

Mona-Cygnus stood in front of a very grimy mirror and combed out her wiry grey locks to the sound of M. Belvoire snoring loudly in the bedroom. She smiled happily to herself as she trotted through to the kitchen to prepare him some supper. Since

Goldoor had eaten his way through her kitchen there was nothing left to cook let alone nibble.

'Damn. Now where's that spell book.'

She made several aborted attempts at a sumptuous feast for her beloved, each less successful and more inedible than the last. On her thirteenth attempt the plates that appeared were very nice, but the only thing that could be said about the food was that it was dead. A dead what she did not care to contemplate. Finally, more by luck than judgement, she ended up with a supper of croissant, jam, honey, a large singed loaf of bread, a pot of tea, a pile of broken biscuits and a very dead rabbit.

'Damn. No milk,' she muttered. With a sigh she filed the rabbit in the appropriate jar for later use, piled the bits and pieces onto the very nice china and set off for the bedroom.

As she opened the door, a magnificent firework display of flashes and variously coloured smogs greeted her.

'Damn,' she muttered. 'Not again!'

Sitting herself on the edge of the smouldering bed, now empty of the snoring M. Belvoire she pondered while she ate on whether the Mona-Cygnus Rubber-Band Effect were in any way patentable. Either way she would get him back tomorrow. First a good night's sleep and then a fresh start in the morning. Very surprisingly the croissants tasted pretty good.

★

Before going to bed Ortolan Apus, following his well-honed instincts for survival in a cruel world, though not quite so cruel since the early departure of darling Pyxis, balanced a bucket of strangely mixed ingredients above his partially open door in the Queen's apartments. The bucket contained any number of nails, horseshoes, vile smelling concoctions, tar, lead shot and a rusty old axe head. Satisfied that nobody could enter without being at the very least severely injured he threw his bedding from the window to the roof below, jumped the ten feet onto it and made his way to a comfortable corner of the Armoury to sleep the sleep of the innocent and good. The evil smile on his spotty little face did nothing to encourage this, but nonetheless he slept.

All was quiet in the dungeons of Camelopardis Castle, except for the loud and noisome snoring of Chef Bootes and the loud and noisome smell of the little dung cart man. Deidre Dobbs stifled a scream as a brightly coloured cloud appeared before her eyes. As the smog cleared she was confronted by a very bemused M. Belvoire. Noticing the quivering mass of Deidre Dobbs on the narrow pallet, his eyes lit up.

'And what's a darling creature like you doing in an awful place like this?'

'*What*?' she whispered.

'How shall I compare thee to a summer's day,' sang M. Belvoire.

'I'll call my husband!' she said defiantly as the strange man began to unbutton his pyjamas.

'Don't let's talk about inconsequentialities my dear. The night was made for love.'

'You must be mad,' she exclaimed.

'Quite possibly. Mad for you, my darling, mad, mad, mad.'

Climbing into the narrow cot, M. Belvoire smothered any further objections by pressing his lips firmly to the lips of the mountainous Deidre Dobbs.

★

Staggering up the castle driveway from the Dog and Ferret, Fornax was humming to himself a series of disgusting verses from a disgusting song the barman had been playing on his penny whistle. Creeping in through a side door to the West Tower with all the clumsy fumbling, bumping into furniture and objects that the habitual drunk believes to be stealth, he weaved his way across to what he thought was the door to the Reception Hall. He missed by a good six feet and half-staggered, half-crawled up the stairs. It is some credit to the quality of the beer served in the Dog and Ferret that he was not even aware he was going upwards instead of down as should have been the case.

'There wunce... hic... wus a leddy... Hic... fom Verona,
Well... hic... known fer... hic... her... hic...'

His voice petered out as he realised that there was something wrong. On hands and knees he peered about in the gloom. With his much impaired judgement working at full strength he decided he was going in the right direction. Despite the fact that he was on yet another upward bound staircase. Then, having conquered the summit he found himself once more crawling along what seemed to be an endless corridor. He began to sing again.

From his corner of the Armoury, sleeping as lightly as a cat, Ortolan Apus heard the raucous voice on the floor above. He smiled in the darkness, an appalling smile, a smile as close to humour as a rabbit is to a fox.

Spotting the door standing ajar, Fornax surmised that he had reached his goal. Soon he would be able to crash out on his comfortable little pallet and rest until morning.

'There wunce... hic... wus a leddy... hic... fom Verona...'

The bucket full of slop fell squarely on his head and shoulders, spreading out in all directions and spattering the walls and curtains with muck and gunge. When the rusty old axe head found its mark in his skull, Fornax the gamekeeper achieved his lifelong ambition. The ultimate cure for a hangover.

Ortolan Apus heard the crash from above, smiled happily, rolled himself into a comfortable ball in his bedding and drifted off to sleep. He would find out who his victim had been in the morning.

*

In the Hall of Fire, Lacertus was buffing the cutlery for the royal breakfast when the stiff footfalls of the butler approached.

'Good morning, my boy. Glad to see you're feeling better.'

'Much better, Mr Glimmergoyne, thank you. A good night's sleep did me the world of good.'

'Marvellous. So pleased to hear it. Going to the village today, my boy?'

'Don't know yet, Mr Glimmergoyne. I shall be sure to tell you if I do.'

'Fine. See you for breakfast then.'

Glimmergoyne turned and strode off towards the Servants' Hall. Adjusting his tie in the shiny surface of a polished suit of armour the vision of a small cottage surfaced again.

'Soon. Very soon,' he whispered to the image.

Reaching the kitchen he peered into the smog. It was so much more peaceful without the great lard-ball screaming and shouting.

'Morning, Ethel,' he called.

'Morning, Mr Glimmergoyne. Time for breakfast?'

'It certainly is. See you in a moment.'

'Righto.'

'I say. Glimmergoyne. Jus' want hyew to know I is on hduty.'

'Very good, Sergeant Tucana. Glad to know that such an able soldier is available to protect us,' said Glimmergoyne without a trace of sarcasm. 'Keep up the good work.'

'Sah!'

★

Glimmergoyne entered the Servants' Hall and greeted Matron Beamish. He had been sitting at the table sipping his morning tea for more than ten minutes before he realised what was wrong. 'The drunken old fart still sleeping is he?' he asked, glancing at the empty chair by the fire, 'Or does the Dog and Ferret keep longer hours these days?'

'No idea,' said Matron Beamish.

When the long-suffering ladies' maid, Pettigrew, screamed it shattered the peace of the entire castle. Even down in the depths of the Servants' Hall it caused Glimmergoyne to drop his teacup.

'What on *earth* was *that*?' said Glimmergoyne.

'Sounded very much like a scream,' said Matron.

Glimmergoyne groaned.

'*Not again!*' he muttered. When the scream pierced the still morning once again he pushed himself wearily to his feet and moved towards the stairs.

'Sounds like Pettigrew,' stated Matron simply.

'How do you know that?' asked the butler mystified.

'How many staff are there left? Most are in the dungeons. Or the meat chiller.'

'True. Very true,' said Glimmergoyne resuming his measured tread.

What he found was not a pretty sight. Pettigrew had slumped

into a dead faint beside the badly mutilated body of the finally eternally sober gamekeeper.

'Oh dear,' said Glimmergoyne, 'I always said you could rely on Fornax to make a complete mess of things!'

Behind him Matron, closely followed by Captain Parsus arrived.

'Move away, men!' said Parsus. 'This is my pigeon.'

'Very apt for a gamekeeper I would have thought,' mused Glimmergoyne.

'Shut up!' said Matron. 'Hello dear, still with us are you?' wafting a potion of smelling salts, the power of which Ortolan Apus would have been proud to be associated under the collapsed woman's nose. Waking for a few brief seconds Pettigrew looked at the messily demised gamekeeper, screamed and fainted once more.

'She'll live,' announced Matron. 'Now, who's going to clean up this mess, that's what I'd like to know!'

'Private Second Class Gramm. Get your useless great hulk up here. Now!' bellowed Parsus. 'It will be dealt with,' he said simply.

The sounds of the Mighty Wurlitzer coming to life in the room next door made Glimmergoyne cringe.

'That's all I bloody need!' he muttered.

Nobody seemed to notice the maniacal glint in Captain Parsus's eyes, nor the twitch that was developing very nicely above his right eyebrow.

'I have everything in hand,' he said and cackled.

'I'll believe it when I see it!' muttered Glimmergoyne.

Ortolan Apus watched the scene from a safe distance, amazed at the success of his little scheme. Before anybody noticed him he crept around the pillar he was hidden behind and wandered off in search of breakfast. It had been a very exciting morning so far.

★

'An whot is that there that hyew is amakin'?' asked Sergeant Tucana.

'Mousse de champignons de bois. My own recipe!' announced the young cook proudly.

'Sounds good. Gi' us a dollop on me toast there, boy. Hi mus' check everythin' y'know!'

The Sergeant took a large bite from the slab of mushroom covered toast, chewed slowly, nodded his assent to the waiting cook and took another large bite. Whereas Mona-Cygnus would probably have appreciated the flavour of the powerful toxins in the mushrooms, as probably Ortolan Apus would, Sergeant Tucana, not being a failed witch or budding toxicologist did not.

The convulsions that wracked brave Sergeant Tucana's body would have stunned a seasoned epileptic. He rolled about on the floor, retching and coughing while the poor little cook looked on stunned. As Sergeant Tucana's body finally collapses with a wheeze of escaping breath the petrified little cook turned and bolted. By the time Glimmergoyne reached the kitchen on his way to finish his breakfast, the body was cooling fast and nothing in the kitchen moved.

'Oh dear. It looks like being one of those days,' muttered the unflappable, conscientious butler.

*

Mona-Cygnus pursed her lips, leaned over the blackened cauldron and uttered the required verses. The tremendous thunderclap that followed surpassed anything she had yet achieved.

Blinding white lightning filled the small kitchen.

'By Satan's left titty that was a good one!' she exclaimed.

As the smoke cleared she was confronted by six bodies in various states of repose, blinking and befuddled by the sudden change of environment.

'I say,' said Goldoor.

'You!' bawled Mr Fred.

'Morning people. When's breakfast?' asked the dung cart driver.

Lying atop Mrs Fred, M. Belvoire looked very, very sheepish.

'Well hello again. What's a nice girl like you…'

'Deidre!' bellowed Mr Fred.

'Oh. Hello dear.'

'You utter creep!' screamed Mona-Cygnus. 'Here I was

expecting you to be suffering unimaginable horrors and you turn up with that, that, *slag*! Men! You're all the same!'

'I beg your pardon. I'll have you know…'

'Shut up dear. We'll discuss this later!' said Mr Fred.

'That bit about breakfast. Have you got anything in or shall I nip down to the corner shop?' asked Goldoor. 'I must keep my strength up you know.'

'Shut up all of you and get yourselves as far away from my pretty little rose-covered cottage as fast as your legs will carry you. Now!' shrieked the little witch. 'Or by Mummy's bones I'll turn you all into frogs!'

The scramble for the door as thunder and lightning rolled and crackled around the small kitchen resembled the rush for the bar following the call for last orders in the bar of the Dog and Ferret on a Saturday night. When the rumbling had died down, Mona-Cygnus found herself very lonely and very cold. Why couldn't life just have a few good points?

'I say. Do you think you could possibly send me back. Only Lyra was just about to give me breakfast and…'

He could not understand why the little witch burst into tears and began to pound at the tiled floor with her fists.

★

King Vulpecula of Camelopardis was not a happy King.

'I am not a happy King!' he announced to the assembled gathering of surviving staff and family. 'What the hell is going on here? Parsus?'

'Seems to be a plague, Sire,' said Parsus with a giggle. 'Could even be an epidemic.' He giggled again.

'I believe there to be anti-monarchist activists at work, Sire. The "accident" that occurred with the gamekeeper was obviously intended for Ortolan Apus and…' said Glimmergoyne.

'I told you so. I told you so!' sang Captain Parsus and he giggled again. 'You wouldn't believe me would you. Hah!'

'My little Orty!' sobbed Matron Beamish. 'Who could possibly want to hurt my poor little Orty. Come to me, baby.'

'Any takers?' asked the King. It would have been impossible to cut the ensuing silence with a cut-throat razor. 'So. That sums *that* up. Now, I suggest we bring all the prisoners from the dungeons and question them all, and separately.'

'Gone. All gone. Gone, gone, gone,' sang Captain Parsus.

'What do you mean by that? They were your responsibility. Find them!'

'Going to find prisoners. Yes Sire. On my way. They won't get past me this time,' Parsus cackled and ran out of the door.

'I must admit to being worried about the Princess and the Queen, Sire. Neither of them is here,' said Lacertus.

'Sod them!' snorted the King, 'The pair of them have been a pain in my backside for longer than I care to—'

'Peccy. I've warned you about that sort of language before.'

'Sorry, Mummy. Private Second Class Gramm, you are now *Private* Gramm. Your new duties are the protection of the Queen and the Princess Andromeda. You start now.'

Private Gramm spluttered a mouthful of semi-masticated sandwich over the assembled group.

'What? Now? I was just 'aving me breakfast.'

'Give me strength,' muttered the King, head in hands. *'After* breakfast then.'

'Very forceful dear,' said the Dowager.

'Shut up, Mummy!'

'Well really! Your poor dear father would never have spoken to me like that!'

'Probably never managed to get a word in edgeways,' murmured the King.

'Now people. Things are getting out of all proportion here. Let's all calm down and consider the situation very clearly,' said Ethelreda, the flour-dusted pastry cook.

'Time to get the hell out of here?' suggested Glimmergoyne jauntily.

*

Ortolan Apus was still puzzled. It could not possibly have been Fornax the gamekeeper who had given him such a run for his money in the Armoury. The prat had never been sober. Ever. He crossed and recrossed all the lines, chains and tracks of thought that could possibly be of some use in identifying the perpetrator of

Pyxis's downfall. Wandering the corridors of Camelopardis he mentally ticked off all the names still available, or indeed still living. Standing in the entrance hall a sudden movement caught his eye. The portrait of Queen Xenophobe was watching him. He *knew* it. Who could possibly know the secret of the portraits? Who was so base cunning as to know of their existence let alone lithe enough to get through the passageways?

Suddenly he grinned, the flash of inspiration that burst into his mind was intense in its clarity. Ortolan Apus winked up at the portrait knowingly.

'Elementary, my dear Lacertus!' he whispered softly.

Thirteen

The first class royal coach, much repaired and repainted at
ruinous cost after the collision with the solid archway, was
despatched to Leophus replete with the cadaver of Sergeant
(Honorary Captain) Tucana in a small ceremony before the gates
of Camelopardis Castle.

The small, blue clad driver was singing one of Fornax's
favourite dirty ditties as he lashed the horses into motion but no
one had the heart to tell him to stop. Getting rid of one unwanted
cadaver was to everybody's benefit.

Nevertheless, King Vulpecula was worried. His worries were
threefold in essence and overwhelming in their entirety.

First, would the Duke of Leophus want his 20,000 ducats
back? Second, would the Duke still pay out on bets against Her
Royal Ugliness being married since he no longer had an interest
in the castle so to speak, and third, what the hell was to be done
with Captain Parsus? The man was becoming impossible.

With a sigh, the King turned his back on the assembled group
and marched off to his office to try and see a way out of the
current mess.

★

The council of war convened in the back bar of The Artisan's
Arms had a distinct air of sour grapes about it. Following the flight
from the terrors of the pretty little rose-covered cottage, the spirits
of the gathering had lifted quite considerably due, in part, to an
infusion of several bottles of spirits.

'Well, I think we should all go and see the King!' said Mrs
Fred.

'Don't be silly dear, he'll only get that slimy chap to lock us up
again.'

'They did before,' said M. Belvoire, 'for no understandable

reason or purpose.'

'Ah fur vun vill geh nicts mehr in the bloody place,' snarled Chef Bootes. 'Crowd 'o loonies, thae lot 'o 'em.'

The group of white coated, white hatted minions standing in rank behind the great white linen blob nodded in unison.

'Now, people. We must have a purpose in mind before we attempt anything,' said Mr Fred. 'After all we cannot take on the King of the Castle and all his minions.'

'Wha' minions?' snorted Bootes, 'A coupl' o' overweight guards, a Cap'tn 'oos gone round th' bend an' a coupl' o' ancient bloodsuckin' servants. Wha's they tae uss?' he glared around the table anticipating comment, but none came. Nobody seemed to notice that the cultured accent had degenerated to gutter speak, but all listened intently.

'Wha' ah suggest is we aw goes tae they Polis an' meks an official complaint an' gets the auld bugger arrested.'

'Arrest the *King*?' muttered M. Belvoire astounded. 'Never heard of such a thing.'

'I say. Didn't somebody mention breakfast?' whined a small voice through the partially open window.

'Shut up and get back to the compost heap ya smelly old git!' shouted Mr Fred.

'Sorry. I only asked,' came the soft voice again.

'Forget it!' bawled Mr Fred. 'You'll never be served in *my* bar.'

A loud hammering at the door stopped the conversation dead.

'It's 'im. Tha' bloody nut case o' a Cap'n come tae get uss,' muttered Bootes.

Dark looks were exchanged around the table, for several long moments before, as a man, the mob made a dash for the window.

'Where is everybody?' called a raucous voice from behind the front door. 'Who shuts a boozer at ten thirty in the mornin'? I don't know what this realm is coming to. Cassius, stop that, it's disgusting. Leave the cat be. Carina, leave Eric alone. You *know* worms make him sick. Hello! Is there anybody home?'

The mad scramble at the window halted abruptly.

'It's not him,' hissed Mr Fred trying to extricate his head from between the thigh of Chef Bootes and the window ledge. 'Ow, get off of me, let me out you slobs. Sounds like customers. Can't afford to turn away customers. *Will you get your foot out of my ear please.* Thank you. Won't be a sec'.'

'Hello!' bawled the voice as Mr Fred reached the door, 'Carina, I won't tell you again, put your knickers back on. Norma, help her. She's got stuck again. Cassius, I'm warning you. God give me strength.'

'I'm terribly sorry to keep you, madam. Now, how may I be of service to you?' asked Mr Fred suavely, swinging the door wide.

'At bleedin' last,' said a small, wizened old woman propped on the doorstep, a huge black handbag causing her to list.

Mr Fred looked around aghast. Everywhere he looked there were children of every shape, size, colour and description, running riot over his flower beds, digging up the lawn, molesting the cat and peeing into the ornamental pond.

'Oi! You kids! Get out of my garden before I clout the lot of you!' bawled Mr Fred.

'Don't you talk to my children like that, laddie, or my Cassius will sort you and no mistake,' muttered the old woman.

Mr Fred took in the broad-shouldered, heavily muscled figure of the indicated avenger and swallowed hard.

'I'm terribly sorry, madam. Now, how may I be of service to you?' he said hastily.

'The name's Crater. Agnes Crater. I understand my boy is here.'

★

Goldoor cleaned the last of the dripping from his plate with a huge hunk of bread and stuffed it into his mouth.

'Hrummphh hrm phrum?' he said.

'Eat first, speak after,' said Mona-Cygnus patiently, watching the huge jaw rolling and chomping as Goldoor followed instructions and wondered just what she was going to do now. A world-weariness had fallen on her wizened old shoulders in the last twelve hours and she felt tired to her very bones.

'I said, "Do you think you could manage to send me back?" Only Lyra was just getting my breakfast ready for me and I do feel that I'd be better off there than here...'

'You ungrateful little toad. You come in here, eat all my food and you *still* want favours! What did I ever do to deserve you?'

'Sorry,' mumbled Goldoor, 'it's just that I can't think of anything else to do. It's not that it's not nice here in your cute little rose-covered cottage and all that but I just don't belong here. I just want to go and get my darling beloved and return home to Mummy and Daddy.'

Mona-Cygnus sobbed aloud, covered her face with a large, dingy handkerchief and burst into tears. Bemused, Goldoor watched her, not quite sure what to say or do. The smile went on to automatic pilot as he waited for the little witch to cheer up and send him back.

★

Private Gramm sat in the hallway outside the Princess Andromeda's apartments and looked at the mountainous plate of fresh cut sandwiches on the small table before him. Within ten seconds five of the quarters of thick cut bread and ham had been stuffed into his gapping maw when suddenly the door to the tower burst open.

'Aha! So this is where the action is, is it?' shouted Captain Parsus. 'Guard them well lads, the very safety of the realm lies in your hands. Ha. Ha! For England and King Harry!' And he was gone.

Private Gramm stared at the still open door, a hunk of sandwich halfway between plate and mouth, and shook his head slowly. It came to something when a simple soldier couldn't eat his elevenses in peace.

'Wotcha Gramm. How's it going?' said the cheerful voice of the large blond head that was poked around the door.

'I was just 'avin me elevenses,' spluttered Gramm, 'an' that loony comes in here an' ruins it for me!'

'Gi' us a sandwich, Gramm,' said Private Volans bringing the rest of his body into the room to catch up with his head, 'I'm starved!'

'But it's me elevenses!'

'Come on now. Us Privates've got to stick together. Specially with the Captain going out of his tree, big time.'

'I suppose...' started Private Gramm but got no further. The shriek that erupted from the Royal Bedchamber of the Princess Andromeda drowned not only conversation but thought as well.

'Where is she? The tart! What has she done with my bleedin' rollers this time?' bellowed the Princess.

'Bloody Hell!' muttered Private Gramm as the still loaded plate slipped to the carpet. Before he could gather all of the scattered remnants of his elevenses onto his plate the heavy wooden door slammed open and Her Royal Ugliness stood glaring at the two stunned soldiers.

'Where is she? What have you done with her? I want my—' She caught sight of Private Volans's short blond hair, straining biceps and stuttered, 'My... my... stupid, big breasted... my... my... Oh boy! My Hero!' she screamed, grabbed Private Volans by the arm and dragged him bodily into the Royal Bedchamber. As the door slammed shut, Private Gramm shook his head slowly, gathered up the rest of his sandwiches and carried on eating contentedly. He could always go in and rescue Private Volans when he'd finished his elevenses.

*

'Right laddie, before you lob me out of the window again I think you and me should have a quiet chat,' croaked Serpens.

Lacertus eyed him warily, wondering if it would be possible to squash the slimy little creep before he could escape.

'No you couldn't,' said the frog, reading his mind. 'Besides, I've left a sheaf of documents relating to your, how shall I put it, *unusual* behaviour, in a safe place to be opened only if something untoward should happen to me.'

'So what do you propose?' asked Lacertus, narrowing his eyes even further.

'You take me down to Leopardis, get the little witch to return me to normal and I get the hell out of here, never to trouble you again.'

'Why should I trust you?'

'We must trust each other, laddie. I have sufficient funds secreted in the bottom of the moat to set me up with a lovely woman I know in Barton Regis for the rest of my days. If you do this for me, I shall give you the number that opens the King's private safe. Do we have a deal?'

Lacertus smiled, narrowing his eyes to slits. The contents of the Royal Safe could be very useful in his quest for ultimate power. 'So what are we waiting for?'

'I knew you would see reason,' said the frog as Lacertus slipped the slimy little amphibian into his jacket pocket and opened the door.

★

On the top step of the Main Door, Glimmergoyne leaned against a great stone lion and sighed deeply. He really was getting too old for all this excitement.

Suddenly, far above his head a window slammed open loudly and the megaphone voice of the Princess Andromeda bellowed,

'Oh no you don't, Big Boy. You're all mine!'

Sounds of a scuffle at the top window echoed around the stone courtyard for a while, before a heavy silence fell. The large, red, shapeless jacket and black uniform trousers of Private Volans floated down to drape themselves over the statue of King Monoceros, and the high window slammed shut.

How on earth did I get myself into this mess? mused Glimmergoyne.

The gang of scruffy little urchins that ran tumbling and shouting through the gate took him completely by surprise. 'What the…'

Everywhere he looked there were children, climbing the walls, swinging from the statue of King Monoceros, digging up the driveway, jumping into the fountain.

'Bloody hell…' muttered Glimmergoyne.

'Cassius! I told you to leave that cat back at the pub. Put it down *now*, or big as you are I'll belt you. Otto, you just get yourself dressed. No, Carina does *not* want to swap clothes. Ah, I say, you there, my good man, you with the natty black jacket. The name's Crater. Agnes Crater. I've come for my boy.'

Glimmergoyne stared at the small, wizened creature in terror. With a speed that belied his previous thoughts of being too old he had leapt through the huge wooden portal, slammed it shut and thrown all of the bolts before the first fists began to hammer on the outside.

Leaning back against the door with a deep sigh, Glimmergoyne summoned all his remaining strength and bawled,

'Summon the Guard! Enemy at the gates! Prepare to repel boarders!'

★

Lyra massaged the broad shouldered back of our hero as he lay on the narrow pallet in her tiny room. An air of discontent hung over him, despite the soothing manipulations of the large-breasted ladies' maid. With a start, Goldoor realised what was wrong. He did not belong here. He never would. His dream of moving Mummy and Daddy into a sumptuous castle like this was not right. He was, after all, only the son of a poor woodcutter from the forests of Picton.

'I think it might be time to go home,' he murmured into the pillow.

'I think you could be right,' sighed Lyra.

'You mean, you'd come with me? Gosh! And I thought a girl like you would be bored in a small woodsman's cot in the forests of Picton.'

'Look at it this way. With all the things that have been going on in this horrible castle in the last few days, a girl just doesn't feel safe. Now with a wonderful person like *you* to protect her, a girl *could* feel safe.'

'I say. Does that mean…? Well what are we waiting for. Get your gear together, dear. Let's go and see Mummy and Daddy. I'm sure they'll just love you.'

'We don't have to go straight away do we?' asked Lyra silkily.

'I say!' muttered Goldoor.

★

The Princess Andromeda sighed and stared lovingly at her hero.

'Look this is all very nice and all that, Princess, but I am supposed to be on guard duty. You know, all sorts of strange people wandering through the castle and, and…'

'I need somebody to protect *me*. I pick you. I shall tell Daddy the new arrangements next time he comes up. Give us a kiss, gorgeous,' boomed the mighty vocal chords of the Princess.

'Um, I think there has been some mistake, you know. I would be failing in my duty if I, you know, if sort of... well you see, a soldier must, you know, guard and things, like, and not get um get um involved with, uh, female type persons, like, that he is supposed to be, you know...' babbled Private Volans as the formidable body and face drove him into a corner of the room until he was trapped.

'You can protect me just as well here as anywhere else,' rumbled Princess Andromeda as her fingers sought out the buttons on his chest and removed the smart red jacket with less trouble than undressing a doll. Throwing it casually to the floor she turned her attention to the buttons of the beautifully pressed black trousers.

'No. Please. This is not right. What if somebody should come in? My career would be over. *Stop it*. Please!' The Private's voice rose sharply, becoming more hysterical until the roaming hands pushed the offending trousers around his ankles.

'Help!' he squeaked.

'Ahh! What have we here?' asked Princess Andromeda huskily, taking in the knee-length leather boots, pale white thighs and tight white shorts covered in printed lipstick marks.

'Look, I can explain. The pants were a present, you know, and the boots, well, the boots are just very comfortable to go riding in, like. You won't tell the Captain, will you?' whined Private Volans. 'Only he may not understand you see...'

'I won't tell if you won't,' growled the Princess and barked playfully at him. 'Just you wait here a moment, Big Boy!' she breathed.

As the piggy eyes and bloated body receded from him, Volans let out a huge whistle of relief. As she opened the door to her changing room he made a desperate leap for the exit, careless as to who saw him, the desire to escape this desperate situation overriding everything else.

'Ah, ah, ahhh. Naughty boy!' teased Andromeda waving the large brass key in front of her face. Totally beaten, Private Volans slumped into the corner and rested his head in his hands in utter despair.

He did not notice the passage of time, but in what seemed like only seconds the Princess had returned and was standing over him.

'What do you think, Big Boy?' she rumbled as if from a great distance.

He cringed, throwing his arms up to defend himself.

'Come on. Be honest now,' said the muffled bellow.

Slowly, Private Volans eyes opened, one by one and focused on the bare, thick-soled leather boots planted on the elegant Persian rug. Unwillingly his eyes swept upward, took in the black leather garters, black leather panties held up by a black leather braces, the bright red rubber cummerbund and nippleless, red leather brassiere almost lost in the folds of white flesh and the whole ensemble topped off by a black velvet riding helmet.

'Wha... Wha... Wha' the... Wha...' blubbered Volans.

'Nice isn't it? I chose it myself!'

The Princess did a messy twirl in front of him, the rubber boot soles indelibly marking the priceless Oriental rug. Private Volans made one last attempt at escape, leaping for the window and throwing it wide, but for her size the Princess Andromeda could still move fast when she needed to. It was far from graceful and lithe but it was effective.

'Oh no you don't, Big Boy. You're all mine!' she said, grabbing the waistband of his tight shorts from behind, twisting them in her fist. Private Volans yelped in pain and clutched at his constricted region while Andromeda stooped to sweep up his uniform jacket and pants in her other hand. Lazily she threw them out of the window and slammed it fast.

'Now then, I think it's time for the *fun* to start!' she growled.

*

Lacertus approached the door to the little rose-covered cottage whistling happily. If this worked his ambition could well be fulfilled very, very soon. The confusion at the castle when he left was developing nicely. Who the strange woman and the raucous children were he had no idea, but he felt sure that they could only aid his cause.

Before his hand could tap on the door, it swung silently open.

'I was expecting you,' said the little witch, gazing up at him.

'I felt sure you would be,' answered Lacertus.

'You want me to help your little green friend I take it?'

'And myself at the same time of course,' grinned Lacertus.

'My boy, I like your style. Follow me.'

In the kitchen of the rose-covered cottage the cauldron was bubbling and spitting, its unmentionable contents swirling wildly. The little witch pulled her spell book from under the cushions on the grotesque sofa.

'Now. The only problem that I can see is really twofold. First, the original spell was not mine, it was Mummys.' Thunder rumbled around the little cottage. 'And second, I'm not really very good at this sort of thing.'

Mona-Cygnus stopped. Maybe I should try a change of profession, she thought. Maybe that's where I've been going wrong all these years. I'm in the wrong bloody job.

'Hello? Are you still with us? Can you help or not?'

'Help? I'm a witch, you pea-brain! Witches don't help people.' But maybe that too was wrong. Maybe she was just not hard-hearted enough to do the job properly.

'All right. Get the frog out and I'll see what I can do,' she said abjectly.

'Great!' said Lacertus depositing Serpens on the kitchen table.

*

The hammering at the doors of the castle penetrated as far as the King's personal office.

'I knew this was going to happen as soon as Captain Parsus started his private investigation. I've been expecting something like this,' said the King, spinning the dials on his private safe.

'So what happens now, Sire?' asked Glimmergoyne.

'You and me have known each other a long time, Glimmer-goyne. We have both seen this castle in all its good points and every last one of its bad points. There comes a time in a man's life when a small cottage by the sea with only gulls spinning overhead and the sound of the breakers on the shore to disturb the peace seems like utopia. Have you never felt that way, Glimmergoyne?'

'I know exactly what you mean, Sire,' said the old butler dryly. 'And are you suggesting what I think you're suggesting, Sire?'

'I do believe I am. Pack a small bag, pick up your savings book and get the hell out of here. It's what I intend to do,' said the King, stuffing thick wads of cash into his jacket pockets. He slipped the remaining unsold crown jewels into a small, black rucksack and hefted it onto his shoulder.

'Well *Mr* Glimmergoyne, it's been a pleasure knowing you. Maybe we shall bump into each other again on a deserted beach somewhere, sometime and have a damn good laugh about all this.'

'Maybe, Sire. Maybe.'

'Just plain Mr Vulpecula will do fine.'

Slipping a pair of very plain dark glasses onto his nose the Ex-King held out his hand to Glimmergoyne. The butler took it, smiled once, then the funny little man was gone, disappeared through the private bolt-hole built into the wall many years before for just such an emergency as this. It was a few moments before Glimmergoyne realised that the Ex-King had put something in the palm of his hand. Looking at the round, gold ring he smiled to himself. It was the Royal Seal of King Multiceros the Wise.

Glimmergoyne moved to the small window and peered out into the courtyard. The gang of marauding children had dismantled a good portion of the stable block and had piled the wood across the doors. It had been sprinkled with the contents of some of the older tins of paint from the paint shed and as great gouts of flame spluttered and licked around the great doors and tinder dry beams the children performed a limited form of tribal dance around old King Monoceros.

'Resourceful little buggers,' he muttered to himself with a grimace. 'Bless their little cotton socks.'

Fourteen

The Dowager Duchess sat in her favourite armchair in the Queen's chambers listening to the awful noise emanating from the Mighty Wurlitzer. The pair of Royal consorts were completely unaware of the commotion going on below. Even when the doors slammed open and Captain Parsus strode in clanking loudly from the heavy suit of armour he was wearing.

'Never fear, ladies!' he cried in a loud, clear voice. 'I shall save you from the mob. I will defend you to the death should such be necessary. Fear no fire or foes whilst I am here…'

'Who on earth is that?' bellowed the Dowager Duchess to the Queen who merely shrugged her shoulders and kicked a few more duff notes into touch.

'Ladies, I must warn you that your virtue is in danger if you remain—'

'Listen, sonny, I don't know who you think you are, but I gave up all pretence at virtue years ago. So you just sit down and enjoy the music or bugger off,' said the Dowager Duchess.

'But ladies I implore you to reconsider—'

'Bugger off!'

Parsus dejectedly clanked his way to the door.

'I'll be downstairs guarding the entrance to this precious enclave if you should need—'

'Can't you take a simple hint, sonny. Bugger off!' bellowed the Dowager Duchess. 'Very nice dear,' she said turning her attention to the Queen and applauding enthusiastically at the dying of a barely recognisable George Gershwin tune. 'How about 'Danny Boy', now? You know how much I like that one.?'

'Well, if you're sure…' simpered the Queen.

'Go on, dear, give us both a treat.'

At the bottom of the tower stairs Captain Parsus brightened. He would defend the Royal ladies anyway. They would appreciate his efforts when the enemy were vanquished.

Ortolan Apus turned from the window where he was gleefully watching the now raging fire before the main doors and stopped dead, his mouth hanging open. The sight of Captain Parsus of the Royal Guard dressed in shining plate armour stunned even him into silence. In a flash Ortolan was beside the Captain.

'The enemy are in the Hall of Fire. Quick, we must not let them through!' cried Ortolan. 'Take up your sword and defend your King!'

'Yes, yes I will!' shouted the Captain, his eye twitching wildly. 'Where away, boy?' he bawled, clumsily pulling an enormous double-handed sword from its wall bracket.

'Down the stairs!'

Ortolan deftly slipped a small vial of stink bomb mixture number five into the neck of the armour and pushed the metal-clad madman towards the stairs.

'Aha! I can smell the accursed pigs now!' cried the demented Captain Parsus. 'For England and King Harry begad!' And dashed down the stairs.

Ortolan Apus shook his head sniggering happily and quickly loped off after the clanking figure. Settling himself on a step near the top of the stairs Ortolan watched the wild-eyed Captain as he began, single-handedly, to decapitate every suit of armour in the Hall with clumsy swinging strokes of the heavy sword. First he laughed then he began to guffaw. Before Parsus had even halfway finished the tears of enjoyment were streaming uncontrollably down the little Prince's spotty face, while the great doors burnt steadily on from without.

*

Goldoor and Lyra made their way carefully up the long staircase from the Servants' Hall to emerge into the noisy Reception Hall. Dropping the stack of heavy suitcases he carried, Goldoor sniffed the air cautiously.

'I say, beloved, do you smell burning?'

'It smells like the Hall of Fire on a cold morning, when the great fire has just been lit,' said the charming Lyra, wrinkling her nose sweetly.

'Oh. It's not me then. Good.'

Once more Goldoor gathered the pile of suitcases together. A sudden loud crash from the Hall of Fire resounded through the Hall, followed by a virulent curse.

'That still doesn't sound right to me!' said the muscular hero and he promptly dropped the suitcases again.

Lyra grabbed his arm and said wildly, 'No. No don't. It's probably just mice or something, you know. Don't let's get involved!'

'Involved with *mice*. What piffle!' he exclaimed, dragging the poor young girl clinging desperately to his arm effortlessly to the top of the stairs.

Ortolan Apus, curled up on the fourth step and clutching at the painful stitch in his side was bawling, 'Stop it. Stop it. I can't take much more of this.'

Glancing down into the Hall of Fire, Goldoor was just in time to see Captain Parsus vanquish the heaviest and most menacing suit of armour with a wildly swinging, double-handed blow. His great momentum swung him around on his heel several times before causing him to trip, stumble and fall flat on his face on the stone flags.

Goldoor gazed at the scene with an uncomprehending smile. His mind, unable to make head or tail of the astonishing sight, put the smile onto automatic pilot and let it wander off to have a cup of tea and put its feet up for a while.

'Come on!' hissed Lyra. 'It's only the obnoxious Ortolan playing silly buggers. We must go. N*ow*!'

Goldoor did not move, despite her insistent pulling at his arm. Suddenly Ortolan spotted them. Recognising the blank gormless expression of Goldoor from the night of the intruder he smiled back; an evil, calculating smile.

'I say, Parsus. You missed one. There's a nutter on the loose up here,' he shouted in a voice fit to wake the dead.

With a speed of reaction that belied the weight of the armour, Captain Parsus jumped to his feet, swung the huge blade twice above his head and started a clumsy run towards the stairs.

'The nutter? I've got 'im this time, Sire. Never you fear. Charge!' bellowed Parsus, eyes blazing fanatically, the heavy armour clattering as he picked up speed.

Ortolan Apus had to roll quickly out of the way to avoid being trampled by the metal shod feet as Captain Parsus thundered past, gathering speed all the time. At the top of the stairs he swung the broad-bladed sword at Goldoor's head, missed by about three feet, stumbled, spun round a few times, bumped into two very solid pillars and slashed a unique, priceless wall hanging before he eventually made contact with the doors.

In normal times the doors would have been more than capable of stopping his berserk progress by their sheer physical presence, but these were far from normal times. The fire-weakened timber, reduced to less than one eighth of its earlier thickness, allowed the deranged Parsus's body to pass straight through scattering hunks of blazing stable walls and throwing up vast clouds of ash before, with a final cry, the Captain fell, head first, into the child-filled Romanesque fountain.

Glimmergoyne, dressed in one of His Ex-Majesty's more tasteful suits and sporting a shiny black bowler stepped out of the shadows near the Servants' Hall doors just as the Captain made his spectacular exit. He put down his suitcase and trudged slowly forward.

'What in the name of…'

Suddenly the gap was full of children leaping through the smouldering beams and shrieking with delight as they started to rip the upholstery from the antique furniture, pull the racks of fine, old, razor-sharp lances from the walls and swing from the great curtains. Glimmergoyne swallowed hard and closed his eyes despairingly. When he opened them, after what seemed like eternity but was in fact only about thirty seconds, he was confronted by the wizened little face of an indescribably ancient woman.

'Hey, you there! Gormless!' she called. 'The name's Crater. Agnes Crater. I believe my little Caelum is somewhere here in this monstrosity?'

*

The Princess Andromeda sighed and rolled over in her large expanse of a bed. Stretched out beside her Private Volans lit a cigarette and let his eyes take in the bright pink complexion of the supine Princess and was pleased to discover that, on second thoughts, maybe things weren't quite as bad as they could be. He could not say exactly that she was his dream girl since that was the only type that he had ever had. In spite of that, her skin colour did remind him somewhat of his favourite doll. Admittedly the face was pretty horrendous, but that was a minor point at this stage of the game.

'I want to run away from here,' boomed the Princess, opening her piggy little eyes abruptly. 'Will you take me away from this horrible old castle and care for me?'

'Well, I suppose I could, you know, arrange something.'

'I have some savings. Enough to buy us a nice little cottage away from all this at least. We'll really teach Daddy a lesson. Just you and me and those *wonderful* biceps?'

Private Volans swallowed hard. If he refused he could well be thrown out of the window. She was perfectly capable of such a thing, that much he knew. He rose from the bed and strolled across to the window. The smouldering woodwork scattered around the courtyard down below was sending small, listless columns of smoke heavenwards. Maybe now *would* be a good time to leave this outdated stone monstrosity. He would still be carrying out his duty in a sense, guarding the Princess, defending her honour. If it wasn't for that face he would have assented without a second thought. The body at least was as close to his idea of the perfect woman as he was ever likely to find.

'I suppose we could have a go,' he said noncommittally, and sighed deeply.

In truth he had been thinking seriously about moving on for some time. The Duke of Philbert had almost promised him a position as Corporal the last time he had been here. The chances for advancement in this derelict old pile of stone had diminished considerably of late. A man had to think of his future, when all was said and done.

'How do you fancy the Duchy of Philbert?' he asked softly.

'Anywhere. I just don't care any more I'm so happy!'

Private Volans winced at the happy-go-lucky, little girl joyfulness but shrugged and said simply, 'Go pack your bags then old gel.'

'Oh you wonderful, wonderful man!' bellowed the Princess. 'I knew you would. Quickly now. We must go before anybody notices!'

★

'So now, having got that bit sorted, we now need to bathe the frog in fresh pig's blood, at least I *think* that's what it says. I'll kill that cat one of these days. Right, come here young fella-me-frog and jump in that bucket over there.'

'This is not going to hurt is it?' asked Serpens, eyeing her warily.

'Shhh! Don't interrupt, this is a very delicate process. *This* one goes to *that* one and that one goes to that one. Bloody hell, what's that word supposed to be? A pinch of *cinnamon*? Most unusual, I never use cinnamon in my recipes. I'm not even sure if I've got any. Hey, did I ever tell you about the time I tried to conjure up a storm over that penny-pinching prat of a butcher after he short-changed me over half a pound of sausages and a couple of pints of bull's blood? Took me many days of effort and a lot of head scratching and *still* it didn't work. And do you know why?' she cackled insanely.

'No. Why?' asked Lacertus dryly, wondering if he was going to regret asking.

'Turns out I was using Mummy's Christmas Cake recipe.'

Thunder rolled and crackled around the tiny kitchen as Mona-Cygnus almost collapsed from cackling so insanely.

'I'm getting out of here!' croaked the frog.

'Oh no you're not. We've got a deal, remember?' said Lacertus as he casually picked up the frog by its neck and shook it.

'Aha! Or eureka or somesuch!' exclaimed Mona-Cygnus, and cackled again.

'I don't like the sound of that either!' said the frog.

'Shut up and don't interfere,' snapped Lacertus and lobbed the frog into the bucket of pig's blood and slammed down the lid.

'I think I've got it!' enthused Mona-Cygnus.

'I really don't like the sound of that 'I think' bit!' said the muffled voice of the frog.

'Right, now. This experiment requires precision timing,' said

Mona-Cygnus.

'Experiment?' croaked the frog.

'When I give the word you grab the little fella, put him in that pentagram over there and pour this over him. Got that?'

Lacertus nodded wordlessly.

'I'm *really* not going to like this, am I?' muttered the frog.

'Go!' shouted Mona-Cygnus.

★

Mr Fred stood at the corner of his bar and surveyed the large crowd of customers with a deep sense of satisfaction. When the great Artemis Bootes had suggested taking over the catering at The Artisan's Arms *personally*, he had been more than a little sceptical. Such a scheme involving so many stray bodies could not possibly work in a village of this size, he had been adamant on that point. Deidre though had been very persistent, nagging at him about his lack of ambition, his lack of foresight. In the end he had relented. The past two days had surpassed his wildest dreams. Never had he seen such a diverse range of customers in his humble little pub.

M. Belvoire it appeared was a natural Maître D'. How he could sweet-talk the little old ladies into parting with so much of their savings just for a plate of egg and chips was something that he would never understand.

Despite still smelling pretty disgusting the dung cart driver had had his pot-washing sink brought another ten yards towards the back door of the kitchen. Luckily only two of the great man's assistants had elected to stay on as there had really not been the space in the tiny kitchen to accommodate all of them.

Mr Fred watched the elegant figure of M. Belvoire, coat-tails flying, white bow tie immaculately in place, glide up to the serving hatch and call, 'Two egg and chips, one over easy, an Artisan burger light on the onions and a basket of chef's special fries!'

'Mais oui!' called Bootes from the depths of the fug-filled kitchen.

Life could really be worth living some days thought Mr Fred happily.

*

Ethelreda emerged from the stairway to the Servants' Hall and stopped. The place was a total shambles. Kids ran, jumped, fought and tumbled over the furniture, carpets, curtains and banisters.

'Dear God, what's been going on here? The place looks like a bomb's hit it. Several bombs. Very large ones at that.'

'Ah! Hello dear,' said Glimmergoyne, turning to her with what a genuine smile of relief on his face. 'Might I introduce to you Mrs Agnes Crater.'

'Hallo dear. Nice to meet you,' said the wizened old woman. Ethelreda felt the blood drain from her face, and she closed her eyes. Her earnest prayer that all this would be a bad dream and that by the time she had counted to ten things would be back to normal failed ignominiously. Slapping on the best smile she could find in her repertoire, she decided to brave it out.

'Hello Mrs Crater. How very nice to meet you.'

'Stop that, you disgusting little beggar!' bellowed Mrs Crater only inches from Ethelreda's ear. 'Cassius! Otto's peeing in that bleedin' flower pot over there. Stop him, *Now*. So sorry 'bout that but boys will be boys. Now, if you'll just tell Caelum we're here, we can give 'im 'is birthday present and be on our way.'

'You only came to give him a *birthday present*?' muttered Glimmergoyne through clenched teeth. Ye Gods, what kind of damage would they have done if they really had come to rescue the little runt?

'I'm afraid that he is not actually in the castle at this time, Madam. He has proved such an invaluable member of our little team here that the King has taken him along on a visit to some Royal relatives…'

'You think I've come to take 'im back, don't you?' she said and cackled raucously. 'Lawd love a duck, that is rich. Take a good look around you, sonny. I've got more than enough to cope wiv' wiv' *this* little lot. But Caelum has always been one o' my favourites. 'Is Dad was a bit of a bad lot mind. Come to fink of it so were Eric's. In fact, come to fink of it even more, they all were. Bastards the lot of 'em. But that's life for you, there's never a good man around when you need one. Right, well then, if 'e's not 'ere then 'e's not 'ere 'an I'll take up no more o' your time. Going somewhere nice are you?'

'Church,' blurted Ethelreda. 'We're just going down to that nice little church at the top of the village.'

'That's nice. Can't say as I go often mesel' but you know 'ow it is. Anyway, I'm glad 'e's behavin' 'is self. 'Es a good boy really. One o' my favourites as I said. So, if you could jus' make sure you gets this to 'im, I'd be most grateful.'

Glimmergoyne stared distastefully at the crudely carved, horrendously painted atrocity of a model sailing boat and grimaced.

'Of course madam, it will be my pleasure.'

'An' if you'll tell 'im Cassius made it for 'im special 'e'll be ever so pleased.'

'Cassius?'

'My eldest. Good lad. Bit rough an' ready but I expect 'e gets that from 'is dad. Right you lot. If you wants any tea tonight I wants to see you all lined up, outside them doors. Now!'

The sound of axes, pots, pans, spears, expensive vases and costly glassware being dropped to the floor in the rush to get out was deafening.

'Right, goodbye to you then Mr, er Mr…?'

'Glimmergoyne.'

'Mr Glimmergoyne. Nice name. Very nice to 'ave met you an' all that. Give my love to Caelum an' tell 'im Mummy says to behave 'isself an' be a good boy.' Agnes Crater hobbled after her unruly brood and painfully eased herself out of the gaping hole.

Ethelreda looked at Glimmergoyne and grimaced.

'Exactly what happened there?' she asked softly.

'Hey, Mr Glimmergoyne?' called the old woman's voice from the hole in the door, 'I think I got 'em all, but if you do find any strays once we're gorn, you can keep 'em. Sorry about them doors. An' the carpets cum t' that. But kids will be kids. You ought t' see my place sometime. Ta ta.'

The wizened old head cackled wildly and withdrew.

'Um, all this socialising is very nice and all that but I do feel that we ought to be going too. What do you say, dear?' said Goldoor in the ensuing, stunned silence.

'That sounds like a *brilliant* idea,' breathed Lyra. 'Let's go!'

'Well, bye all!' called Goldoor smiling broadly as Lyra dragged him quickly through the hole in the doors.

Stunned, Glimmergoyne watched them leave.

'Wasn't that the nutter everybody's been so fanatical about?'

'I've no idea. Could be somebody else entirely.'

Glimmergoyne's eyes took in the battered wreckage of the Reception Hall and he shuddered. He looked at Ethelreda standing at his side, dressed in her Sunday best, a well-stuffed suitcase at her side.

'Well, old dear. If we stay around here much longer we shall only have to clean up this mess. Shall we follow suit?' he said, proffering her his arm.

'I always said you was a gentleman, Mr Glimmergoyne.'

★

'It didn't work, did it?' said Mona-Cygnus quietly.

''Fraid not,' muttered Lacertus.

'Damn. Too much juice probably. Mind you, he does look quite cute like that. I've always fancied a small stone frog beside my goldfish pond.'

'Be my guest,' said Lacertus listlessly.

'I've been considering giving up this game you know,' said the little witch despondently.

'Don't be silly. What on earth would you do instead?'

'Well it just so happens I've been offered a job.'

'But you're a witch. Witches don't take jobs.'

'I know, but this sounded too good to miss. Have you ever heard of the Lost Church of St Reticulum the Barbarian?'

'No.'

'Didn't think so. It's been lost for a very long time. But I found it, quite by accident really. I won't bore you with the details but it appears they have a position going for a Junior High Priestess. Very prestigious. Not much money of course but that's par for the course.'

'How could you possibly give up all this?' asked Lacertus, a bemused smile on his face.

'All *this*? *All this*! Just what exactly do you think I've got here? A nice, cute little rose-covered cottage? A millstone, rather, that just so happens to be a bugger to run. Stone cold in winter, an oven in the summer. And look at me. I mean just look. Old, grey, wizened. Everybody and his brother's idea of a witch. How would you like to live in a cliché like this? Be honest now.'

'I see what you mean,' he said slowly. 'Don't they mind about the witch bit? At the Lost Church of wherever it was?'

'No, no. They were actually quite impressed I think. To tell you the truth they've been lost for so long now that they wouldn't know the difference between Catholicism and a bucket of tar. Besides, I'm no good at it. See, I've even upset you now, haven't I? Turning your poor little friend into a garden ornament.'

'*My friend*? Please, let's be realistic about this. He was no friend of mine. It's just that he was my best hope of getting into the Royal Safe up at Camelopardis Castle.'

'Is that all?' she exclaimed. 'Why didn't you say so. I could have helped you without all that messy, mind-numbing, mumbo-jumbo back there. Hold on a sec. Let me just go and have a look…'

'No more magic, please. I don't think I could—'

'Piffle boy. You don't honestly believe us witches do every-thing by magic do you? It's difficult, dangerous and can be downright messy if you cock it up. I mean, just *look* at me! No. For simple problems, even witches prefer simple solutions.'

Lacertus watched Mona-Cygnus digging around in a vast wooden chest, cursing and swearing as she rifled the contents.

'Aha!' she exclaimed suddenly, rising and handing him a small, tightly wrapped bundle.

'What's that?' he asked.

'Six sticks of Harmon and Grob's best. Enough dynamite there to shift the most tightly bound of old maid's corsets!' she cackled again, hysterically. 'See what I mean boy. I'm even beginning to *sound* like a cliché. What a pathetic way to make a living. So what are you going to do now?'

'Me? No problem there. I have nothing against clichés. I have a kingdom to inherit!'

★

Private Gramm, perched dangerously on the small milking stool in front of the Princess Andromeda's Royal Bedchamber was in a bit of a quandary. The empty plate lying on the floor beside the stool stared up at him like a huge, red-rimmed, accusatory eye. Private Gramm looked from door to plate then back again.

Since the shouting and peculiar noises emanating from the room had died down it was obvious that Private Volans had managed to get the situation under control and would not, therefore, be in need of rescuing. He was free for a few moments to go downstairs and collect his lunch. Having made what he felt to be the most logical assessment of the situation, Private Gramm rose and picked up the empty plate.

'I'll be little use in defending anybody if I'm distracted by hunger, will I?' he said to himself defensively. Private Gramm waddled to the outer doors and quietly let himself out into the staircase. He hummed a tuneless little song as he bounded down the stairs to the kitchen.

★

Goldoor dragged the carriage bodily out of the stable block and pushed it to the gate. With the heavy repairs made to it since the collision with the gate it was not a pretty sight, but at least it was standing on its own four wheels. Guiding a horse from the stables Goldoor manhandled it between the shafts and hitched the unfortunate creature in place. He then repeated the procedure with a second.

'Get in, beloved,' he said, finally ready, to the pretty, young ladies' maid, proffering her his arm.

'Why thank you, young sir. I shall indeed!'

Beside the fountain Ortolan Apus half-dragged, half-hauled the dead weight of Captain Parsus, including fast-rusting armour, from the water, in between gales of laughter.

'The nutter, Captain,' bawled Ortolan Apus through floods of tears. 'He's getting away!'

'Wha... Wha... Who?'

Parsus coughed up a large volume of water at the young Prince's feet, dragged himself from his knees and elbows and staggered towards the castle doors, stood upright, lurched drunkenly and swung his sword at both of the stone lions in turn.

'No Captain. The nutter. Over there!'

Ortolan Apus was laughing so hard by this time that he could barely get the words out.

'Begad boy but you're right. For England and St George!' screamed the demented Captain and ran straight towards the stables. The coach lurched into motion and cleared the gates in one smooth arc under the steady guidance of Izakiah Goldoor of Picton, a man on a mission, leaving Captain Parsus to fall noisily into the woodwork of the stables with a mind-numbing crash. Ortolan Apus was no longer in any condition to control his voice, he could only point wildly in the direction of the gates.

'Where away?' bellowed Parsus, saw the pointing finger and galloped, clanking and swaying, in the approximate direction in which it pointed.

The armour clanged loudly as the Captain managed to collide, like a billiard ball, with each of the four columns on the corners of the gate in turn before fatally hurtling over the parapet ten feet beyond. By this time, Ortolan Apus was so lost in tearful, all consuming laughter he could not stand, let alone follow.

Glimmergoyne, standing on the top step of the doorway, took in the whole scene. When the sounds of the metal clad Captain plummeting down the hillside finally faded, he shook his head slowly and turned to Ethelreda and said tiredly, 'Let's go. I've had more than enough of this!'

'Yes dear.'

He doffed his (Ex-King Vulpecula's) natty little bowler at the little Prince but the boy took no notice. He was sobbing uncontrollably with laughter.

'Thick as pig shit, the lot of them,' muttered Glimmergoyne.

'Yes dear.'

Fifteen

Lacertus started off towards Camelopardis with a confident stride, convinced by now that he had enough in his private armoury to take on the whole castle garrison and win. He had paused by the roadside to take time to wrap the six sticks of dynamite in nice packaging, just in case the challenger at the gates wanted to be difficult. When he reached the lower gates he found them deserted. He wrinkled his brow in puzzlement.

Where was Ernie Pavo? What had happened to the normal guard? Twenty feet inside the gates the dilapidated royal coach drawn by two scrawny looking nags thundered past, almost knocking him from his feet and pushing him into the near side wall.

'The nutter!' he muttered, recognising the blond hair and grinning teeth too late. 'What has that stupid idiot been up to in *my* castle?'

Lacertus began to trot up the steep gradient, losing more hope with every step. A clang from above made him stop warily, expecting the worst. Another louder clang and the patter of falling stones that followed caused him to look skyward just before the suit of shining armour containing Captain Parsus bounced on the road in front of him and disappeared over the steep side before his very eyes.

Impatient now, Lacertus hurried on. Too late now and there may be nothing left to inherit!

He literally charged into Glimmergoyne and Ethelreda as he turned the final bend.

'Whoa, there! Whoa!' said the old man.

'Mr Glimmergoyne? What are you doing here? Shouldn't you be—'

'I should, but I'm not. I'm afraid she's gone, boy.'

'Who?'

'The luscious Lyra. She's done a runner with the nutter I'm

afraid. Shame really, but there you go. Girls will be girls. Here, this is for you. Keep it well and remember me of a time. I shall be watching you, just as Our Gracious Queen Xenophobe always did.'

'You knew about all that then?'

'As I kept on telling you, my boy, I came here when I was eleven years old. There is *nothing* I don't know about that grotesque old monstrosity up there. Oh, by the way, don't bother with the Royal Safe. *Mr* Vulpecula emptied it before he left.'

Lacertus opened his palm and looked down at the hard object Glimmergoyne had placed in it. It was the Royal Seal of King Multiceros.

'You know what this means, don't you?'

Glimmergoyne shrugged, smiled and bowed low.

'Yes, Your Majesty. It means that you may do as you please, just exactly as you bloody well please. And may your gods be merciful to you.'

'You old bastard!'

'Less of the old please. Well, you'd better be off before the obnoxious Ortolan moves in on you. Shall we go, dear?'

'Yes Mr Glimmergoyne. We've wasted enough years already.'

The two old retainers turned their backs on the young Lacertus and walked sedately, arm in arm, down the long winding driveway.

Lacertus gave a small whoop of delight and bounded on up towards Camelopardis.

*

'Are you sure we're going the right way?' asked Private Volans in worried tones.

'Just shut up and follow me!' grated Andromeda, nastily.

In the narrow tunnels of Camelopardis that Lacertus was used to running through, the unlikely pair of elopees were having immense difficulties. The Princess Andromeda, though not actually obese, had trouble with the tight corners and the vast height of Private Volans meant that his head kept making painful contact with the low ceilings. He was gradually developing a very nasty headache.

When the pair finally emerged into the stable block it was virtually empty. The cold wind blowing through the gap, caused by the cannibalisation of the wooden planking, was filling the air with stray wisps of straw.

'Dear God!' bellowed Andromeda. 'I knew that Daddy was cutting costs to the bone but this is ridiculous!'

'What do you mean, dear? There's a horse over there, look. For as long as I've been here there's only been four horses – two for the coach and two spare.'

'But there used to be twenty horses here. Plus grooms and tackmen. I just don't understand it!' she bawled.

'Get yourself on the back of this one here and then we'll be off,' he said testily, throwing a saddle over the thin ribs of an elderly nag.

'But what about—'

'Look, just get yourself on the back of this horse now or the deal is off!' shouted Private Volans angrily, pulling the saddle straps so tight in his exasperation that the horse winced.

'Yes dear, of course, I only asked—'

'Well *don't*!'

'Yes dear.'

The horse seemed to bow in the middle as Her Royal Ugliness boarded it and Private Volans strapped the bags onto its sides.

'But what if—' she bellowed meekly.

'I said don't. Now shut up!' screamed Private Volans.

'Yes dear.'

*

Private Gramm, finding nobody available in the Servants' Hall to cut his lunchtime sandwiches for him, set about making his own. It took quite a while since, being just a common soldier, he knew little of fridges or knives, ovens or hotplates.

Finally he managed to accrue a pile of what on the surface appeared to be normal sandwiches but was underneath three loaves of bread and a half hock of ham. Even without the pickles and lettuce it would have kept an impoverished family of four alive for a week.

On his return trip to his guard post, eyes firmly fixed on his plate of food, Private Gramm missed a turning or two, wandered down several passages and round several corners until he found himself surrounded in thick, white steam.

'Er... Hello?... Hello, is there anybody there?' he called into the fug hopefully.

Silence.

Private Gramm took a bite of sandwich to fortify his courage.

'Mr Gramm!' boomed a voice directly into his ear, so unnerving him that the pile of food scattered across the floor.

'What the... I was just havin' me lunch,' he said petulantly.

'Sorry Mr Gramm, but we don't very often see you down here in the Laundry,' said Hydrus conversationally.

'That was me *lunch*!'

'Sorry about that I'm sure. Let me help you pick it up.'

Private Gramm stood and watched as Hydrus gathered all the scattered hunks of bread, bits of lettuce and ham and put them all back onto the plate.

'So where's everybody gone?' asked Private Gramm peevishly. 'I had to make them meself!'

'I'm sure I don't know, Mr Gramm. But who are we to question our betters, eh? You and me are just the workers. Who cares about us, eh? Nobody, that's who. Would you like a cup of tea? I've got a fresh brew on the go. We can have a natter and a sandwich before you're back on duty?'

'Well all right, but just you remember, that's *my* lunch.'

'Of course, Mr Gramm. We can always make some more you know.'

Private Gramm's face lit up at the suggestion.

'Of course we can. I hadn't thought of that! Pour the brew, Mr Hydrus. Pour the brew!'

'My pleasure, Mr Gramm.'

★

Mona-Cygnus turned and locked the door of the pretty little rose-covered cottage and grinned happily, if somewhat lopsidedly. Decision made, she had no regrets. She looked down at the two suitcases at her side, thought about putting a spell on them to follow her to the church of St Reticulum the Barbarian, then decided against it. They would probably vanish in a puff of smoke to Timbuctoo or somewhere similar.

Picking up the bags in her wizened old hands she hobbled to the gate and opened it. Turning one last time she took in the overgrown garden, the late summer roses, the pink door and the cute little stone frog on the wall of the cute little wishing well and sighed wistfully.

'Goodbye cute little rose-covered cottage. Goodbye and good riddance!'

She lobbed the door key accurately into the round, brick-lined well and turned away. Flashes of lightning and sulphurous gases enveloped her before imploding gracefully. Carefully she looked over her shoulder at the large hole in the ground that had until so very recently been her home.

'By Satan's left titty! It *does* works. Now I never knew that,' she muttered. With a shrug she turned to face the approaching clattering racket.

Abruptly she was confronted by two steaming, stomping horses between the shafts of a once magnificent carriage.

Goldoor, perched on the rotting box, idly twisting the reins in his hands smiled with a mouthful of teeth and opened his mouth to speak.

'Why thank you, young man, I was expecting you.'

'But how…' began Goldoor.

'Shift over, you, and stop asking stupid questions,' she said effortlessly throwing her two cases onto the roof rack and deftly climbing onto the box beside him.

'Hit the gas, boy.'

Goldoor smiled at her broadly.

'Yes ma'am!'

Nobody seemed to notice that the concussion from the imploding cute little rose-covered cottage had caused the little stone frog to fall into the deep waters. Had they done, they probably wouldn't have cared much anyway. Such is life.

★

Lacertus bolted the last few hundred yards up the driveway as fast as he could go. The sight that greeted him was awe-inspiring. The great doors still smouldered slightly and the burnt out hole in their middle made Lacertus wince. The impregnable fortress had been breached, a concept he had never ever considered possible. Warily he approached the hole, wondering feverishly what he would find within.

'Hello my dear Lacertus. Good of you to honour us with your presence. Here, catch!'

Before Lacertus could pinpoint the voice of the obnoxious Ortolan he knew exactly what to expect. By the time the small vial of blue liquid made contact with the statue of King Monoceros he was safely within the protection of the paint store walls.

A childlike giggle of joy followed the massive explosion that shook even the thick stone of the solid walls around the cowering kitchen boy.

When the reverberations had died down, Lacertus cautiously poked his head above the lintel of the small window, now uncluttered by opaque glass, above his head and gaped in awe. The once magnificent statue of old King Monoceros had been cut off at the knees. The thousands of tiny shards of marble and marble dust that had once been the bold King covered the courtyard. Shreds of red jacket took on the aspect of pools of blood at the scene of a massacre.

'Come to my office later on and we'll sort something out between us. What do you say?'

'Over my dead body!' bawled Lacertus.

A faint boyish giggle was the only answer he got.

Lacertus crept out through the door and loped warily across to the stables. Once in the inner passageways, instead of going directly to the King's office as would be expected, he trotted off in the direction of the kitchens, listening with senses on full alert for sounds of pursuit or unusual doings ahead. It was now stunningly clear that the spotty little Prince knew the layout of the tunnels at least as well as he did. Now was no time to become careless.

*

'Well dear, I have to love you and leave you,' said the Dowager Duchess to the Queen Berenice. 'Got to go and see Matron for some more of my lotion. Not that it hasn't been lovely to hear some proper music for once. I really do think you're improving!'

'Oh, do you?' simpered Queen Berenice. 'Do you really?'

'Of course dear. Don't listen to a word that idiot son of mine says. He's tone deaf. Always has been.'

'Well I think I shall play for just a *bit* longer. It's such a wonderfully soothing instrument.'

'Don't let me stop you, dear. I'll see you later. For cocoa.'

Opening the door to the stairwell, the Dowager Duchess smiled as the Mighty Wurlitzer bellowed into life behind her, an unrecognisable string of duff notes making the door tremble.

'Ah, 'Danny Boy'. How lovely,' muttered the Dowager quietly to herself. Slowly she made her way down the steep stairwell and through the lower tower to the Reception Hall.

The sight that greeted her one good eye as she opened the door stopped her dead. The devastation was so overwhelming that she could not quite take it all in.

'Servants! Can't even keep the place clean nowadays. My poor dear husband would *never* have let things come to this sorry pass!'

Picking her way gingerly across the jumble of armour parts and discarded weaponry, she muttered and cursed the lack of her son's management skills and resolved to have it out with that idle, good-for-nothing butler herself, personally. Just as soon as she had consulted Matron Beamish.

★

Sitting in her tiny office below stairs, Matron Beamish woke from a very pleasant nap to the sound of deafening silence. The normal, everyday sounds of a busy Servants' Hall were thunderous in their absence. Matron Beamish crossed to the door and opened it warily.

'Hello? Is there anybody there?' she called hopefully. A glance at the tall, ornate grandfather clock showed her that it was nearly five o'clock.

'That's not five in the morning is it?' she muttered, noting the cold ashes in the great fire. 'I must have slept the whole night through in here.'

Footsteps sounded on the stairway from the Hall of Fire. Slow meticulous footsteps.

'Mr Glimmergoyne? Is that you? Where is everybody? What time is it?'

Lacertus crept into the long hall and glanced furtively around.

'Matron!' he said, recognising the rotund face peering at him, half-smiling. 'Not seen Ortolan, have you?'

'No. Not recently dear. Probably amusing himself with his toys or playing in the Armoury. He does so love that old room.'

'*That's* one of the things about him that worries me,' said Lacertus edging warily around the outskirts of the room, staying close to the wall.

'Are you feeling all right, dear? You look very pale. Can I mix you a pick me up or something?'

'No! Er, no, I mean, no thank you. Just a bit of indigestion I think. I shall go and lie down for a bit, have a nap. Make me feel lots better.'

'Sounds like a good idea,' Matron said watching bemused as he finished his wall hugging trip around the room to the Servants' Quarters.

'Um, just one thing. Is that five in the morning or five in the afternoon, only I seem to have lost all track of time.'

'Afternoon,' he said bluntly over his shoulder as he sloped off to his room.

'Have a good nap, dear. Come and see me later, won't you? Just in case it's something more serious.'

She turned back to her armchair, closed the door softly behind her and put the kettle on. Maybe by the time she had made a nice cup of tea someone would have started to get dinner ready.

★

Lacertus felt, rather than saw, the very slight angle at which his door was standing. Since the frog was long gone, and so for that matter was Lyra, there could only be one explanation. Cautiously he pushed at the portal with an outstretched foot. The clatter of the bucket full of lead shot, rusty horse tackle, several old axe blades and a head sized lump of masonry hitting the stone floor was deafening.

'I should have expected no less,' muttered Lacertus.

As the din faded he pushed the door gently again, letting it swing wide. When nothing else appeared about to deluge him, he quickly stepped inside, kicked the nasty debris out of the way, slammed the door and threw the bolts. Pulling the gaily-wrapped package from his coat pocket he began to concentrate his thoughts on his next move. Somehow he had to think of a way to get this package to the obnoxious Ortolan without being in the vicinity personally. It promised to be a long night.

★

Private Volans led the heavily laden horse through the Gatehouse and onto the westerly road in the direction of the Duchy of Philbert. He was quietly pleased at not having to go down the High Street in such an undignified fashion. The horse seemed to be bowed at the stomach and the legs slightly splayed as it doggedly followed him. When the group of scruffy, dirty little children spotted them and started to dance in a large circle around, Volans grimaced in embarrassment.

'Ha ha. Better to put the nosebag on 'er 'ead than on the poor old 'orse's!'

'You'd be quicker walking.'

'Where'd you find the mask Missus? It's not 'Alloween yet is it?'

With a grunt Private Volans swung a very well-aimed leather-covered foot at the nearest urchin and smiled as the lad screamed and fell to the ground, clutching at his groin. The rest of the group stopped in dismay and stared hatefully at Volans.

'Run along home now. I'm sure it must be time for *little boys* to be having their tea,' he said nastily.

Strolling as nonchalantly as possible away Private Volans ignored the abuse and catcalls as the stricken boy was carted away, still screaming horribly, by his comrades.

'Kicking children now. Very masterful I must say,' muttered the Princess.

'You can shut up as well, otherwise you *will* be wearing the nosebag!'

He ignored the Princess's aggrieved grousing as he led the slowly buckling horse ever onwards towards the rapidly setting sun.

Climbing clumsily out of the cute little stone well in the grounds of the once pretty little rose-covered cottage Private Serpens swore vehemently. His naked, still a touch greenish, skin shivered with cold as he looked around for something to cover and warm himself. On a bank beside the hole in the ground he found a pile of burnt and tattered clothing, the once best suit of Izakiah Goldoor had he but known it. But be that as it may, Serpens pulled on the shreds of clothing and mentally made a list of all the people he was going to do some very nasty things to by way of retribution for the indignities he had suffered in the past few weeks. It was a long list.

He strode purposefully down the High Street of Leopardis in the direction of Camelopardis, but more importantly towards the castle moat where he had sufficient booty to fund his schemes.

Mrs Frobisher in Barton Regis could wait just a little bit longer.

*

Matron Beamish flounced unhappily into the Servants' Hall in search of some signs of life, or rather of some food. She had been devastated at the scene of carnage in the Reception Hall and frightened by the cold feel of the castle as a whole. That there was a perfectly logical explanation to all this she had no doubt. She would go and speak with the nice young kitchen boy and together they could sort something out. And if he still had indigestion she could sort that out too.

Before she even reached the passageway that led to the staff quarters she was drawn to the murmuring of voices emanating from the kitchen. If there was somebody in the kitchen, then there may well be some food coming up fairly soon.

Pushing the large double doors aside she spotted first the large red blob of Private Gramm set against the grubby white blob of Hydrus the laundryman. Private Gramm was observing closely as the great paws of Hydrus deftly cut huge chunks of bread from a large, round loaf.

'Well hello, Mr Hydrus. Do you have any idea where everybody's gone? It's nearly dinner time you know.'

'I had realised that, Matron. Would you care for a small snack in the meantime?' asked Hydrus solicitously moving the bread aside and replacing it with an enormous joint of cold roast beef.

'What a wonderful idea. I'll make some tea, shall I? There must be some biscuits around here somewhere too. We could all have a nice little picnic. My, but that beef really does look good. Won't the others be upset when they find out!'

As the vast blue cloud of Matron Beamish drifted away Hydrus smiled gently.

'A lovely lady don't you think, Mr Gramm?'

'Who?' asked Private Gramm closely watching the huge slabs of dead cow being laid onto even thicker slabs of sliced bread.

'Never mind,' said Hydrus quietly.

Sixteen

Glimmergoyne and Ethelreda arrived at the entrance to The Artisan's Arms to be effusively greeted by the white tie and tails of M. Francis Belvoire.

'Welcome to our hostelry, good sir, if you would care to step inside I shall endeavour to find you and your lady a quiet table…'

'Dear God no thank you. What time is the next coach out of this noisome little burg?'

Puzzled at getting such a negative response M. Belvoire stopped open-mouthed. He stared hard at the smartly dressed pair for a long moment before he finally recognised the leathery old face with the piercing eyes under the black bowler.

'It's Mr Glimmergoyne isn't it? I'm so sorry. I didn't recognise you without the uniform. What a pleasant surprise,' he said, his voice tailing off.

Suddenly he noted the two stuffed suitcases at the old couple's feet.

'Going away are we?'

'*We* are going away. Whether you go or stay is of such little consequence to me that I shan't even bother to contemplate the question,' said Glimmergoyne coldly.

'Well really I don't think that is very…' blustered M. Belvoire, only to be drowned out by the loud clatter and rumbling hooves of a fast approaching coach and horses.

The entire ensemble ground to a noisy halt only feet from the wide-eyed, open-mouthed Maître D'.

'Cap'n Tuc'na delive'ed safe an' sound, Mr Glimgoy' sah!' slurred the little blue clad driver.

'Quite an achievement considering he was far from safe and well when he left,' muttered Glimmergoyne to Ethelreda. 'I say, my man! We need to get to Aqua Scutum, out on the west coast. Will the horses make it?'

'Cours' Mr Glimgoy' sah. 'Op in.'

'Shall we, dear?' he said, offering Ethelreda his arm.

She glanced at the worried face of M. Belvoire, the open door of the inn and the rickety old coach in turn before deciding on the lesser of multiple evils. She smiled at Glimmergoyne, took his arm and murmured, 'I think it is *way* past time we were on our way. Lead on, Mr Glimmergoyne.'

M. Belvoire smiled weakly at the back of the once stately royal coach as it picked up speed on its way down the High Street, causing all it its path to leap for cover.

As the last sounds died away and peace returned to the little village, he turned and re-entered the bar of The Artisan's Arms switching on the charming smile of the elegant, charming Maître D' as he went.

*

Following the destruction of the statue of King Monoceros, Ortolan Apus was in a state of mild elation. The result had even improved on the conflagration in the Servants' Hall that had so distressed everybody. Wandering the hidden passageways on his way to his father's office to check on the contents of the safe, a sudden whim diverted him down to Lacertus's hutch where he set up the old 'bucket above the door gag'.

That the young kitchen boy would not fall for that one Ortolan had no doubt; he was not as stupid as he made out to be, that one. At least it would keep him on his toes.

That completed, a masterly example of the art of the murderous practical joke on a par with the one that had done for the drunken gamekeeper, his mood remained buoyant as he bounded surely down the narrow passageways to his earlier objective.

A cursory search of the Royal Safe revealed what he had suspected all along. Dear old Daddy had done a runner with all the loot. Sitting himself in the Royal armchair behind the vast carven desk he put his feet up on the highly polished tabletop and surveyed his new domain. Since there was no money freely available he would need to sell off a few of the more valuable items to raise some funds. The shelves of books that lined the walls of the office would be a good place to start. The desk alone had to be worth a good few ducats of anybody's money.

Once the enemy had been vanquished and he could move around freely he would see what could be done. Then the *real* party could begin.

★

The Dowager Duchess hobbled into the Servants' Hall and glared around. The three vast shapes, the red, the white and the blue were sat at the long polished table stuffing their faces with what looked very much like bloodstained pillows. When none of the heads turned at her arrival she tapped her stick on the stone flags impatiently. Still they ignored her, engrossed in their feast.

'Harumph!' she snorted loudly, glaring even harder. If there was one thing she could not abide it was to be ignored by servants. Matron Beamish turned heavily at the sound, sending the plates nearest to her sliding gracefully along the highly polished wood to crash noisily to the floor at the same time as her chair ungracefully clattered behind her.

'That was me dinner you just—' began Private Gramm.

'Your Highness!' said Matron, frantically. 'I'm so terribly sorry. I didn't realise, you were—'

'That much is obvious. Get me some more of your dreadful lotion this minute! It doesn't do much good of course but we have to do something to justify your extortionate salary.'

'Yes of course, Your Ladyship, right away. How are feeling in yourself? Where does it hurt?'

'It hurts all over as bloody usual. Just cut the cackle and get on with it will you!'

'Yes Your Ladyship!' simpered Matron Beamish as she hurried off to her little office.

'And what are you two staring at? Get that mess cleared up and get back to work before I go and see His Highness. Honestly, this place feels more like a bleeding holiday camp every day!'

The cold, narrow eyes watched the two corpulent figures as they somnambulantly brushed the remains of their supper into a dustpan and polished the already gleaming table.

The Royal foot continued to tap out a tuneless melody of impatience on the cold stone floor as the breathless matron bounced up to the shrivelled Ex-Queen and handed her a dark brown bottle.

'About time too. Make sure these two get the job done properly! And since that lazy great plank of a butler is nowhere to be seen, organise my little Ortolan his cocoa and biscuits. The lad is getting far too thin. He needs feeding up at his age. See to it!'

'Yes Your Ladyship, of course I will,' murmured the matron.

Without another word the stately old lady turned and hobbled away towards the stairs.

★

Lacertus paused at the entrance to the Servants' Hall and glanced shiftily around the darkened Hall of Fire for signs of life. Nothing stirred.

Breathing out slowly he deliberately began to pick his way across the room. Stepping circumspectly over the scattered debris of arms and armour and of once valuable furniture and carpets he shook his head sadly. Calculating the damage even vaguely upset him. There would be so much for him to do when this stupid game of cat and mouse was resolved.

He found what he was looking for draped over a decimated sofa. The leather and chain-mail jerkin was heavy in his hands and it promised to be very hot and tiring to wear but, nevertheless, he removed his shirt and put it on.

At least it would offer some protection against some of the nastier weapons in obnoxious Ortolan's repertoire.

Replacing his shirt over the shining steel rings he spotted a long thin-bladed knife stuck into the leg of the sofa. He smiled to himself, a smile as close to jollity as a camel is to a lobster. Wrapping the ultra sharp blade in a fragment of heavy curtain he slipped it beneath his shirt, up against the steel rings. Now was not the time for caution.

Bold action was required. With the personal protection measures he had just implemented, Lacertus felt ready to take it.

He strode purposefully towards the stairs that would bring him to the doors of the Castle Armoury.

★

The silence below stairs was deep and soulless. In her 'Executive Staff Suite' Matron Beamish sat on the edge of the bed and stared at the wall, a six-month-old letter hanging listlessly in her hand. It was a letter from her niece, Vela, announcing the imminent arrival of sprog number six and requesting that she, the elderly, caring nanny should come to Leophus and assist with caring for the children of her own family instead of for the children of strangers, as she had spent most of her life doing. The tone of the letter was much the same as the five previous communications from her fecund niece that had been arriving punctually every year for the past six years.

But this one was different. This time the old matron felt a real need to go. Since Pixie had still not returned from his extended 'Tour of State' to the surrounding Kingdoms and did not look likely to be for quite some time yet, according to what His Highness had said at their last interview together, and little Orty seemed to be spending more and more time on his own projects, so much so that she was beginning to feel desperately worthless. The prospect of being landed with the job of companion to the crabby old Dowager Duchess was such a bleak one that her thoughts slowly came to their inevitable conclusion.

With a tremendous effort she pushed herself to her feet and purposefully crossed to the small writing desk set against the opposite wall. Pulling a sheet of official headed notepaper from the beautifully proportioned antique escritoire she began to write,

Dear Vela, Eridanus and family,

I should be most pleased to accept your invitation to come and visit with you and all of my lovely little great-nephews and great-nieces for a time. I have a short holiday pending that would seem to me to be the ideal opportunity to…

The shadows in the hallways were spreading and darkening profoundly as the corpulent nanny wrote. The idea was becoming more and more appealing with every word.

*

The difficulties Corporal Serpens encountered in securing his funds from the cold and rancid moat were nothing compared to the problems he encountered when he attempted to buy some better clothing. The owners of all three of Leopardis's better clothing emporia, on seeing his singed and moat-stained rags promptly ejected him bodily from their premises as a down and out despite his assertions that he was a soldier, a Corporal no less, of the Royal Guard. Fat lot of good that did.

The small grubby owner of the small grubby cobbler's shop behind the Dog and Ferret had finally come to his rescue by selling him a jacket and a pair of breeches that despite being at least third if not fourth-hand were rather comfortable and a pair of rather tight-fitting shoes that were cutting unmercifully into his heels as he picked his way up the driveway to Camelopardis very, very slowly.

The burning desire to right the wrongs done to him was rapidly replaced by the severe burning pains in his feet.

Contemplating the pair of nice sharp throwing knives and heavy short-bladed sword hanging from a belt around his waist brought him some comfort, but it was only short-lived. The man in Leopardis Hardware and Armoury had no problem accepting him or his money. Besides the shoes, it appeared that the breeches had also been occupied by several large families of fleas before he, rather foolishly in retrospect, bought them. The little buggers had not yet vacated the premises and were driving him to distraction as they celebrated an early Christmas by feasting en masse on his legs. Never had the driveway to Camelopardis seemed so long – to anything other than a frog of course.

*

Tentatively Lacertus approached the Armoury doors. He paused for several long seconds as his sharply-honed instinct for self-preservation took over. Releasing the handle he sidestepped quickly and kicked the door open with an extended foot. The three heavy steel-tipped bolts that thudded heavily into the tapestry on the opposite wall came as no surprise.

'Greetings, Lacertus. You found me then!'

'It would seem so.'

'Come and join me. Let us drink a glass of wine and talk of the future,' called the voice of Ortolan Apus. 'We have more in common than you may think.'

Lacertus grinned to himself. This would be the turning point, the point of no return. Stepping carefully around the edge of the door and keeping out of line of fire of the three chair-mounted crossbows, Lacertus picked his way towards the far end of the room to where Ortolan Apus lounged in a large and ornate armchair. As he approached he noticed a similar chair beside the first. Between the two stood a small table decked with a ghastly striped cloth and two tall stemmed, wine-filled glasses.

'Come to join me?' asked Ortolan, affably.

Gingerly Lacertus perched himself on the second chair, his eyes fluctuating between the spotty young Prince and the diabolical tablecloth.

'Pyxis's?' asked Lacertus delicately.

'As if you need to ask. A nice touch, don't you think?' Ortolan said with a shrug. 'I found the beloved nightshirt behind the wardrobe in your very own room would you believe! Very careless of you.'

'And the glasses?'

'Exactly where you left them, dear boy,' he giggled happily.

Lacertus's throat was so dry that he could have drained both of the glasses of ruby red liquid without a second thought and still have asked for more.

'So which is yours?'

'Take your pick!' grinned Ortolan.

Lacertus dropped his eyes from the spotty face and concentrated on the glasses. He knew that the wrong choice, or rather the *right* choice in his own best interests, would lead to other consequences. His hand hovered first over one glass then the other. Instinctively he picked up the glass nearest himself and took a long swig, relishing the deep rich taste of the wine as it filled his mouth.

'Touché, Mr Lacertus.'

Ortolan giggled again, picked up the glass nearest himself and drained it in one smooth motion. Suddenly he leapt from his chair and disappeared into a secret panel in the back wall.

'We will meet again very soon!' he called, but before the panel was fully closed Lacertus was up and running. The agonised creaking of the trapdoor rapidly dropping away beneath the two very comfortable antique armchairs resounded loudly and violently around the room followed by a loud double splash as the doomed furniture entered the foetid moat, far below.

Lacertus reached the thick doors and slammed them shut behind himself.

'The little sod will *definitely* have to go!' he muttered.

★

Deep within the castle, Private Gramm and Mr Hydrus sat huddled over a small table in the back of the Laundry. The cards on the white cloth before them were the only points of colour visible in a world of white smog since Gramm had removed his red jacket. Neither said a word as the steam from the huge copper boilers filled the air and swirled as ostentatiously as Queen Berenice's rendering of 'Danny Boy' around them.

Every so often a great fist from one or other side of the table would absently reach out and pick up a hunk of sandwich and stuff it into a waiting mouth.

Not even the ticking of the great clock in the Servants' Hall could penetrate this far. The peace and quiet that was so strikingly absent in the rest of Camelopardis seemed to have made its home down here until all the fuss had died down.

'Hah!' grunted Gram suddenly. 'Rummy!'

'Oh well done, Mr Gramm!' smiled Hydrus pushing the pile of coins in the centre of the table towards him. The big paws of the laundryman gathered the cards together, splitting and shuffling them with the dexterity of a Louisiana Riverboat card sharp.

'Another hand?' he asked pleasantly.

'I suppose I really ought to go and see what's going on upstairs.'

'I don't imagine for one minute that the castle is going to fall to pieces without you for a few hours, Mr Gramm,' said Hydrus jovially.

Private Gramm looked greedily at the pile of coins on the table in front of him and considered the situation. He tried to assess in his mind the wealth accumulated there, but his mind stumbled over the numbers and so he just licked his lips instead. Must be a month's pay there at least, he speculated wildly.

'No, I suppose you're right there. Deal 'em up then, Mr Hydrus,' he said decisively, his hand reaching for the plate of sandwiches.

★

Lacertus was thinking hard. The safest place for him to be at the moment would be the top tower. Nothing could fall on him or be thrown at him up there without his being aware of the attack at least for those few precious seconds before it happened. The situation itself could be managed if he could ascertain the time it took for the number two acid to work its way through a quarter inch of cork to compound number five from the Junior Chemistry Set recipe book. The blue one that had so devastated young Crater and the poor old statue of the now very, very late King Monoceros. If he could work the delay time down to three minutes the job could be over and done before anybody even noticed.

His luck held as he reached the open skies of the highest point in his small realm without trouble. Bolting the door to the stairwell from the outside, he spread out the contents of his small backpack and set to work.

It took over four and a half hours of his precious time, energy and single-minded obsession and the light was fading fast by the time he wedged the penultimate portion of cork into the final test-tube, but he could sense the oncoming jubilation.

He pushed the final portion of cork loosely into the mouth of the test-tube before laying it gently into the cotton wool bed ensconced in the nest formed by the six sticks of Harmon and Grob's best and covered the whole in a very tasteful, but rather over-the-top, wrapping paper. All the while he smiled to himself. It was the smile of the child who knows exactly what he wants and exactly how to get it, making it a smile that could have annihilated a Panzer regiment should such have been its whim.

Now all he needed was an appropriate vehicle to transport the goods.

★

Once more ensconced in her favourite armchair in the Queen's music room, the Dowager Duchess was carrying on a diatribe on the vagaries of her own family and their many, many faults, mainly to herself since the long fingers of the Queen were hammering to death a beautiful, centuries-old, folk melody on the keyboards of the Mighty Wurlitzer. As the last set of violently molested chords made their way towards silence the Queen turned to the Dowager and simpered. 'Oh, very nice dear. Very nice. But as I was saying, the sooner Peccy abdicates and darling Pyxis assumes control, the sooner I shall feel safe. I mean can't you speak to him?'

'He doesn't listen to me!' whined the Queen hopelessly. 'All he ever does is come in here and complain about money, money, money. Money and my music. But I need my music you see, he just doesn't understand…' the thin, toneless voice tailed off into the distance.

'I know, I know,' muttered the Duchess. 'I honestly don't know why you married him.'

'What would you like to hear now?' asked the reedy voice in embarrassment, trying to change the subject.

'Whatever you fancy my dear. You always did the Vivaldi so splendidly!'

'Oh I say, how kind of you to say so.'

The Wurlitzer that would normally have drowned out most ordinary conversation as it burst into life did not stop the Dowager Duchess.

'But he is such a wimp of a man. Not the boy I brought up at all. My little Peccy was always so sweet and kind, so helpful to his mummy.'

The tones of the Mighty Wurlitzer droned ever onwards destroying yet another fine and sentimental old ballad.

*

Corporal Serpens reached the Upper Gatehouse in pure, unremitting agony. Leaning against one of the stone pillars he made one of the first of a series of extremely stupid decisions – decisions that in hindsight were possibly even worse than the one he had unwittingly made in upsetting the long-dead mother of the witch Mona-Cygnus. He removed his shoes.

The cool breeze that made contact with the raw blisters and contusions was heavenly. Serpens stood for a few moments merely enjoying the sense of having rid himself of an indescribable burden. It seemed even the mites in his trousers had stopped their feast in honour of the occasion. That they were fully sated and sleeping off the effects of their revels was not of any great importance at that particular moment in time.

The second stupid decision was when he decided to charge the very doors of Camelopardis itself. The long minutes of recovery also stimulated his vengeful instincts. Drawing the sword from his belt with one hand and one of the ultra-sharp throwing knives in the other he made his move.

If anything, the pain of the crystal sharp shards of marble that littered the inner courtyard were worse than anything the damnable shoes could have done to his feet. Stumbling and swaying drunkenly across the courtyard, cursing and swearing vehemently Serpens finally arrived at the stone steps and fell heavily forward onto their solid sanctuary. The pair of stone lions stared down at him impassively as he passed out cold.

*

Totally ignorant of the poor Corporal's plight outside the doors, Lacertus entered the Hall of Fire. The obnoxious Ortolan was ensconced in the King's office. A peep through the eyes of Queen Xenophobe had confirmed that. But how to deliver the package? Matron Beamish was whistling happily to herself as she strode through the servants' entrance from the kitchens, carefully balancing a tray of cocoa and biscuits in her hands as she negotiated the mess that cluttered the once beautifully polished floor.

'Matron!' beamed Lacertus, grinning owlishly. 'What a pleasant surprise.'

'Oh. Hello dear. Feeling better now, hmm?'

'Much better thank you, Matron. I say, is that for the Prince Ortolan? Only I have a small present for him. Work being what it is, it would be helpful if you could just take it to him for me?'

'Of course dear boy, of course. A present for my Ortie. Oh, he will be *so* pleased!'

'Just a moment, I have it here,' said Lacertus ducking behind the door to the cloakroom. Swiftly he removed the slug of cork, gingerly poured in the acid and stoppered the phial firmly.

'Just one minute, Matron!' he called, his voice muffled by the thick walls.

'All right dear, but I musn't let this cocoa go cold.'

'Be there in a second, Matron,' he called, bundling the lethal package back into its ostentatious wrapping and sealing it heavily.

'There we are then,' said Lacertus genially, appearing at her side, his fervid eyes watching the nearest exits warily.

'Thank you, dear boy, I shall make sure—'

'Look, I really must go. Work to do and all that!'

Desperate to get away Lacertus was hopping from one foot to the other'

'Yes dear, but I was just going to say that I should be grateful if you could just take this letter to the post for me when you go into—'

'Yes, yes of course, Matron. Glad to. Bye.' So saying Lacertus snatched the thick envelope from her thick fingers and bolted.

'Oh! Yes. Er. Bye.'

Lacertus galloped over the debris of the statues and reached the door to the Servants' Hall running flat out.

'I don't know, the young people these days!'

Still whistling happily Matron Beamish pushed open the heavy office door forcefully with her foot, carefully balancing the laden tray in her great fists so as not to spill the steaming cocoa, and stumbled forward suddenly.

'Lacertus, what a nice surprise,' said Ortolan. 'Oh God. No!'

'It's only me dear, I just brought—' called the kindly matron stumbling blindly into a storm of falling horse-brasses, axe heads, miniature gargoyles, blunt instruments and razor-sharp five-pointed Aikido stars. As the dust settled Ortolan Apus seated behind the Royal desk, feet resting nonchalantly on the expensively lacquered surface, stared down wide-eyed at the unfortunate Matron Beamish.

'Nanny! I wasn't expecting you, I… I…' His eyes caught sight of the brightly coloured package in the midst of the wreckage.

'The parcel! Who gave you the parcel?' he demanded hysterically, but the poor old nanny was no longer in any condition to respond to even the simplest of questions.

If an explosion can ever be described as beautiful, in the terms of pure aesthetic beauty within the true context of the word, then the ensuing detonation would have been a siren of the most outstandingly voluptuous proportions. In the event it substituted a concussion of such thunderous magnitude that it caused the ancient desk to exit the small room via the tall windows that had once so successfully shed light upon it, the heavy flagstones of the ceiling to fall to the floor like the stones they were and the thick wooden door to part company with its safe haven of frame and hinges only to impact violently with the third pillar from the left in the so recently magnificent Hall of Fire. The massive flare of flame that ensued succeeded in consuming all of the oxygen in the vicinity regardless of others' needs or comfort. Loud and long resounded the ear-splitting sounds of destruction through all levels of Camelopardis, a worthy rival to even the Mighty Wurlitzer many floors above, but sadly of a far shorter lifespan. Indeed, the massive jolt did cause a few extra duff notes to hit the air, but not nearly enough to make any real difference to the formidable way in which Queen Berenice played.

*

Lacertus felt the dull thud at his back as he leaned against the inner wall of the strongest, safest tunnel he knew of. The cold wind, laden with stone dust, that whistled as a back draught through the passageway shortly afterwards caused him to cough and splutter uncontrollably. He waited just long enough for the air to clear and then he was off, running in the direction of the King's office.

The opening in the wall that had at one time been directly behind the eyes of the much-painted Queen Xenophobe was empty and fire-blackened. Cautiously he drew his eyes level with the opening. Lacertus almost giggled insanely at the scene of utter destruction before him until he remembered the biography of Caligula Caesar he had read recently and stopped abruptly.

'Been done before!' he muttered enigmatically.

Stretched out face down on the stone steps Corporal Serpens woke to a rumbling noise at close hand. So close that his whole body bounced five steps downwards in the resulting shock wave.

A loud crash behind him caused him to cover his head with his arms and cower in absolute terror. Whatever was going on in there it was far more devastating than the simple revenge attack he himself had been planning.

After the dust had settled and an uneasy silence fell heavily on the much abused courtyard, Corporal Serpens dared to look up just in time to catch sight of the great doors falling slowly, as if in slow motion, directly down towards him. With a yelp of horror he rolled himself over the broken glass and shards of marble spread over the steps to come up hard against the pedestal of a remarkably unscathed stone lion.

The solid wooden portals missed him by inches as they fell, sliding gracefully down the wide steps. Corporal Serpens gibbered in terror and clutched the tacky third-hand jacket close about himself. Mercifully he passed out cold again at that point and knew no more.

★

Lacertus admired his image in the huge, heavily-framed mirror and smiled to himself. The ambience of the Royal Bedchamber that surrounded him in the reflection only added to the deep sense of satisfaction that showed itself in his casual stance and gleaming eyes.

The smart black dress suit he had found at the back of the Royal wardrobe was a little big but still in very good condition. Obviously the old boy had outgrown it so quickly that it had not been worn very often. He adjusted the white bow tie and brushed some imaginary dust from the broad silk lapels. He nodded to himself, slipped a broad white silk scarf around his shoulders and pulled on a long black cape. Finally, he added a shining top hat and set it at a jaunty angle. He turned and bounced happily out of the room. It felt strange and not a little disconcerting to be using the more conventional corridors rather than the hidden routes he was so used to.

Reaching the top of the staircase that descended to the Hall of Fire he stopped and surveyed his domain. He no longer saw the shattered suits of armour, the shredded curtains and abused furniture. He saw instead images of what would be. Beautiful girls in low-cut dresses sat at round, baize-covered tables and dealt cards to wealthy clients. Against the far wall a number of glittering, fast spinning roulette wheels held the greedy gaze of more wealthy clients. Everywhere from the ornately carved and painted Cocktail Bar to the rank of cashiers' booths shone and glittered in the light of three great chandeliers.

More pretty girls darted in and around the crowd of expensive suits and rich evening dresses with salvers of exotic, expensive looking cocktails.

The funding for such a venture would not be easy but he felt sure that at least half of the surrounding Dukes and Earls would be more than willing to contribute for a percentage of the returns. Anyway, they could hardly refuse their King outright, impoverished as he may be.

Lacertus's happy reverie was broken by a loud cry from behind and the sound of running feet. Turning abruptly he was astonished to see a very badly dressed, bare-footed man bearing down on him brandishing two very sharp blades. With a sigh that indicated long-suffering patience, he adroitly sidestepped as the knife-wielding maniac hurtled past him and plunged down the long staircase.

With a clatter of steel the man stumbled over a number of the larger pieces of armour and fell flat on his face.

Shaking his head slowly, Lacertus strode nonchalantly down the stairs to the prone figure. Huge sobs wracked the body of the little man and his hands pounded feebly at the priceless Oriental rug beneath him. With a great deal of effort Lacertus assisted the distraught figure to his feet, moved him across to a sofa by the wall and settled him there.

'How nice to see you again, Corporal Serpens,' he said without a trace of sarcasm. The sobbing stopped when Lacertus spoke the long lost title and the eyes opened wide. 'Now, as you can see, things have changed somewhat since you were last here. I have a proposition for you, *Captain* Serpens, that will be advantageous to both of us.'

Serpens eyed him warily.

'And just what may that mean?' he asked suspiciously.

'Well, you see as I said, things have changed in the set-up around here—'

He stopped abruptly as the Dowager Duchess Harmonia hobbled into the Hall of Fire and cried haughtily, 'I say, you there, I demand to see the King immediately. Go and fetch him.'

Lacertus smiled wickedly.

'My dear Duchess. How jolly nice to see you. As I was about to explain to this gentleman here, things have changed.' He lazily flashed the Great Seal of Multiceros the Wise in her direction, laughed and said confidently. 'As to the King?

You are looking at him. How may I be of service to you, my dear?'